PRAISE FOR NICOLAS FREELING AND
THE SEACOAST OF BOHEMIA

"A delight....A lively adventure.... Castang [is] full of Gallic charm, wry humor, and long-suffering patience."
—*Booklist*

"Freeling writes with heart and unfailing intelligence."
—*Publishers Weekly*

"Freeling's characters are cynical, deeply intelligent types.... His books are always a treat—well-written, full of interesting philosophical digressions and observations."
—*Boston Herald*

"If you've never heard of Nicolas Freeling ... you're in for a treat.... Read one and you'll want to get all the Freelings in print."
—*Cosmopolitan*

"Nicolas Freeling is a master of his trade."
—*Sunday Times* (Trenton)

"In depth of characterization, command of language, and breadth of thought, Mr. Freeling has few peers when it comes to the international *policier*."
—Marilyn Stasio, *New York Times Book Review*

more ...

BY THE SAME AUTHOR

You Who Know • Flanders Sky • Those in Peril • Sand Castles • Not as Far as Velma • Lady Macbeth • Cold Iron • A City Solitary • No Part in Your Death • The Back of the North Wind • Wolfnight• One Damn Thing After Another • Castang's City • The Widow • The Night Lords • Gadet • Lake Isle • What are the Bugles Blowing For? • Dressing of Diamond • A Long Silence • Over the High Side • Tsing-Boum • This is the Castle • Strike Out Where Not Applicable • The Dresden Green • The King of the Rainy Country • Criminal Conversation • Double Barrel • Valparaiso • Gun Before Butter • Because of the Cats • Love in Amsterdam

NONFICTION

Kitchen Book • Cook Book

THE SEACOAST OF BOHEMIA

NICOLAS FREELING

THE MYSTERIOUS PRESS

Published by Warner Books

A Time Warner Company

MYSTERIOUS PRESS EDITION

Copyright © 1994 by Nicolas Freeling
All rights reserved.

Cover design by Jackie Merri Meyer and Rachel McClain
Cover illustration by John Howard
Hand lettering by Carl Dellacroce

The Mysterious Press name and logo are registered trademarks of Warner Books, Inc.

 Mysterious Press Books are published by
Warner Books, Inc.
1271 Avenue of the Americas
New York, NY 10020

 A Time Warner Company

Printed in the United States of America

Originally published in hardcover by The Mysterious Press.
First Printed in Paperback: July, 1996

10 9 8 7 6 5 4 3 2 1

FOR
Andrea/Jean-Luc

Chapter 1

The city of Brussels: a winter morning. Seven forty-five by Central European time, an hour after the Greenwich meridian. Over there in Greenwich, a little to the north of us, nothing much is moving as yet: a few trucks perhaps, on their way to markets; some dawn-bird cleaning women. Here the streets are crowded and edgy. At every intersection is a queue of nervous, irritable cars: every pavement holds a scurry of anoraked and ponchoed schoolchildren, thickened still more by their large square bags full of paperwork. Trams grind on the curves and clank on the junctions: one cannot see through the windows because of humidity. Neither can one see out, but commuters know their stop by instinct.

Henri Castang is on his bicycle, in no particular hurry, pedalling stolidly. There is no especial virtue in the bicycle. True, it causes less pollution than cars; it gets there quicker; it creates less nervous tension; it provides exercise for deskbound legs and sedentary abdominal muscles; it wakes one up. All these things have merit in the eye of a man of fifty, no better now than fairly trim, relatively spry. One cannot claim it affords fresh air, out here breathing all the exhaust gases. Such air as there is, is vile.

As vile, just about, as it ever gets. On dark grey screens, like outsize television sets, clusters of bright green dots shape letters; the time is now 7.51 and the temperature is 0 degrees. Follows miscellaneous information about available

parking places and some municipal self-congratulations; a
concert, the Theatre of the Monnaie, to which nobody will
give any heed. Temperature zero is all you need to know.
The January Sales, we all know about already. That will attract another crowd, a little later, and where they are to park
God alone knows; it's for sure that the municipality of Bruxelles doesn't.

There are hills to climb, and also to go down, in large
curves where the cars hurry with a shriek of accelerating mo-
tors before blocking again, braking and even bumping, unch
and crunch at the next red light. Castang takes his foot off
the ground and the other foot heaves at the pedal. Zero degrees means raw. Also it is raining, in the fine, dense and
greasy rain of Flanders; the city of Bruce lies within the
province of Flanders, a great cinder in the throat of every
Belgian government since about seven-tenths of the city is
French-speaking. The Rue de la Loi is also named the Wet-
straat by decree: there is a lot of Law around here by any
name and in any language: Castang, an Advisory Expert on
criminology, penology, and kindred concepts, within the bureaucracy of the European Community, is part of all this
Law. Great rubbish it all is, but he is not paid—rather generously—for saying so. There is also some fog this morning. A
Dickensian image of the Law. It is over a hundred years later
but the scene is quite true to the opening pages of *Bleak
House*. And over there in Greenwich still more so, but that
fact is not on Castang's mind.

The bicycle is an old Raleigh, solid, durable, reliable; built
in the days when such things still were. When Castang ar-
rives at Star of the Sea (the Communauté rents at vast expense many large buildings with lyrical names but
forbidding aspect) he will secure it with an enormous chain,
since they'll steal the milk out of your tea around here, and
Old Raleigh Bicycles are desirable. It has only three gears
but a large comfortable saddle, soothing to the legal behind.
Its chain does not come off in traffic. Castang has an oilskin
hat, held on with elastic, and a rain-cape with a nasty habit of
catching the wind, with reflecting bands on the back like an

autobahn roadworker. He has also several lamps, for cars make the road dangerous. He has leggings which draw on over his trousers and end in braces, and he has boots. So that he is warm, dry, and as comfortable as could be expected, and much more placid than he would be in the car. In a nasty frame of mind still. He 'thinks' but it is not thought; neither properly a daydream; it is more the ridiculous interior dialogue which is so difficult to suppress.

'I am not really being scatological. Not like all those Great Authors, uh, Shakespeare or uh, James Joyce. My existence is covered in shit. I've lots of paper but there are moments when paper is insufficient. You have to sit on the bidet, mate, and have a good scrub. Because of Crime—there's no getting free of it. Look at that idiot there. First he double-parks and then he opens the driving door without looking, at the exact moment I prepare to pass him. Now that man is a fucking Criminal, an assassin of schoolchildren. Though he'd be most surprised to be told so.'

"Enculé!" said Castang, going past.

He has arrived, neither late nor early. Well, early, since if half an hour, even an hour later, nobody would feel perturbed and in fact few senior officials arrive before nineish. But these are the disciplined habits of a lifetime. Even if

> 'The Working Class
> Can kiss my Ass—
> I've got the Foreman's job at last'

he still likes to come in early. Feels more comfortable that way. Take your time putting the bicycle away carefully; come lurching in like Frankenstein's Monster on top of the concierge who is accustomed to this apparition and greets him as always with beaming smiles.

"Good morning, Monsieur Castang." Quite aside from his own opinion, which would certainly accord with this estimate, the concierge is the most influential person in the building. A master of intrigues and invisible threads, an air of corridors of power and whispers behind the sofa. Monsieur Josselin is generally known as Monsieur Charles, which is quite appropriate since he looks like the manager of a palatial hotel. His hair which is of an auburn colour is combed sideways, thin but polished, across a white brow, his white shirts gleam with cleanliness and just a little starch, and his voice is ecclesiastical. Vera says that he gives one absolution so beautifully.

"A woman is asking to see you. A lady." He is punctilious about the difference. "A young woman" might hope to become a lady at some future date; "a young female" never.

"Asking to see me?" Both unexpected and unwanted. "What have you done with her?"

"Sent her for a cup of coffee since you wouldn't be in for a little while yet."

"And what's she like—young, pretty, eager?"

"Middle-aged. Respectable. Well dressed, for a day like this."

"Did she leave a name?"

"Madame—ah—Groenendaal."

"Means nothing to me. State her business?"

"Said personal, and private."

"Any clues?"

"Och, Monsieur Castang. I'd say reasonable enough. Quietly spoken, polite. Not a troublemaker to go by the look . . . Some good diamond rings."

"You'd make a good cop," a joke he makes fairly regularly.

"Oh Monsieur le Commissaire," falsely deprecating and that too has often been good for a laugh. Castang makes no secret—it would not stay a secret for long—of having been a Divisional Commissaire in the Police Judiciaire. Indeed he still is, if very distinctly off 'the active list.' Hors Cadre, as is said of Prefects or such who have smudged their copybook— 'outside the frame.'

"Well, I'd say better give me a quarter of an hour; to Get Undressed." Monsieur Charles' smile stops just short of a giggle.

Fourth floor: 'middle management.' A line of not-very-large and not very luxurious offices. Some doors are shut and some are open as the cleaning women have left them. Secretaries are down at the end but aren't in either. Castang stowed his bicycling things, put on Italian moccasins, combed his hair; routine. The window didn't open and the radiator was too hot as usual. His desk was as he had left it the evening before, tidy, well Fairly tidy. An unknown woman left a prickle, a very faint prickle, of interest. The housephone tinkled.

"The lady's back, if you're able to receive her."

"Send her up."

A heavy tread on the corridor carpeting announced the rubber-soled boots of the security man. Discreet tap and entrance of same, blue-bloused, black polished belt holster, big cowboy gun—a 357 magnum; oh well, it impressed visitors.

"The lady, Monsieur Castang, your visitor you know," with a habitual fussy pomposity.

"Obliged to you, Monsieur Gandin. Do come in. It's quite warm here, shall I take your coat?"

"Thank you." Composed. Fur, a standard sort of ranch mink; nothing grandiose. A bourgeois appearance, nice-quality Italian gloves and handbag. Fur barely spotted by damp; she'd come by car.

Under it a wool frock, a dab of perfume, a big cashmere scarf which had protected neat fair hair beginning to grey. One of the diamonds was an engagement ring, a nice look-at-me solitaire, the other a pretty Victorian half-hoop.

The habits of a lifetime are not quickly lost. As an adjunct commissaire, chief of staff to that old bandit Adrien Richard, he had 'received' a lot of people, the undotty like the dotty. A lazy as well as a wary old bastard, Richard always wanted a report, first. As a Principal Commissaire with his own 'antenna' criminal brigade, Castang had made many and many more. Now, the Divisionnaire but kept well away from a contagious public, excluded—politically—from what he used to think of as his career, he saw few people he didn't know already. But he hadn't forgotten how. So one gains time, for further study of an unknown quantity.

"A cold morning; you'd like some coffee?" gesturing towards the little tray on a side table: present from Vera, Saint-Germain Limoges with a tiny pattern of forget-me-nots. Sober and pretty, typical Vera.

"I've had some, thank you." Good legs. Had changed into high heels, getting out of the car. He had her in that very low armchair. He tucked himself behind the desk, quite the reassuring house doctor. So what's the worry, Mrs. Chose?

"How can I be of service to you?" A menopausal woman. Vera would sniff loudly, likely utter a yap at this denigrating definition. Can't help it, it's true. The jaw and the corners of the eyes were blurry, not lifted. Well cared for, but this handsome face, barely beginning to go over the hill, had taken a stroke of age. Coup de vieux; she had been crying recently. Had taken some massive shock and wasn't over it. And had come very early in the morning. He could feel pretty sure of her errand.

"Monsieur Castang you are quite literally my last hope."

No marks for having got it right.

"Madame—is it Groenendaal?"

No. I live out that way. I gave a false name. You'll understand why. It's Rogier."

"Madame, I must tell you—"

"Oh I know what you're going to tell me. But you'll listen to me?"

"Certainly I'll listen."

"My boy was stolen, my Maurice. The only boy I have, my only son."

"The police—"

"Will you listen, damn it? Don't interrupt. This was—four years ago. Of course I've been to every policeman in Bruxelles. I've gone high up. I've seen senior officers, magistrates, the Procureur du Roi. We are not influential but my husband is a well-placed man, widely respected, a wide circle of friends. We did all that could be done. They too, I've no doubt. But nothing ever came of it. Four years—four years. No ransom demand, nothing like that. There was never any trace. In the end they said it was a fugue. A fugue—the boy was eight years old. We've had to live with it. A friend in the Communauté mentioned your name. I won't say who, you'd only think him indiscreet. But he said you were like Parsifal; that you were 'Durch Mitleid wissend'."

"A fine compliment."

"That you were a proleptic thinker."

"I don't think I know what that means," disconcerted.

"It means that you imagine things, anticipate things, that you have one of those minds which are able to make a jump into the unknown."

"Oh dear. I can do nothing that the police cannot do better."

"Monsieur Castang, two days ago my son telephoned me. I heard his voice . . . No, I can see you don't believe me. Nobody believes me. As I live and breathe that was my son."

"What did he say?"

"I gave the number, we always give the number, he heard my voice. The child was trained to ring home if ever he was in any trouble. He said 'Hallo, Mama, it's me, it's Maurice, I'm fine, don't worry' and then the phone went dead, cut off. They're all saying I've imagined it. Will you believe me?"

"I have to say I'll be slow to. There are people with crippled minds who use the phone to persecute, and to intimidate."

"Yes I've heard all that too. A mother knows her child's voice."

"Think carefully. The voice as it was then? In four years might it have changed quite a lot?"

"It was a free, a happy voice. Under no constraint. And then it broke off. That was no tape, that was no fake, that was actual and alive."

"Madame Rogier, assume that I believe, and of course I have the fullest sympathy, understanding. Ask yourself then what I could possibly do. The police have resources, human and mechanical, a wide complex network, powers of search and enquiry I don't have. True, I was once part of all this but now I'm cut off from all official capacity. Further I'm rusted, outdated—in brief I'm now only an advisor; I'm happy to advise you but my only counsel could be to renew your effort in the right quarter. I have some friendly relations with the Central Commissaire in the CID here and I'll gladly give him a call on your behalf." He might as well not have wasted his breath. Her fine pale grey eyes, reddened on the rims, as though bruised in the orbits, stayed steady.

"Will you come and see my husband? That is all I ask. Chaussée de Groenendaal." He did not see how he could well refuse. "Just tell me you'll do that. This evening. When he gets back from work. I'll call for you here. I'll drive you home after. Here outside. Cream-coloured thing, a coupé, I think it's a BMW." And cutting through his hesitation she left, with decision and dignity; she didn't let him fetch her coat.

Castang has habits of prudence too, to be sure. Check the phone.

"Three three one, seven five three one."

"Good morning. Could I have Monsieur Rogier please, Arnold Rogier?"

"No I'm sorry, you could get him at the office."

"Then perhaps Madame?"

"No luck I'm afraid, she went into the town."

"Is this one of the family, at all?"

"Oh no sir, this is the cleaning lady. I could take a message."

"Thanks, I won't trouble you . . ."

He dialled another number. "Pass me Mertens if he's there. Henri Castang . . . Good morning . . . Yes, quite so . . . Oh, you know, lounging round and suffering . . . She's fine, thanks, sends her regards. No, it's nothing naughty, leastways it is of course; my ear got bashed. Just tell me whether the name Rogier means anything to you at all? . . . Yes that's right, I've had the woman swarming all over me . . . I quite agree; preposterous. No, of course not; blank faces and polite murmurs. What could one do but listen politely? What would you do? Come to that, what are you doing? . . . Right, you'd be upset too when it said suddenly this was your long-lost daughter from Singapore . . . no, of course I won't be getting in your hair, it only occurs to me it's been some time since we had lunch together . . . By the fishmarket? You make the reservation, you'll get a better price . . . Lovely, see you." Commissaire Mertens is a very sensible sort of man.

Behold; when he came out of the office (lacking in enthusiasm, hoping that at the least he would be offered a Sustaining sundowner because he was feeling the need right now) there she was, right in front of the door and what's more sitting at the wheel of the car as though that would save time: in rush-hour Bruce!

"Don't worry, I'll bring you straight home."

"No you won't," said Castang, a little tart. "You'll be kind enough to bring me back here, because I have to pick up my bicycle." This discouraged conversation.

But she was an excellent driver, agile as a jack-rabbit in the hummocky tussocky hazards of heavy traffic. He admired this gift, since a gift it is, to anticipate which file will be the first to move and be at the head of it. Would that be proleptic thinking? (He had looked up this word in the dictionary.) The gift of getting lights to go green for one is something else. This (Castang's lights go red, which is one good reason for the bicycle) is akin to the gift some people possess for winning money: why is it always the same people who gain lotteries and for whom silver dollars come spewing out of slot machines? Good, the little coupé was an eager, even fierce piece of mechanism. But it's like a computer; without talent behind it the thing stays dead stupid.

So that he didn't try to talk. Most of the time indeed he was wondering whether jack-rabbits existed outside the North American continent (perhaps in Siberia?) and is it the same as a hare?

And then they were whipping in at the gateway of a large square ugly villa. About 1910. Only ten metres back from the roadway but standing in a respectably large piece of ground with grass and trees. (These people had money: had a

ransom demand been intended?) Come on; it is time to wake
up. Amazingly ugly house with balconies and shutters
painted a horrible crimson colour; but covered largely with
wisteria.

She noticed this police eye. It is not of course a normal police eye; a fat lot they care about aesthetics. It is that across a
lot of years now. Vera has made him look at such things. A
year in 'Fine Arts' with as teacher that very bright young
woman Carlotta Salès had done more. He had, he supposed,
some natural sensibilities to begin with. But he has never
been tempted to write any poetry.

"It was my father's house," she said abruptly. "My grandfather built it. I agree it's pretty dreadful. I'm used to it."

Inside were more monuments to bad taste, the sort one can
never quite get rid of in a house like this. A hallway floor of
chequered black and white marble, in winter impossible to
warm—but it was very warm; had they gone underneath with
electric wiring? Immense curtains of plum-coloured velvet,
such good quality that a hundred years later one could not
bear to throw them away. Enormous cast-iron radiators.
Massive chimney-pieces like the bishop's tomb in St.
Praxed's Church. But she led him through to a back room
furnished in a lighter, clearer style, yellow and white and
early daffodils in a vase.

And then he understood things better because she opened
big double mahogany doors and a man came in propelling
himself in a wheelchair. Explanations were made. Monsieur
Arnold Rogier was paraplegic, and this sort of house is very
suitable for wheelchairs. One can move around freely and
there is a chairlift on the big easy-paced generously curved
staircase. The heating bill here must be something shocking.
But Monsieur Rogier is a computer engineer of great talent
(analeptic thinker?) and the firm pays a lot of money, and
contributes toward that special car which brings him to work;
various gadgets that will ease the strain.

Looking at this man, Castang knew he would have to go
through with this. It was not—not so much—the worn look
on the face; the look of much suffering patiently born, for the

most part patiently and cheerfully accepted. Afterwards Castang would know that it was the very slight smell, so slight that he would not have noticed it and probably not have recognised it. But twenty years ago Vera had been in the same boat. Not a true paraplegic thank heaven, but chairbound for two years with a spinal injury. So that he knows the bland smell of talcum powder and rubbing alcohol. (The French say 'fade', a word for which there is no satisfactory translation.) If one has not total control over the bladder, even when one is very scrupulous there can be a slight taint of urine. There is the smell one notices in hospitals, of pains taken to overcome the hospital smell.

Castang remembers the thin boy's buttocks (she had been very slim) that were so difficult to keep from getting sore; the wasted legs she exercised with such a concentration of effort; the contraptions of weights and pulleys and springs. Lubricating oil. Embrocation. The 'manila' smells of the ropes fixed for her to hold to, when she began again to walk, just a little.

She walks freely now. A little limp when tired. Remember the car. She said 'I'm going to learn to drive that'—a Renault mechanic fixed an automatic gearbox.

There was some conversation. Formal at first, with a lot of polite phrases, some bourgeois formulae. But then Castang got down to brass tacks: odd phrase. An upholsterer uses brass tacks, but how did this metaphor come to be widespread?

"I'm going to say, bluntly, I accept it all. So just remember I'm a cop, will you?" He had had a drink, a good solid Scotch even though the woman had—without asking—put in iceblocks, which he detests. But Arnold ('Never mind about Monsieur Rogier; just say Arnold') had said "Come on dear; open a bottle of champagne for your guest."

"What do you make of this tale?" Rogier's voice was quiet, the tone level and composed, that of a business man, determined to keep his detachment.

"There's no pattern to it," answered Castang. "Commissionaire Mertens tells me they could find nothing sequential, nothing to suggest a line of enquiry. You know this, it's what they told you at the time. You didn't accept it, you suspected laziness and inefficiency, and that's very often the truth. But the police aren't magicians; they're overworked and at best it's a heavy-handed bureaucracy, tends to lumber to a stand-still without the stimulus of something to go on. Nothing to do but wait, one concludes, for something to surface. I've been in this position," apologetically.

"Something has surfaced," said the wife, crisp and acid.

"But they're not very likely," suggested Rogier, "to re-open a dossier this old on the base of an unsupported state-ment. Which is why we turn to you, Monsieur Castang. A fresh mind."

"I don't have much to offer. It was thought an insanity, a pathological compulsion, mm?—women who steal babies outside supermarkets. A criminal kidnapping of the usual crapulous kind was dismissed since there was no message, no ransom demand. But now . . . I can dismiss the sex ma-niac, I can speak of that now knowing you've faced that, lived with it, these long years, because of the phone call." Castang is studying 'the pattern of the carpet.' There is no very good way of saying that Mertens had only made a face: 'Come on Castang, you're not swallowing that.'

"Let's just say," looking up, "that I accept the phone call. I'm assuming your boy alive—well-cared for—can I even say happy? Something must have been told him that he could accept. A child has trust." The woman covered her eyes. Ro-gier fingered his jaw.

"I'd look, still, for an insanity factor—how else are we to account for this? You ask for my opinion and I'd look for a missing wheel, and if it's to be found it would be among people who know you well; close friends, family alliances."

"But they looked," said the woman. "They investigated us. They found nothing."

"I'd still suggest that you searched in your family circle. Cousins? Knowing you well." He was stumbling, awk-wardly, with two pairs of eyes on him, sharp and steady. "Families have secrets. Things concealed, obscured or obliterated because something caused shame. A piece of family history perhaps, buried, and the police did not know of it. I've met cases like this. Some grievance behind an obscure happening. I think you might find something. If you decide not to tell me about it, then there's no more to be said. It might be something painful, to you both. You'd have to make up your minds whether you can trust me. But if I'm to get anywhere, it's what I'd have to know."

There was a silence, oppressive, so that he had to make another effort.

"I used the word insanity. If a child is kidnapped, and the obvious answers don't fit, one must look for something motivated by a piece of logic, however perverted or dotty it might appear."

Silence, still. Now he had to extricate himself.

Rogier looked up at him. "You are helpful, and I am grateful."

The wife busied herself. "Did you have a coat? I'll drive you back. My husband has a driver, but I don't like to ask him this late. And this is personal—I hope it will stay between us."

"I can give advice," said Castang, "and forget I gave it."

Chapter 2

A few days passed. Ten, perhaps; he hadn't counted; he hadn't forgotten but he'd pushed it out of his mind. Excuses made to himself: there was much to preoccupy and much to distract him: he had—he still had—no wish whatever to get involved. One didn't regret a moment of generous spontaneity but one had a sneaking sort of hope it would come to nothing. What could it be but a lot of grief, meaning bother, to himself, and more, real grief and prolonged suffering to a family with a bad wound, slow to heal.

For it was not a clean wound from knife or bullet. Those he knows about, and 'modern surgery is wonderful'. Marvellously skilled, since a bullet has a small entry but a big horrible exit, taking with it the pound of flesh exacted; of bowel and bone and muscle all smashed into a paste of catfood. Even these you can recuperate from, they can shortcut you, hitch the wagons up closer to the locomotive and carry on, almost as before.

Castang knows, and from direct experience. A police pistol took his elbow out and in the old days he'd have lost the arm; no two ways about it. Now it has metal and plastic pieces, and he can use it. 'Silicone' is the police joke-word for this. You can do anything with silicone (they say) from a new elbow to the ten million francs so unaccountably missing from the trust funds: you 'silicone the gap in the accounts.'

But to lose a child, not even knowing what has happened,

that is a dirty wound. A jagged shell splinter that tears its way through your flesh and bone, and also your spirit and soul, your memories of a past and your hopes of a future. It leaves an unmendable trail of destruction.

Do not think Castang is sentimentalising his sympathies. Looking at Monsieur Rogier in the wheelchair, even while remembering Vera determined that not only would she walk but she'd become pregnant and carry the baby to term, he had wondered whether the man was or could be the father of his wife's child. An obvious line of police enquiry. Even if one had to ask nasty questions. But 'We went into that,' said Commissaire Mertens. And so did private enquire agents hired by the man himself. The real as opposed to the putative father—'First thing anybody thought of. But the car accident came after the child was conceived. Oh we've been into it all thoroughly, I'm afraid.'

Now—sitting here with her opposite, in his own living-room—he says suddenly, "Madame Rogier, what is your name?"

She was taken aback, went red and then pale again, and unsmiling said, "Anita."

"You see, I have to get to know you better."

"Yes . . . I agree." He is listening to her carefully but his mind is in three places. Here in Bruce, and also in New York where Lydia has found a job as a secretary. And in Berlin where Emma is a student. One can go hot and cold thinking of those streets. Lydia of course is a fussy and a careful girl for all her affectation of casual negligence, and Emma is un-usually hardheaded. But does one ever know? And what could one do? Nothing. Castang, nothing. Concentrate upon this woman; it cost her a lot to come here.

The air is full of violence.

Violence is not just Dirty Harry on the television, the in-numerable versions of the perverted cop chasing the crooks through every aspect of the Robin Hood Syndrome (the Law is no good, so I can take it into my own hands, disregarding all rules).

Violence has been done to this woman and violence is in

her. She has come here to sit down in front of him (and of
Vera too) and spit out a further and more deeply infolded
area of her fear.

"It cost me a lot to come to your office, and more to come
here."

"I can see."

"I've thought a lot about what you said that evening."

"I hadn't wished to push you."

"I realise that and I'm grateful. God knows there's enough
pressure on me already—can I have another drink?" And
good Vera gets up, knowing he has to keep his eyes on the
woman, holding her. Like the trainer watching a tennis
player. Only eye movements are allowed from the side of the
court; you may not speak to the player. But there are codes,
of course.

"I didn't believe it. I don't think it's true. I'm still refusing
to believe that it might be true."

Violence.

"Call him Arnold since you now know my name—he has
pushed me. He has the computer mind. Linear, perfectly log-
ical."

"Legal." Ghost of smile.

"Women's minds just don't work like this." (Vera cough-
ing in the background.) "And family loyalties—with us these
are very strong. Very close-knit." The capacity to do herself
violence. "Ever since you came, saying we should look further into ourselves, Arnold has been hammering at me. Saying 'Old Klaas' but I've been refusing—it's my father. Easy
for Arnold. But my blood and bone, he made me." Silence.

"I see," said Castang gently.

"My father was an SS man."

"Is he still alive?" mild.

"Very much so." Strained, artificial smile. "He's seventy-
three. Tough old boy . . . It's all so long ago." Desolate.

Pride, and shame, and obstinacy. Blood . . . One had
thought that all this had at last been allowed to sink into
oblivion. And then this stinking policeman comes and drags
it all out.

She is dabbing at words now, barefoot on surprisingly hot bricks.

"I suppose you know that in Flanders . . . Hitler was popular."

"Words to this effect have reached me."

"He was no murderer. He is no foul person. They were Waffen-SS. They had clean hands."

"Not always they didn't," suddenly too upset to bother about his grammar. "Who killed the hostages in Tulle? Who massacred the civilian population of Oradour? Who set the entire village in flames?" He stopped himself, horrified at her distraught face and furious at allowing emotion to swamp his training. "I am sorry—I am proud of being a European and I find myself French in obscure dusty corners." But oddly it helped her, in spite of her shaking face.

"Do you think I don't understand? They were never sent to France. It was in the East . . . I must be grateful you are not Latvian, Lithuanian—that the Russians did even worse is feeble, it's no defence at all. I must say this: my father is not a bad man and I won't allow anyone to . . . He was tried and retried. These beastly denazification tribunals, while every real criminal escaped judgment. He was penalised, for years a pariah, deprived of civic rights. Nothing was proved, no proper accusation was ever even brought. No witnesses. Rumour, prejudice, hearsay—from people anxious to whitewash their own stinking skins."

"I'm aware. It was so everywhere," sadly.

"He has lived with it ever since. And so have I."

"All right. Stop tormenting yourself. Come to the point." That this stale old story can still call up this atmosphere of violence . . .

"If we—Arnold says—admit your supposition, then those years are where we—you—must look."

"And you just said it," muttered Castang. "Where would there be any evidence?"

"But you trust your husband" put in Vera quietly. "He is not the one who whitewashes." Anita turned to look at her, neck and head stiff. There was a silence.

"You understand. I'm torn, you see. I suppose I must say that it's possible. Everything is known—everything is unknown."

"You are saying" said Castang briskly "that your father wouldn't have known anything of a plan to abduct your child. But that it's possible that he did something in wartime and was somehow identified, and that all across these years, a distorted act of vengeance—is that it?"

"I'm certain he wouldn't know. He loved the little boy . . . From forty-three to forty-five, all across Europe. The blood and the snow and the ice."

Castang had known and witnessed many scenes of violence. He needed no fevered imaginations of television script writers. He had rarely known more than was in this quiet room at this minute.

"One time in Russia, on a tour," said Anita, "we were on the road up to Leningrad. There was an old man in the group. Shaky. Parkinson's—you know? We wondered why he had come. Suddenly he said out loud 'I know this road' And the Intourist girl said yes, that was the old supply line of the besieging troops."

Vera simply tipped up the bottle, emptying it; went off—limping a little—to fetch another, go through the stale social movements of opening the tiresome thing. But he was grateful; he wanted it.

"It's what, from Bruce to St. Petersburg—a thousand miles? Not far, when you look at Russia. But Napoleon asked one day—how far from Madrid to Danzig? General Rapp answered—'Too far'. "

"We don't know," said Anita softly. "He doesn't know himself. He was an officer in a tank squadron. Around that time they gave away Knight's Crosses like Purple Hearts so I'm not going to talk about the decorated hero. There came a moment at the end when they put all their medals in the ditch and said Now we're free, let them come and we'll make them pay for it. Drowned everything in blood. But he came out alive, and I'm proud of him."

"It is just barely possible," said Castang who had been ruminating. "I remember a case of a paternity suit. *Bild-Zeitung* took it up. They have some stores of archives, of German soldiers wandering about in the East."

"You could ask him," suggested Vera. "Something might come back. I mean, if it's clear that he's nowise held to blame."

"You think so? How does one go about that?" That's the *Winter Reise,* he was thinking. A whole goddamn Schubert song cycle.

"There's just one thing I know of," said Anita. "I mean that's documented. Some time in forty-three he was wounded badly. Put in a field hospital, back to rear échelon and a military hospital, and some pretty good surgeons. Convalescence before some leave back here, patched up and the chest full of medals. He never speaks about it. My mother told me. She might have known. But she's dead, you see."

"It would be a starting point. Any idea where?"

"They had these rest and refreshment places, didn't they? Reichs Protectorate somewhere. Czechoslovakia, I believe."

"Really?" Vera too was looking across the room with the glimmer of personal interest. "I suppose I might try. He can only throw me out, when all's said. You give me permission, to have a word with him?"

"I suppose it can't do any harm."

Castang rubbed his elbow, which was hurting him.

Chapter 3

It was one of the old Flamand streets of the Ville Basse, enclave in the bourgeois, bank-and-insurance Bruce, where they talk platt in defiance of the over-pronounced and -pointed French of the Ville Haute. And, they say, may the Devil fly away in a high wind with all promoters, speculators, lawyers or financiers, and most especially with the government, the Wallons, the French and the bureaucrats—while a particularly pious wish is held to the last for emphasis and launched in anathema upon the Communauté. What have they ever done, ces cochons-là (if you must insist on speaking French not understanding honest Vlaams), but put up prices, drive up rents, abolish jobs and feather their own nests? Man, I'd rather have hair growing in the palm of my hand and lice in that. It is a pretty safe assumption that Castang will not be popular in these quarters.

Still, as a cop he'd had to go into a lot of houses where the police were not popular either. So be polite. Respect them and show that you respect yourself. The police have been taught to wipe their boots and take their hats off crossing these thresholds. Keep your voice down, be neither arrogant nor surly. The thing they hate most and detect quickest is hypocrisy.

'Nicolaas de Roodt' was cut in four-square letters on a nice piece of wood. It didn't say his trade. If you didn't know, then what business have you here? Inside the door a bell went tingling. There is nothing to pinch; a lot of junk, a lot of dust, not much light and apparently nobody interested. Castang looked around. 'Old Klaas' is an artisan and still at it. There are smells of plaster, glue, wood, canvas. He makes picture-frames and gilds mirrors, and sells these to expensive decorating shops. He mends, cannibalises, restores and refreshes old things or pretty things which have got broken or wormeaten or are just tumbledown. He doesn't apparently work with metal but knows those who do. The klokkemaker will do the movement of that old grandfather ticktock, but he'll do the case. He has stocks of old ivory and onyx and mother-of-pearl, bits of inlays and veneers, and—delighting Castang—a wall full of little drawers, as in one-time ironmongery shops which held hundreds of sorts of screws and nails and hooks and sockets.

A voice is grumbling back there in the workshop that he won't be but a minute, and three minutes later a tall old man came out and switched the light on. Washed but not recently, shaved but not for the last three or four days; you couldn't see whether he needed a haircut because he had a funny hat on, but it was probable.

"Dag Meneer." Mijn heer on Mon sieur or just Mister; Castang can be polite in several languages, if not much else: he can talk a bit of Vlaams or Nederlands (only the accent really is different) and understand quite a lot, but he can't carry on a conversation.

"Whatyawant then?" expecting the hand put in the pocket, some small battered object diffidently withdrawn, the 'Can you fix this?'

'Kunst,' thought Castang, and also 'Silicone.'

"No, it's not that sort of business. Sorry, my Vlaams is not up to much. Okay in French? German if you prefer it; I've an introduction from Madame Rogier, from your daughter if you'll allow me to speak of her."

"My daughter. So you've been told that. How well d'you pretend you know my daughter?"

"Just fairly well, so far. I hope to get to know her better. I call her Madame, I don't call her Anita. I hope to know you, that's all." Big battered loose folds of eyebrow wrinkled at him; red-streaked but shrewd and sharp old eyes took him as though in tweezers.

"Never mind my daughter, state your business." Lies won't do because they won't be forgiven or forgotten when he finds out the truth. So shade it as close to the truth as you can.

"I'm a writer. I think it's time the truth was told about some ancient history. To get rid of the propaganda and the brainwashing. To hear it as it really was. Not to say oh, it didn't exist, it was all an invention of the Jews. Nor of course that it was civilisation's crusade against the Bolsheviks. It's possible now. But there aren't many good witnesses left."

"The truth," said the old man softly. He was standing behind the shop-counter which had been scarred by a good many burning cigarette ends. The big scarred hands were resting on some shelf behind it. He made a loose easy movement and a pistol was pointing at Castang. It was the classic wartime souvenir, the well-shaped, marvellously-designed, simple, efficient, nine-millimetre semi-automatic, known all over the world as 'the Luger.' An old one with a lot of bluing worn from the metal. The butt was unseen sitting solid and comfortable in the accustomed hand. The foresight stayed absolutely steady on Castang's midriff. "This is the truth," he said softvoiced. "All the truth I have for nosy parkers, so you run off home, boyboy."

"You know," said Castang conversationally, "in America, in Wyoming, an armourer called Casull, makes a thing he calls the Rolls Royce. Calibre four-fifty-four, he says it has double the power of a forty-four magnum, Jesus, the thing's even got a telescopic sight. Jesus, just imagine. Legally, you can carry a pistol in Wyoming but it mustn't be concealed. I don't know how you'd conceal a thing like that. You know, it's ten years since I had one of those pointed at me."

It still is pointed and he holds quite still. This phrase does not tell the truth because his belly is oozing and lurching about inside, a dinghy in the wake of an aircraft carrier.

"You're a cop."

"Was a time," agreed Castang, wishing it would stop.

"You're another of those fucking enquiry agents."

"They're lazy cops. Want an easy life."

"You look like an owl in daylight. You frightened?"

"Yes."

The old man broke into a hearty guffaw. He shook; the gun didn't.

"So who are you really?"

"Put it down and I'll tell you." There were violent twitches all down his abdominal wall, like a horse which has had a hard race. He rubbed it to try and stop them. The old man lowered the pistol until the weight rested on the counter, but he didn't let go of it.

"Spit it out," cupping his free hand behind his ear, grinning with evil yellow teeth.

"It's true I'm ex-PJ. I do legal work for the Community. You know, senior police officers don't like guns pointed at them, they prefer peaceful bits of paperwork."

"More." The foresight beckoning at Castang, to sort of encourage him.

"Your daughter came asking for my help. I told her there was very little chance indeed of my giving her anything useful and you've just proved me right." Old Klaas put down the pistol and shook all over with laughter.

"Not bad at all. Gassing away there about some cowboy in Wyoming—where d'you hear all that or did you make it up?"

"I read it," truthfully, "in the *National Geographic.*"

"The things Americans get up to!" putting the gun away. "I liked that," appreciatively, "I really did. Hold the shooter at him and he starts telling me what he read in the magazine."

"Next time I'll come in with my own in my hand. Shut up!" addressing the stomach which was still troubling him.

"I wouldn't recommend it," leaning back now with his hands in his pockets. "I'd pop you and they'd pin a medal on me. Now we'll have a drink to settle your gut," bringing up a bottle and two glasses, and a pair of spectacles. What else has he got down there? Castang wondered. "Now tell what you really want," pouring—Calvados, there was a lovely applejack smell. "I know about my daughter. She's upset, thinks she heard from her little boy. Maybe she did too, how should I know?"

The first taste created a shiver, but it was the last.

"I'll tell you it straight up. They've all been foxed, all those police and detectives and whatever, they never got anywhere with it, right? Looked at the husband, chap in the wheelchair, looked at all the friends and relations, big handful of nothing. Looked at me too. As though I'd make away with my own grandson. But," bitterly still, "they'll believe anything of me. Fifty years on and I'm still the war criminal, I burned Jews," pointing at Castang with a fingernail which looked as though it had been cleaning pipes out. "That your idea?"

"No. But I think it possible you started something without ever knowing, without ever guessing. Like was there ever a moment, back there in the East, when your name and where you came from was known? You did something quite ordinary. In the line of duty. Say burned a house down. So what, so did Julius Caesar when he invaded Belgium. But somebody has a grievance, gets handed down like a vendetta. Fifty years is nothing, in Sicily or Corsica. But they'd have to know who you were, and want to hit you where it hurt."

"I get your point," scratching with the fingernail, which made a loud noise. "Pretty far-fetched but it could happen. I don't see nothing like that but it ain't altogether stupid."

"The whole point," said Castang, "is that it had never occurred to you and never would if I didn't ask."

"So now you want to hear, do you, all about the campaigns of the wicked Waffen-SS in the East, do you? How we were BAD?"

"No. I was a schoolboy, had to do Latin, shows how old I am. Had to read Caesar, all about the Gallic War. Pretty dull stuff, he left out all the funny bits. Or if I wanted to get sexy, go to Spain, ask ol' Leon Degrelle how he got his Knight's Cross in the Smolensk pocket, golden oakleaves on it."

"I had it too. He made a lot of money. While I stayed here and got fucked."

"You've got a point there. But no writing it down in little books. No haha neither with your cop friends."

"It's your daughter, and it's your grandchildren. It's nothing to me and if you ask, then no, I don't get paid and I get no medal."

"I gotta lot of work," said old Klaas. "But all right. I'm getting old, I suppose I'm getting soft. Maybe that's good too. I don't love much, I don't have much to love. My daughter . . . they were all ashamed of me, when she got married. Didn't want Dirty Harry sitting down at table with them. She's been a good girl."

Not the moment, thought Castang, for any helpful comments. "You and Julius Caesar," with a snigger. "And the cowboy with the great big gun in Wyoming. You made me laugh . . . You come and see me tonight, when I've shut up shop. Say after seven. We'll go and eat some frites, and have a couple of beers."

"Entertaining old man," said Castang, chuckling rather; he should have known better than to be self-satisfied but he thought he'd managed quite well.

"Really?" Vera sounded absent, and even a bit edgy.

"Violent old villain, face like a battlefield." It would be tactful, and prudent, to avoid all mention of the gun. Vera is happy that nowadays he has nothing to do with guns. She likes this Bruxellois world, which gives her a sense of security, and has no regrets for the Police Judiciaire, from which she has inherited a revulsion to violence in any form, a shrinking of the skin, the fiercer because she had always taken such pains to master it.

"I might get somewhere with him tonight. Some grub and plenty to drink. I'll try not to be late, but don't bother with supper."

"And what about my concert?" glacial. "That had slipped your mind, just a little? I went to a lot of trouble, to get those tickets."

"Oh God." Never become even in the slightest puffed up because women always know where to find a sharp pin. Now one is going to feel guilty, gottverdomme. "I'm sorry." But she had stalked away and could presently be heard on the phone with one of those women friends known collectively as the biddies, being gently ironic about men "qui font faux bond"—Letting one Down.

Shit, and where was his train of thought? Yes, what had the grandchild been told about Old Klaas? He would have to cross-examine Anita more closely, catch her tits in the wringer just a bit. Not a phrase Vera would approve of. She came back, perched on the arm of a chair and said (considerably curt), "You should stop this kindhearted act which is only vanity anyhow because people wind you up in it and you don't get free and one never sees the end of it. And Don't Get Drunk."

"I truly am sorry." He was, too, penitent.

"Your loss. She's a beautiful singer. And doing a Schubert cycle. Magali will go with me. Only too delighted. The *Winter Reise,* lovely. Oh well," relenting a little, "I'm going out early and having a bite with Magali in the pub, okay?"

"So you take the car," doing penitence.

"While you eat mussels and drink a lot of beer chez les Flamands. And talk about the war. Men! . . . He'll tell you a lot of lies."

"Never known anyone yet who didn't," reverting to police days.

"But war memories more than most. How the hell else would they make it sound exciting?"

And where was he? There'd been a phrase; struck him at the time; one let it go on by, but one tried to catch it and keep it, to think about later.

Vera had gone upstairs to change. The house was very silent, the more with the two girls gone. Then, it had always been a hurricane of activity and noise. Too silent, now. The house was too big. It would do very well until he retired, and at that happy moment one would sell it, and the proceeds . . . It would be winter, then, and there would be

Winter Journeys, such as Schubert—there are winter journeys right now. Vera said things when in a dudgeon; she knew very well that it had nothing to do with being kindhearted. One had to make these journeys; they were discoveries within oneself.

He had got it—'They looked at the man in the wheelchair and came up with a big handful of nothing.' I suppose that's so, thought Castang. What else could it be? One still wonders.

And what did one make of the father being the old-freedom-fighter? Nine-tenths positive. He was no criminal, but could one ever be quite sure? Castang remembered a famous television piece that the Germans had made.

A series of interviews with the children of national-socialist notorieties. Some had come to terms; others hadn't. Some showed their faces; others couldn't bear to. One woman—a fine face, too—had made a really gallant effort, and had won, and right at the end could even laugh. Another sat in total darkness. Literal, as well as figurative. One man said, in a dry level voice, 'I'm against death penalties in general but if ever one was justified it was my father's.' And one, quiet and controlled, found that 'thinking it over' he could feel, well, ninety per cent of 'positive' emotions. Anita would agree? There is just that small area of not-knowing.

Poor old Hess; ninety per cent dotty to say the least. Old Klaas is very far from dotty.

Castang felt oddly touched. The old man had washed and even put on a suit, and made an impressive figure. When the hair was brushed one could see a big scar running from the temple to back behind the ear, where no hair grew. A close call, and perhaps it was like that with guilt. Times there's a scant millimetre in it. He had even stopped feeling guilty himself about the concert ticket. And in the warm, smelly, furry atmosphere of a Brussels pub—there was no 'choiseuls' to eat but there was a Liègeoise veal kidney—after a few drinks the old boy got into a good frame of mind. "I'm damned if I find anything to feel guilty about."

The Flamand sense of humour is mostly scatological and on this premise very funny indeed. There are numerous clas-

sics including the one of the canal boat whose master decides
to have a shit with one foot on the bank and then discovers
the boat to be insecurely moored. These gain on the whole,
when translated to a Russian winter temperature of thirty
below zero. There is also a long-standing debate in all European countries as to whether it is advisable to put beer before
wine, or vice versa. But do not add any sort of schnapps.
Castang didn't and managed to obey the Vera-command not
to get unmercifully pissed. The old man did and it made him
funnier. They had dinner and some hours later they felt like a
little supper. By this time Castang had got him on to the documented bit. The wound—oh, That wound. Yes, it had been
quite a bad one. The old boy stood up, pulled his shirt out of
his trousers and displayed a hairy stomach: it says something
for Brussels pubs that no one paid this any attention but there
was light enough to count five machine-gun bullets. At the
back they were a good deal larger. They'd all gone on
through. And that said something for a Russian winter. One
wouldn't have survived that in Africa, while three, four
months later this man had gone back for more.

"And mark, I've the digestion of a boy of twenty." In that
cold it was clean and scarcely even bled. One can find more
miracles from those years, in Russia . . . yes, the nurse. Not
pretty, you know. Young, that yes. Got into bed with me, I
couldn't bloody move, and I thought what's this, barbed
wire, what's that doing here, but it was only her fan. Remembered that afterwards, had my life saved by a woman
with a barbed wire fan.

And convalescence—yes, there is Czechoslovakia, down
there by the Danube somewhere. I suppose I could find it on
a map. No barbed-wire there. Ingrid—and afterwards, yes, in
Prague, Ingrid, Ingrid. Yes, that leaves its mark. Like these
five silver pennies on my belly, I haven't washed off Ingrid.

Sure she had a baby. They all did. That was the right thing
to do, to have a baby for the Reichsführer. Have one by an
SS tank captain, poor old Himmler would have tears of joy
in his eyes. Decent old stick, you know, would never take a
penny, hated and despised Fatso and the other greedy pigs,

'Be more than you appear.' Dotty, of course he was fucking dotty, how else survive in that gang?

Castang, who is not quite sure that 'decent old stick' is exactly the right epithet for the Reichsführer, knows better now than to interrupt with nasty questions about the Warsaw Ghetto. Or even 'Silly old sod.' He had to see how they worked it out; whether they had anything better than lunatic ideologies and self-justifications.

"Th' old fool made the fatal mistake early on of allowing all sorts of crooked trash to wear SS badges and uniforms. That's what did for us, you know; not just swine like concentration camp guards whom we wouldn't have touched with a ten-foot pole, but those loutish Gauleiters whose one idea was to make little empires for themselves and fill their pockets, while we got killed protecting them. We refused to cover up, but they got away with every sort of corruption and sadism and called it police regulations.

"People talk a lot now about Europe," with a malicious look at Castang, "and we pay a lot too. Don't you know that we had all those ideas, fifty years ago? That we wanted to get rid of the customs barriers and the tariffs, the fifty different sorts of money and all that national crap, all the talk about sovereignty.

"Oh I can see you coming, that it would all be for the Germans and to aggrandise the Reich. Not a bit of it, we spoke our own languages, we had our own structure and there were German officers, high-ranking ones too, proud to serve with us and under our command."

The eyes were getting very bloodshot and Castang was hoping that neither of them was getting too drunk to stay coherent.

"We had French soldiers who'd won a Legion of Honour fighting against Germany, and wore it side by side with an Iron Cross. Don't talk to me about Europe."

"Hear a lot now, don't you, about Bosnia and Hercegovina. Papers are full of nothing else but how Moslems are oppressed and robbed and raped and murdered by Serbs and Croats too. No idea of history, no idea that it was always like that because you had mixed groups in the same village, Catholics and Islam and Greek Orthodox all hating each others' guts and taking any opportunity for a massacre. It isn't new, you know," and Castang, who didn't know, felt shame.

"Perhaps you didn't know that to put a stop to that, Berger formed the 'Prinz Eugen?' Moslem officers wearing a fez; bloody good soldiers they were too."

"You were a sort of Foreign Legion," suggested Castang helpfully and the old man turned on him, and then collected himself; what was the use, now?

"No way," with much dignity, "were we any sort of Foreign Legion. Viking . . . Nordland . . . Nederland—yes and Wallonia. You can say that living here I've small use for Wallons. But they were my comrades and I fought with them, fifty years before you talk-merchants started quacking about Europe. And over nine in ten of us left our bones there." And at last a tear gathered and rolled down. It was vital to put a stop to this.

"Tell me about Ingrid," and the old man was glad also to let go of these long-vanished ideals. He cheered up.

"Ha, Ingrid. Yes, she was quite a girl." And exactly as one hadn't dared hope, he felt in his inside pocket and pulled out an old sealskin wallet, fat with the débris of a lifetime, rummaged, muttered. "Here you are—that's Ingrid." Had he carried that, in the field? Castang wasn't going to ask: he was feeling lucky. It hadn't been softened or glamourised by any studio; a straightforward snapshot taken up close and with a good lens, a Contax or a Leica, so that faded as it was and grotty round the edges it was still bell-clear after all these years. "There were others—Astrid found those, destroyed them." He spoke of his wife levelly, naturally. It had been a long time ago. It was her right, still; she had been his wife. "I had some of her naked. They weren't porn—they were goddamn sexy though."

Castang could believe it: if ever he saw a home-breaker it was this. A beauty too, and in her full bloom; girlhood was behind her. But not a mark yet on this curved laughing seducing face. In the 'Marlene' pose of the thirties, wrapped in some pathetic wartime finery (did he bring her back a fur coat, some soft, high, lovely leather boots, some heavy, barbaric gold jewellery from Russia?—they would suit her). She had not plucked or painted her eyebrows, and the face had character, yes, and intelligence as well as the fatal charms. The fair hair was swept up at the back and pinned with combs, in the pretty style of the forties which one no longer saw—and alas, because it shows off the grace of a fine neck and ears. Vera does it sometimes . . . this girl too has those wonderful Slav features. Her jaw is a bit too heavy, her eyes are a bit too small. And perhaps a bit too shrewd. Castang shuddered a scrap, for it was a face that cities had been burned for, and how many men had shattered on that rock? Old Klaas had had a month or two, before going back to his unit—with this in his pocket, and a few memories, whose vivid glow had even now not altogether faded. A familiar Hollywood seductress? Or something just a wee bit higher class? Yes—very like Garbo; but who, now, remembers what Greta Garbo's face looked like? And is one going to say of them all, contemptuously 'Just another cocksucker?' Vera would, and so no doubt had Astrid; with a keen naked personal hatred. But would he, himself, say that? The police officer would, but he—the human being? He thought that he felt able to understand.

"She had fantasy," said old Klaas softly. "She could change your world."

Castang did not speak. But now the old man was too far away, too far back, in the secret antique world where one is strong enough for anything and one will never be defeated.

'Waltz me around again, Willy—
Around, around, around—
The music's so dreamy, these peaches so creamy—
Oh don't let my feet touch the ground.'

Never any more can there be any girls like that; never such music, never such feats of arms. She was so funny! So much laughter . . .

The strawberries have no flavour, nowadays.

Chapter 4

"I've come to present my preliminary report."

"Really? I'd thought we were past that stage." Monsieur Rogier was smiling a little. "I did not see fit, of course, to put any pressure on either my wife or yourself. No conditions. No guidelines, even. No forbidden areas." He made a hand gesture. Fine hands, beautifully shaped; the fingernails ovals. "I thought, in fact, you'd come to present your bill. I hadn't wanted to mention it. Naturally we'll see to any little out-of-pocket expenses, but your honorarium—a cheque if you like, but if you prefer it a bank transfer to anywhere you name—and as discreet as you might like . . ."

Castang's turn to smile.

"In the PJ—a crime that's known or simply suspected, we'd be given a generalised authority to look into things. 'Tour d'horizon.' Mostly then, we'd bring our conclusions to the examining magistrate instructing the affair. He—she—might then decide to orient matters in a particular direction, lay down some ground-rule framework for behaviour. He or mostly she nowadays is bound herself by obligations and re-sponsibilities and is answerable to higher legal authority, but we remained subject to the orders she gave—often quite a young woman, which sometimes created friction. But under the code there are strict rules of procedure, and there's a be-havioural code of deontology." If it were really so, thought Castang, but didn't say it. "When we did private affairs—en-quiries, they're termed, in the interests of a family—the same rules governed our contract. In this case, you're the magistrate. I've come to tell you that I'm prepared to go further into all this, but it's at your peril."

"I see." Anita sat by, silent, watching Rogier's face. He is the dominant personality of this couple? Or more simply, in this world it is the man, the head of the family, who takes the important decisions.

He is impressive, all right. Thin, and perhaps getting thinner, or he just likes the collars of his shirts to be rather loose. Obviously a man who hasn't the use of his lower limbs concentrates his force in the head and torso, which is muscular and alert and the head is monumental, sculptural. Great strength there in the forehead and the line back to the ears; especially in the orbits of the eyes and the eyes themselves; large, clear, mobile, and yes, which burn.

"You've found something out. As you suggested—hinted—would in your experience be likely, probably. Even certain?"

"I got on pretty well with old Klaas—after a bit of an initial barney," grinning and getting a grin in echo from Rogier.

"Your family, my dear," but kindly and with no snide sidethrust.

"The name of Ingrid mean anything special?" A faint flush on the delicate skin of Anita's cheekbones.

"Not a great deal. I've heard it mentioned, but it's a commonplace name. I think it may have meant something—special is your word—to Astrid, my mother. And she was a strong-minded woman—a secretive woman—extremely proud, and you might say touchy, and not at all given to publicising her private life."

"Like you," suggested Castang. "But you are obeying a force stronger than these instincts, because you want to know what has happened to your son."

"That is the truth," painfully.

"Ingrid was a very attractive girl with whom your father had a love-affair while in convalescence from a bad wound. As you suggested, in Czechoslovakia. I know when, and I know approximately where, and I know Ingrid had a child. Your brother, as it were."

"I didn't know, I was a small child, as I've told you I lost my mother when I was still very young. I think I may have known something subconsciously—does one ever know what small children hear, or believe they hear?"

"I think I understand. But you've never seen your brother—that you know of? You don't know who he is? Even if he's still alive? Klaas says he doesn't. He may not be telling all of the truth. Okay? It's a piece in a pattern which suggested itself to me, and it might be completely false, one can't build on it. But since it fits, I'd have a look closer. That would mean going to look; to be sure, there'd be expenses, I'd have to take some time off; yes, I'll send you in a bill, that angle's settled. But soft methods make for stinking wounds, say les Flamands. Dutch folk wisdom. If I got into this at all I have to go in sharp and deep, and that's just what the police didn't do. Human respect, laziness, timidity, not wanting to stir up shit—I've nothing to say, no criticism to make. D'you get me?" Because Anita looks like crying.

"It has to be." She brought it out, however painful. "Astrid is dead."

"It has to be, quite plainly," said Rogier. "Just one minute, Monsieur Castang. My wife's life, by the same token my own, was very thoroughly and painfully investigated by the previous enquiries. Naturally enough they started at the beginning, close to home. Did my wife have a lover?—that sort of thing. You aren't proposing to include this area when you come to reopen the book? Because for me it's an open book, I am as you see me, and pretty helpless with it, but I spend much of my life at work, and you're aware that my company gets very paranoid indeed about anything that could be construed as undue interest. My wife's entire existence was thrown open to every imaginable curiosity, and very disagreeable that was to her and even I may say to myself. So that may I ask you to keep a light hand? You're a man of sensitivity, and I'd be grateful if my sex life like my business life remained where it belongs," with a gesture towards his heart.

"I'll give you that assurance," said Castang mildly. Looking at Anita—"Not even your mother's sex life from what I can see. She got married after the war, right? And you were born."

"It all caused an upheaval in the family and a considerable scandal," she said, managing to smile, "and some of my aunts haven't perhaps got over it to this day. He wasn't quite the sort of returning hero they'd bargained for. I'll say this, I think my mother may have had unhappiness in her life, and certainly much strain and struggle, but I think too my father is a good man, and I believe that he gave her much happiness too, in the years left her."

An envelope came in the post, marked 'Personal.'

'Castang, I'm typing this myself. Doesn't concern your office, nor mine—nor the police. You and you only—clear?

I've thought over what you said. Your Czech guess might be good, but if the woman you mentioned is alive, painful areas result, wounds reopen. I want no more bandying about of domestic life. I think I made that clear, but it has to be unmistakeable.

Whatever your findings, they are to be reserved for myself alone: totally confidential. I want this in writing, daily, at this office and marked personal.

Accept this condition of total privacy and the payment I mentioned will be made over at once, whatever the result. If, as is your right, you feel for whatever reason that you cannot accept it, it will be understood that the enquiry is dropped. I will pay you a forfeit for your time and trouble that I believe you will consider generous.

On the other hand, should your findings upon acceptance lead to the knowledge that our son is alive, and might be restored to us, I should propose to double the payment agreed.

Naturally, it is my hope that you will accept the offer here outlined, on the understanding that any breach of confidentiality instantly nullifies the said agreement.'

Castang put down the piece of paper the better to think about it. Wasn't all this rather odd? WhiteMan speak with forked tongue? Being offered bribes is common form, but was he being bribed to accept or to refuse?

The mentality of this man might not be as straightforward as had appeared.

Well, what did one know about computer experts? Precious little; what one reads in magazines, so that any question put to a man, for this is not a world women enjoy, is met with an indulgent smile; polite but inevitably a mix of amusement and condescension.

Feeling the need to sort it out Castang went to see him.

Security? Yes, the duties of a senior consultant would inevitably touch upon this field. But at the bare mention of the word 'virus' Rogier's smile became mechanical.

"A journalist's word. There are large numbers of malicious and indeed highly maleficent programmes written. It is true that these can be most ingenious, highly corruptive, in the pathologic sense criminal. The psychology of the authors is interesting. There have been blackmail attempts, but it's rare for any material gain to be made. A perverted sense of power for power's sake. There are Freudian explanations of the phenomenon."

"Fair to say you have to patrol your networks, in almost a police sense, for safeguard?" The smile vanished.

"There is an aspect with similarities to your suggestion." Primly. "There could be occasions when I might be asked for advice."

"Diagnosis? Treatment?"

"The medical metaphor is inaccurate, you know. These things are not airborne. They are engineering tricks, patterns, mostly invented by over-ingenious students. And that is all I feel inclined to say of the matter."

"I seek only to examine a possibility of someone, known or unknown, trying to gain advantage or leverage, cause malicious damage to your position or reputation."

"It was a police theory. They went into it at some length. It was troublesome. It was also fruitless."

This man has two sides to his head, and to his life, and keeps them rigorously separate.

NOT one of Castang's better days: do these get worse? Or are they more frequent? Bacteria lurk in the office, and the extent of air pollution in cities is in direct proportion to the hopeless talk about cleaning it. He enjoys a sturdy good health, which is most unfair, because everybody else is ill. He is burdened by being French; the French are being tiresome, as Vera puts it 'tedious.' Since the French always are tedious it follows that they are being unusually tiresome, for him to have noticed it at all.

People keep ringing up being humorous. Worse, facetious. "I say, Castang, what's got into you all? The rugby team lost again, is that it?" If it were just the farmers; the agricultural population of France shrinks rapidly but the smaller it gets, the more vociferous. Or the diplomats, who always get everything wrong, as it were deliberately, since they haven't even the excuse of the State Department (which isn't very clear where Madagascar is, anyhow). No, it's the police, and Castang is sensitive on this subject, despite—or because of—lengthy explanations that only in the most technical sense (like a law of 1867, obsolete for a century but somehow never repealed) is he a police officer at all: his is a very French situation. They no longer pay his wages, and are busy with a lengthy siege about his pension rights, but technically he's still French and still a Divisional Commissaire in the PJ. Really he is cross with Anita, who has jockeyed him into this absurd position of being both a police officer and a not-police anything.

What is the matter then? He has been asked this question ten times today already. You'd think he was the only man in the entire city of Bruxelles able to answer it.

"Well Henri, after all, you're one yourself, aren't you?"

You see?

And then a close colleague, if nominally a hierarchical superior.

"I say Castang, what's all this hawking and spitting all the time?" Irritably, and he hasn't bronchitis at all, though the whole of Bruxelles has—it's winter. Or well, just a little. Senior commissaires aren't supposed to spit in the wastepaper basket, though they all do. He has to explain.

The PJ is much vexed because of proposed changes in the code of criminal procedure.

"I can't see that anything has changed at all."

That is because of French bureaucratic language, which is so muddled that nobody can understand anything, ever.

"But it's only a modernisation—overdue, surely—this business of allowing a defence advocate access to his client who is held for questioning."

It makes hardly any difference since the lawyer's access is very limited, but you have to understand the French.

"That's why I come to you."

It's a backhanded slap at police abuses (patiently, if irritably). The suggestion is that people get beaten up inside commissariats. The lawyers don't like this either; say quite rightly it's no part of their job to peep through keyholes at police wickedness.

"And do people get beaten up in police stations?"

"Oh yes, frequently." More cheerfully.

"Have *you* beaten people up?"

"In my younger days, I'm sorry to say, yes, I have."

"Filthy bastard."

"I quite agree. The police are, you know, everywhere."

So that now, much ruffled—if just out of spite, really—he would like to be a bastardly policeman again, and behave like one.

He has been thinking about this. Pottering about, and perhaps nosing about, in Czechland (or was it Slovakia?) is possible. Other people go to ski. There isn't much in the office; a few things need clearing up (like the French Code of Criminal Procedure). What's more, the family Rogier is generous about the out-of-pocket details. Since we do not speak Czech, and have never quite made out how Slovak differs, one would ask Vera to come along, to do any interpreting or translating where needful. This is not a police activity at all, really. Any competent enquiry agent; there'd been plenty but they'd all looked in the wrong places. It was quite possible that Ingrid would be still alive.

He was being a bit superficial here with his paperwork. But any moment now there'll be someone else on the phone asking why the Commissaires of Police in all ranks were demanding, or pretending to demand of the Minister of Justice that they be relieved of their judicial responsibilities. Well, you know, the police are forbidden to go on strike.

Isn't that excessive? Yes, it is. They're just being Ruffled. And I feel like being excessive myself. I'm not altogether happy with Monsieur Arnold Rogier. He strikes me as a bit too good to be true.

Now how would one go about that? One wasn't about to put on a false nose and hang about Lurking.

In Paris one could say—one could pick up the phone and order—one would like a bit of discreet surveillance clipped on. One had people supposed to be good at that. The PJ is not the Paraguayan Army. We've lots of generals, but we've a few soldiers too. But suppose that out here in the wilderness one is just the one man—like the officer, all by himself, in *Dances With Wolves,* deprived of military backing?

Castang with all that weight of police experience behind him, a dreary weight it was too, and a weary one, knew very well that people's motives for something or other—crimes for instance—are rarely as clearcut as they have to be for television serials. More often a bundle or faggot of odd sticks than a nice recognisable log. He was being muddy, he told himself; making a poor job of analysing his own motives.

"Did you enjoy your Schubert concert then?"

"Oh yes," beaming, "it was perfectly lovely."

What a dry old stick I have become. The civil servants, called in French 'Les Fonctionnaires', have been to him throughout his life an object of derision; the police are of course themselves servants of the state and share all too often the talent for obstruction and obfuscation, yes and bureaucratic lethargy. A proper func I am now. Never do anything as long as excuses can be found not to.

Wood sculpture has been absorbing much of Vera's energies, for a year and more. An exquisite material, so warm and so alive. She loved its textures. It could be silk or velvet, bone or stone. She did not deal in dry old dead sticks.

She has been going back lately, to pens and brushes and sheets of cartridge paper.

'The wood is a bit self-indulgent, you know. Leads one into fascinating abstract shapes but you can find those on the beach, and the sea does them better. A stage, perhaps, in understanding form. Clay, and then casting in bronze, that's the only real one. But it's so damned expensive.'

Pressed, she'd say, 'I'm not really good enough.' Neither was he.

Castang did have some idea of why he found fascination in this kind of case. He knew very little about his own origins. As a child he never asked. Then he'd wanted to ask and hadn't. Such a lot of things had held him back. Reticence, instincts; reasons too, later on. Later still it had been too late. His aunt, who brought him up, never said a word.

His aunt—leastways, he supposed she was his aunt. So he had been given to understand. How? He no longer knew. Children take things for granted. He must have been told, just as he was told that his mother was dead and his father was unknown. But she wasn't—he thought—his mother's sister. Some kind of cousin, more like. She was just as he always called her 'Tante', and if he thought about her, in the abstract 'Ma tante Cathérine.' Never mind, she'd been a very good mother to him. Unfailingly kind in that dry, detached manner. Loving, certainly; sometimes—occasionally—cuddling. Severe—it didn't do to mess with her orders or instructions. The 'grocer's' down the road, the 'Alimentation' where she did much of her shopping (there were such little shops then, in central Paris)—la Mère Bardin—he'd borrowed money there once. There'd been a frightful scene. He'd be about fourteen. Never, never, never was he to be unscrupulous about money. He got pocket money. That was it. She never once hit him, she never punished, she would 'go silent': she could be very frightening, ma tante Cathérine.

Her untidy bush of prematurely whitish hair, her large blue eyes, so direct, so very sharp, the perpetual cigarette that was always in the corner of her mouth. He'd found her dead on the steep stairs that led from the shop up to the living quarters. She'd just keeled over, quite typically, in silence. The papers of the shop, of accounts—all that in perfect order as it always was. Of personal papers, not a sausage. Regarding himself, there were the certificates of his birth, of her legal guardianship, his school records.

There are a lot of funny anomalies in French law, and some of these apply to 'secrets.' It is possible for a woman to have a baby, in a hospital, and legally enforce her own anonymity. Paternity suits, he had often come across them in his work, are knots, bristling with insurmountable difficulties. Many French people go about searching in their genealogies, and find gaps that no one can or will close.

Castang was 'un Parisien,' a native, of a type now rare. The big Paris hospitals in the centre of the city, which used to look after 'the poor', are all now split up in specialised clinics, swarming with professors and microscopes and white-coated lab assistants. There are no girls now who come to have a baby on the ward: there are no Parisiens left.

He was French. Was he? Colleagues, friends, yes, and Vera, have detected many unFrench characteristics. Does he even look French?—what do the French look like? Who's "French" among all the Poles or Basques, Bretons or Corsicans? There was a time when 'les Auvergnats' in Paris declared themselves proudly, wore their clan in their heart and on their face.

Ma tante was French all right. There was a legend that she came from somewhere down in the Bordelais. Jokingly he has called himself the Aquitanian Bastard and Vera too has laughed. Presumably his mother was French—was his father perhaps English? In those days—1944 and subsequent, between his being started and his being born, there were a lot of soldiers about. Who knew? Who'd want to try and find out? He was happy enough in his skin and his identity. Clever, cool, balanced Cathérine had seen to that. But when he came across a story such as this one, of a soldier sent to recover from wounds in the Czech countryside, then he could feel a rough edge, as of old scars of his own, left to heal naturally: they had not been smoothly stitched. Cathérine had known, a woman who knew how to keep her secrets. She'd never married, as far as anyone knew; she had no traceable children. The State, and the Municipality of Paris, had multiplied a lot of paperwork and been damned greedy with it. He himself, in the end, had come in for a share (not much) of the heritage. It had kept him going a few years there.

Ach, who cares? All water under the bridge. One might as well be a Parisien as anything else. Nothing to be ashamed of. He had always sat very loose to all notions of nationality. Home is where the food comes on the table, as the Turks say. It was Vera who'd had trouble with her origins and her belongings. As a civil servant with the Communauté, he was on the way to becoming a Bruxellois, nowadays. The genuine article, like 'Old Klaas,' would deny that—and most indignantly!

A fact remains. He, Henri Castang, had been drafted in a few years back, as an expert in the Praxis of criminal law administration and procedure. The place was stiff with experts in the theory, who wouldn't have known how to draw up a procès-verbal for the theft of Granny Lemarchand's chickens, nor the probability of said-Granny having craftily watered Granny-next-door's asters with a dose of nocturnal weedkiller.

He—Castang—had come up, with a law degree and a facility in written-examinations, into the inspectorate, the officer ranks of the Police Judiciaire. Gained promotion, bright lad. Passed out of the School in Lyon as a junior Commissaire, adjunct grade. Years more, in the criminal brigade, what the English would call CID. Principal Commissaire, a small brigade of his own, in a smallish Picardy city, cheek-by-jowl with the country and the Gendarmerie; that had taught him a lot . . . And then a political mistake, and finding himself in bad odour with his hierarchy, and they'd promoted him again, just to get rid of him. He'd barely avoided getting posted to Djibouti. But back in Paris, Bruxelles IS Djibouti.

No, I am no longer a Parisien.

He's the local expert on crime. He doesn't have much to say about crime. There's an awful lot of it about. Lashing, bloody great truckloads, *waves* of it. Earthquake waves; this frightens the Communauté very much. National governments (subsidiarity is our great new witchword) are very frightened too; they get under the bedclothes, without ever stopping talking. The Communauté talks less but churns out immense floods of statistics, in Bruce, in Luxemburg, in Strasbourg; the three working areas about which everyone complains so. Ton upon ton of paper rolls, not only to but fro, along the line of these three pleasant cities. Castang contributes, alack, to much of this traffic. I write more reports, he admits sadly, than the Cambridge *Studies in Criminality*. Which was in thirty-six volumes the last time he looked; and that was in 1976. Big wave. But then it's a big earthquake.

People ring up—a great deal—to tell him about crime.

Tell the police, he says. And what should one *do* about crime; meaning how to stop it happening to them? He tells them to go live in New York. There the chances of *not* being murdered, raped, robbed or otherwise violently aggressed in the course of your life do not offer odds better than around four-to-one-on. They feel better then. He does not tell them that large areas of Europe, 'Greater' Paris or London, 'peripheral' Frankfurt or Milano, aren't much better.

This is all meaningless, because Castang will not mention the statistics are bullshit, since nobody knows the shadow area. These are the cases-reported. Most people think that the 'known' amounts to around 30 per cent. Sir Leon Radzinowicz, the Cambridge guru who writes such beautiful English, caused scandal by saying that in his view it wasn't much better than fifteen.

He doesn't say; you want him to talk himself out of a good job? Greatly worried people ask him what they should do?

Burglar-alarms went off (alternatively, they didn't) just because somebody touched the windscreen . . .

"Buy a dog. Big dog. Bark. Look fierce. Bite people."

"Castang, Christ, do you know how many tons of dogshit are daily deposited upon the streets of Paris?" (Upon this we have excellent, exact, and smellable statistics.) He shrugs.

"I gotta big dog." He does too, inherited from Lydia; a Malines shepherd, a bitch (but her tubes are tied), blonde and beautiful if not really very bright. He has got very fond of her. Name of Gisela, gentle as a lamb but goes Waah if anything untoward is afoot. The exercising keeps him (and Vera too) rather Fit. She has been taught at last not to get her lead under the bicycle wheel. You see? Discipline, self-discipline: the idea appals people.

He can't give the effective answer. "Live in a small, poor, underpopulated village, in a backward corner of Europe." He'd like to do so himself. What can one say to people?

A week or so ago he was in Karlsruhe. The German Supreme Court, the Bundesgerichtshof, sits there, worrying about the Constitution—some of their decisions are of moment to him. There's a fine palace there.

"Rather large," said Castang deprecatingly.

"Ho," said a German colleague. "The Grand Duke of Baden had a hundred and sixty-four concubines. Imagine that nowadays."

"Spacious," agreed Castang. "That would make for a few months of correspondence with the Ministry of Social Security."

And now here he is, wondering whether he's going to get himself involved in yet another crime. And finding the answer is yes.

Chapter 5

Castang went home. Rather early, to tell the truth. Washing, changing—in the bathroom Vera has been ironing—yes but has she exercised the dog? The iron stands in the bidet, which looks odd. Vera is mildly dotty, and so is he. Both are monuments to sober sanity in comparison with the latest crime statistic to have arrived on his desk. Two Lyonnais bus-drivers; colleagues, friends, possibly neighbours. One shot the other. Utter boredom normally, and you'd only be asking which one had been sleeping with whose wife. What was this doing on his desk? But there's a red-ink memo in the margin saying 'Castang, have you got a file on black magic?' He sat up! Occultism. In this context, he would not instantly have thought of Lyonnais bus-drivers . . . But there it was—chap claims the other put the evil eye upon him.

He left a note. He did *not* envy the judge who would have to instruct this case, nor the Procureur who would have to present it in court. Nor the police of the PJ in Lyon, who were now getting told by a cross examining magistrate to go bone up on witchcraft. Really, after that there was nothing to do but sigh deeply and go home.

The house is silent. Vera has gone out with the dog. Various things have been left about in the kitchen, with a view to an evening meal. It looks like sort-of-kedgeree. Two eggs have been hardboiled and peeled. There are also two kippers, wonderful English invention but of course the English fuck them up by boiling them. Of *course* kippers must be eaten raw—would the English boil smoked salmon? But they must be skinned and boned, and to this end Vera has pointedly left the sharp bendy knife called filet-de-sole. There are also two shallots to be chopped fine. The knife is not very sharp . . . Castang sighed; this is all his job. But one can think, while doing it.

Commissaire Mertens hadn't wanted to show him the file on the little Rogier boy. Fair enough; it was voluminous and this would be a lot of trouble. They were in any event 'official documents' and he himself has no official standing. Friendship is one thing but a hint of reserve is perceptible. Castang could guess that the enquiry, long drawn out, unsatisfactory, reflected no particular credit upon the department: Mertens would be a little touchy about that. Some of the work had been sloppy? Or it could be the examining magistrate, mentioned in passing as a dry and rigid soul, and perhaps 'uneatable.' Like a boiled kipper.

Very well, he'd shake up Anita. Take her by the ears in fact—that's a good Flamand phrase. 'Pak ze bij de lurfen.' And he'd look more closely at Monsieur Rogier, who appears to take it for granted that the police will be horizontal in his presence.

One might start with the attendant, the nanny who accompanied him everywhere. 'Monsieur Jean.' When, a long time ago, Rogier had done his stint as a short-service army officer, this had been his 'ordonnance' in the old military jargon; the soldier who acts as personal servant. Been with his gentleman ever since. Rather a military type even now. 'Sofort Herr Hauptmann'—hands down the seams of his trousers. Monosyllabic, surly even. Take it very softly.

"Madame has asked me to reopen this whole dossier, so that this is with her full knowledge and approval. Monsieur mentioned that? Good, it's unofficial, of course. There's no reason why you should refuse. Is there? I see none. You neither, good."

Sticky, chilly, just the one step from being hostile. Nothing to be surprised at there. A confidential man. Knows more, no doubt, about the household than anyone. And like a governess, a servant and yet not a servant. This sort of social unease always makes for awkwardness. He'd been driver, valet, and when Rogier had his accident the man had done some nursing training 'to look after my gentleman.' No, no diploma. Too much theory and bloody paperwork. Castang sympathised—it's just the same in the police. But one could say he had a pretty good grasp of the praxis, and the physiotherapy.

He had 'a flat' in the basement. That's nice about this kind of big house. Own room, and sittingroom, and bathroom. His evenings are all free, and the weekends. He'd be on call, sure, if he was needed. No, there's no other real servant. Madame cooks, and he gets the same food as the family, takes it on a tray. There's a woman who comes in as parlourmaid, and help-cook, if there are guests, or a party. To serve and such, drinks and so on; that's no part of his work. And the cleaning-woman, of course. Old chap who comes each week for the garden. Family can afford it, huh? He looks after the cars, that's his other main job. Madame's little BMW, he keeps it clean, takes it for service. The big car, that's his. It's a Mercedes, special doors and a platform that lets down so Monsieur has no problems with that, wheelchair and all. So he drives Monsieur to the office.

And then? During the day?

That's confidential. You want to know about that, 'Monsieur had better ask Monsieur.' He was a handyman himself and has acquired some lab-assistant training. But sorry, no answers on that even if you do have Monsieur's permission. That's the sensitive area, and before too, he'd told the police they could jolly well lump it.

Castang knows all about this, from 'taking Anita by the ears.' He knows damn-all about computer engineering, but she holds up her hands and screams.

"They're paranoiac—you've seen nothing."

Castang knows nothing—the bare names of the principal firms. Who is it even? IBM, Siemens, Philips. Bull, Nixdorf. Chang or is it Wang? It's not quite Jesus but it's everything but. And talk about tight-lipped! He's done a bit of telephoning hither and yon.

"Monsieur Rogier?—I'm sorry but it's not company policy to disclose any personal information about collaborators." He understands. This is perfectly plausible. It's a field where industrial espionage would run riot if they didn't stay sewn tight.

Castang didn't need any false beard for a straightforward piece of verification. From 'a bit back' and in his own car—it's Vera's car and that's quite enough of a disguise—the Mercedes station wagon is easy to follow. 'Monsieur Jean' lets down the step, the wheelchair mounts on its own electric power. They scoot off to one of the broad streets that lead up the hill from the Central Station. Here on the door there are a lot of obscure business appellations which could be absolutely anything. The car goes down into the underground garage and that's it. Anita was quite open about it.

"Heavens, I'm not supposed to tell, even you, because that sort of work isn't done in the factory. That's the lab and it's deathly secret. The air is scrubbed. They breathe through masks and worry about microns. It's no good asking Arnold, he just won't speak about it. I can't see how even the FBI could ever get in there, so it's no good asking me. They've pots of money. They've a pool in the basement and Arnold swims there and that's really all I know."

"And you? What do you do during the day?"

"Oh, I have part-time jobs. Just to interest myself really. I do some afternoons at the garden centre. I love plants and flowers—I don't really know anything on the technical side: I just sell things." She made him laugh; nice woman.

"Those things that go red on top, I've even forgotten their name, though at work I blind the housewives with Latin, the Dutch growers come up with new ones every year, white, pink, cream now, as well as scarlet, no not potentilla, it's on the tip of my tongue, shit—of course, poinsettia. Cyclamen. Azaleas, they all die but that's just the point; that they'll come back for more!" She is attractively feminine. "And of course, I'm a perfect mine of information about deutzia or spiraea, there's about a thousand of the buggers, Hillier's catalogue is nothing to me." She has got a lot easier, looser, in his presence. That is a good sign: she is beginning to feel trust. And perhaps, now that the story of her father is out in the open, she has no little secrets to hide.

"And then twice a week, evenings, I go to the hospital and do water-therapy, re-education for people with limb injuries—Arnold swims a lot—it's important that I know how to help as much as I can.

"But I go to the stables and ride. And I play tennis. I lead a very Normal Life," emphasising half serious and half in mockery.

"And I won't ask about lovers," said Castang. "I agreed not to, didn't I, but of course the police did, and at some length."

She 'mantled.' That clear fair skin is quick to blush.

"Oh they were horrid! It was nice of you to go easy on Arnold. And I've agreed too to trust you, haven't I. I'm quite normally constituted. Women aren't nearly as much obsessed with it as men seem to think. I've no lovers, men or women either. I do without—do you understand me?"

"Yes I do. If you were to get extremely tense you'd go to the bathroom. The subject's at an end."

"Thank you," she said in a whisper.

"Oh I have plenty of other things to talk to you about. About Astrid, and about the aunts, and how your little boy got on with his grandfather."

"Anything you like," she said thankfully.

Castang is at home, lounging, in front of the television set. He is only occasionally a rugby fan but is a cousin—he suspects—of a lot of people called Castang with folklore accents, from down there in the South-West. But he's not in the least Patriotic, and is singing 'Flower of Scotland' with much enjoyment. The very last thing he wants is to be patriotic. He is thinking about Commissaire Richard, and about the Footprints.

Richard—immensely experienced, had taught him most of

what he knew—was highly Anglophile, a great believer in
material indices. Great care was required, insisted upon;
meticulous observation, exact measurements, lots and lots of
photographs.

"We're much too sloppy about these things. The blood
samples get muddled up, it was incorrectly labelled, the lab
made a balls-up, and some pisspot expert, self-styled, makes
a fool of you in court and a perfectly good case gets thrown
out. Still, one can overdo all that deduction stuff. The English assemble everything, feed it all into the Incident Room
of theirs, quite often there's so much wood they fail to see
the tree. If you're going to get it on the material evidence
you're likely to get it quick. If not you've this huge mass of
material, you sit there staring at it, and get misled by your
own obsessions. They think we do nothing but 'chercher la
femme.' Remains a good idea. Find the woman and look for
the money. And then often there's no proof? That's where
your material indices will come in. If you've got them im-
peccable you can adduce them as evidence, and a jury will be
impressed. And you get a good mark. Meticulous observation, but don't draw too many goddam conclusions from it."

It had earned him that good mark, once. A manhunt in
snow, in wooded country? That sounded easy, but they'd
found it late. The snow had thawed a bit, and frozen again,
and far too many people had gone trampling around. Even
the tracker dog had got hopelessly confused so that next
morning early when Castang went back there were their own
gigantic boots, and 'the footprints of the gigantic hound.'
Beastly snow too, degenerated into coarse crystals and nasty
frozen crusts to slip upon, but he found a different print and
followed it and photographed it. Dead pine needles had
fallen but it was light and fast and with feet that turned out.
Worn rubber-track shoes with soles that left no recognisable
imprint but he'd gone after them and found the feet which
fitted them, and after some careful work with the meteorol-
ogy reports he'd thought he had a case, and Richard thought
so too; and they had, too.

But here—even if the police had found footprints these had long ago melted.

Jawohl!—Scotland scored and Castang applauded loudly and drummed with his feet and Vera said 'Do you have to be Obstreperous?' Go out tomorrow, shall he, look for some footprints?

Everything about Monsieur Rogier was very plausible. Maybe even perhaps a scrap too much so. The police had been about with tracker dogs but these animals too have been known to cast in a wide circle and end up where they started.

Castang liked him. Impressive, that fine straight bar across the forehead, bone and brow in one uncompromising rejection of the imprecise or inexact. The small keen eyes sharpened by pain endured and mastered, the keen triangular face tense and harsh with determination. A powerful intellect, a strong character. In the go-cart or out, a fast wing three-quarter, a scorer of tries.

It was troubling him; he had a sneaking weakness for amusing crooks. Instincts awoke, nudged him. 'The Fiend'— to quote Vera—'Is at my elbow and tempts me, saying to me, Gobbo!' (Deep, raspy baritone.)

He was beginning to think that the police might have been overawed by this man, so evidently brilliant and so atrociously wounded in his manhood and vigour.

Anita had been voluble.

"Goodness, it's all most mysterious, terribly hush-hush. You see, this is a business simply rife with industrial espionage." Plausible. "They're *very* tight-lipped, and when they have a treasure they guard it like the crown jewels. Of course, when there was the kidnap, that was one of the *first* things thought of. That this was designed to force him to part with secrets: there are literally *millions* at stake." Plausible. "The company took it very seriously and there was even an extra guard for a while. There are electronic things on the gate and alarms everywhere. I even think Jean is armed but I don't ask. He was Arnold's sergeant or something in the army—totally devoted."

"Had you told him before coming to me? Did he object or show hostility?—dragging it all up again."

"He threw doubt. Oh I mean, not on you. On whether it would be of any real use. But he's very patient, you know."

"Your grandparents built the villa?"

"They were rich from steel, textiles; rentiers, you know. The villa went to Astrid—my mother—I'm rather vague, obscure manoeuvres. Dodging death duties, you understand."

"Wait a second, Astrid married old Klaas. He was treated as a criminal, disgraced and even recently imprisoned—how did she get away with that?"

"I hardly know—I wasn't born! Oh there was an awful fuss. She had a very stubborn sort of character. Eigenwijs as the Flamand say, a highly Belgian characteristic. But she died you know, when I was small, of a cancer; I really hardly knew her. We don't seem to be very lucky, do we?"

"Had Astrid brothers and sister—these Tantes you speak of?"

"Oh yes, numerous. They never liked my father, still are greatly disapproving and he has no use for them. But we have a sort of tacit agreement, to avoid quarrelling about it. But why don't you ask him?"

"I'll try," said Castang. "And how did you come to meet Arnold—your husband?"

"Oh he was already with the company." And she named it. And there was a record of it; he was with them then; engineering student. But from the personnel management Castang got the deep-freeze act. 'Monsieur Rogier has not been with us for some time.'

'How *much* time?'

'It is not our policy to disclose this type of detail.'

'That's their familiar tight-lighted stuff,' said Anita. Oh yes, it's plausible, all right. "And he doesn't go to the *offices* of course. The research lab is *very* strictly guarded and quite possibly a nobody like that wouldn't even know."

And 'Monsieur Jean?' He might well be carrying a gun—but not while Castang was around . . .

There's never any shortage of fancy rackets, thought Monsieur Castang (been told off, enough times, by Commissaire Richard—and many others!—for this enthusiasm towards fancy scenarios.)

There's always a nice line in forging paper. As fast as it's rumbled the imaginative crook thinks of more—a good computer designer wouldn't come amiss, hm? One does wish one knew more about the reproduction processes. Not just passports but credit cards, residence permits, marriage certificates, driving licenses, all that stuff for creating a nice clean identity within the Federal Republic. And there's a long queue of Poles and Russians anxious to pay in cash. Bills of lading; authentifications for everything you can think of from fine art to weapons systems.

It's not in Castang's line. It's not, even remotely, within his skills. Within the span of his career, the Police Judiciaire had got ever more compartmentalised. He remembered Carlotta Salès showing him how you could use a computer to fake a picture with such accuracy as to defeat an expert and all but the most elaborate of detection methods. That was the trick; such equipment is rare and exceedingly expensive, so that only major museums have it. You wouldn't adopt such methods to try passing a major master. You'd do a minor master so as to fox even an experienced dealer. Or engravings, in 'fairly good' states. You'd need some raw materials (not perhaps very much) and you'd need accomplices.

There was the information market. Since the days when boys of fourteen broke into the Pentagon and found themselves able to manipulate all sorts of goodies, from star-wars on down to confidential medical records, the most elaborate guard systems had been devised. Yet however sophisticated the locks, there's a man who designs, programmes and installs them. Did it follow that another man, equally gifted, could search, detect, forestall, impersonate? He didn't know . . . he knows nothing of these machines but he knows a lot about prisons. There are locks; there are keys; and there are men who keep them. There is no security system that cannot be penetrated.

There are drugs, and isn't that the quickest, easiest, sim-

plest racket of them all? He is no more of a chemist than he
is an electronician, but hasn't it all the same beginning?
Crack, angel dust, all morphine-base, no? You begin with
your poppy juice, your coca-plants, and from there on it's a
question of how much you refine. The purer, then the
smaller, the lighter, the less messy or obtrusive.

You don't have your lab here though, do you? Or perhaps
you do, and bring your product in from Antwerp in a plain
van. But you need chemicals, you've waste, you've a massive stink. You can't just shove it all down the lavatory and
into the air-conditioning: quite a crude police sniffer would
detect it. No, you'd set up your refinery in Sierra Leone or
wherever, and bring in refined product. Everyone knows that
a kilo of that goes a very long way, and that for one carrier
caught at the airport a hundred walk through—your profit is
such that you don't in the least care.

But what is the point then of your computer cover? Sure,
good communications are vital to your distribution network,
but that needs no sophisticated equipment surely? An ordinary fax machine and a code.

The absurdity is that Castang's creating all these fairy-
stories, and on his own television screen is just a rugby
match. Quite good rugby; some skilful running of the ball
out of defence, some good tactical kicking in attack, but
these are two evenly matched teams and nothing much is
Happening. There, the French have scored. They'd kept
dropping the ball; habit of theirs; exactly like himself.

The industrial espionage thing would be the most probable. If the fellow is as brilliant an engineer as they claim, the
idea very likely would be to build a machine more advanced
than were marketed, use it to crack people's codes, and sell
the result to what is no doubt an eager and a lucrative market.

Is this illegal? Since both the civil and the penal codes
were thought out for the days of dipping the pen in the
inkwell he has really very little idea—or interest—whether it
is or not. Other Community brains, more massive than his
own, are occupied with this sort of question.

Quite frankly, whatever Monsieur Arnold Rogier is up to in his electronically swept and scrubbed and micron-filtered basement it is none of Castang's goddamned business!

He isn't any sort of private eye. He is no longer even a practising police officer. He has been asked—in good faith—by a woman to try and find out what has happened to her small son. All else is irrelevant. For Castang to try and 'spy' on her husband is about as sensible as hustling into white shorts and the bullet-proof jockstrap. Jumping out there on to the field and telling the French team it'll be all right now, boys, Stand Tall, I'm your new genius out-half.

Oh a Lovely sweeping movement, that scrum-half is the best there is, they're going to go over—they *have*. I told you so, those clowns out there are going to get beaten. Quite as usual; by their own terror of being beaten even more than by a better and more confident team. Or that marvellous Edinburgh crowd.

He looked at Vera. Reading, absorbed, deaf-to-rugby. Upright, twisting her hair, sitting comfortably as only women can with one leg tucked up under her: his would fall asleep, he'd leap out of his chair Flowering for Scotland and fall straight upon his nose. Not her.

"We're going to Czechland," he said. "Not Slovakia."

"I don't want to go there," said Vera, scratching her bottom.

Chapter 6

Advance like a prudent bureaucrat, hastening slowly. There are colleagues to consult, phonecalls to make. The medical dossiers of Waffen-SS officers?

"That's a—did you say one of the foreign divisions; Charlemagne was it? Oh dear, that might be anywhere. Some were destroyed—the Russians got a lot and the Americans nosed about looking for war criminals. What sentimental novelists called the Odessa Gang spirited away a good few, and then naturally the Stasi, for purposes of their own . . . really, Castang, can't you arrange for something a little less Folklore?"

But not all archivists are the dusty obstructionists of legend. Some are just lazy. Even within the Community some will be helpful. Voices cheered up when he mentioned hospitals, convalescent homes, oho, SS Rest and Recuperation Centres, now which one?

"Czech, Hungarian, they ought to have that. Not computerised of course, no way, quelle idée; you'll have to burrow down like a dachshund into mountains of lovely smelly old brown paper.

"Let's see, can't possibly be Koblenz. Würzburg maybe, hold the line would you, Castang, while I look it up . . . Regensburg's your place.

"I've no idea, my boy. I've an address, for you to address yourself to, and that's it."

* * *

"Regensburg," said Vera. "That's a fearful place."

"How, fearful?" Castang has never been there.

"Just fearful." Vera has never been either. "Ludwig Bemelmans came from there, speaks of pot-de-chambre humour and general smallmindedness."

"That applies to anywhere. It is Ober-Bayern or Nieder-Bayern?"

"Don't know, but very Bayerisch."

Their own archives—the atlas, mostly—spoke of a largish, pleasant and prosperous city on the Donau. Picturesque medieval Altstadt, largely unspoiled. Fine (late-gothic) cathedral, lots of churches, lots of beer: to this last, Ludwig Bemelmans' grandfather a notable contributor.

"Sounds just like Strasbourg". This is one of the Community cities and Castang knows it well; teases French colleagues by referring to it as "Strassburg."

"More or less on our way," deep in the autobahn map.

"Rather less than more." Vera, over his shoulder.

"No, look, it will be Nürnberg anyhow, on the way to your lovely Czechland. Not going to go all the way over there to Dresden. Whip through—here—to Pilsen. Regensburg's only just down the road".

"Nothing on the autobahn is ever just down the road." Cross about the teasing over her 'lovely Czechland' which it both is and isn't.

All of Vera's gloomy predictions came true next day.

They started in high fettle, because of 'some free days' which Castang saves up for occasions when one can't stand the sight of home or work. Not quite to the extent of the Italian bureaucrat who hadn't taken a holiday in the last twenty-eight years, and the tribunal bade him enjoy nine hundred days of paid leave. But he generally has ten or so in hand. And Vera was in a good mood.

> 'I like to climb an apple tree
> Though apples green are bad for me,
> I'll be as sick as I can be—
> It's foolish but it's fun.'

Not that she looks or even sounds like Shirley Temple. Just bubbling a little. And crossing the border into Germany she found a phrase.

" 'What I've always really wanted, being off on the Road again with dwarves.' "

"Who's a Dwarf?" asked Castang, stung.

"No no—paraphrase from Professor Tolkien."

Then there was the car, new enough still to be a pleasant toy. Now that the children are grown up, it can be smaller and more sportive. One would rather like a Mercedes coupé, which even Vera admits to be pretty, but alas, Expensive, Eh? All other cars are condemned for being ugly. A few things to which Castang is mechanically-speaking fairly partial were Hideous. Finally, a small Alfa, denounced and even hated for the first three days, has now awoken love. It doesn't compete on the autobahn with the Fast Brothers but those (Vera consoles herself) will all get stolen soon. It is wiry though, whips along, eats many boring German kilometres. Settled Gloom does not appear until shortly before Nürnberg, where it is discovered that the autobahn map (Castang has been steering point-to-point with success and fair confidence) has unaccountably been left behind. Tedious numbers of Autobahn-Kreuz signs appear, each obscured as is their habit by a monstrous Lastwagen on the slow lane at just the wrong moment.

It has started to pour with rain. Everything is swathed in mist. Nothing can be seen but the Road—discouraging—and a great many pine trees, all suffering from acid rain disease. They keep going uphill. They are somewhere in the Bayerische Wald.

"Did that one say Est, or Süd?" irritably. "Where the bloody hell are we?" Vera is no help. She has got into a fantod of depression. The Road winds ever on and on, as Professor Tolkien unnecessarily reminds us, but she was in a black pit. There is nobody alive left in the world, and she is about to fall off the edge of it.

"Oh do stop in a dorp."

"There isn't any dorp. Oh good, that one said something.

Kept on saying Pilsen. Don't want to go to Pilsen; not yet anyhow."

This is not a helpful part of the world. There are no rest stops by the side of the road, not even a petrol pump, not even that so-English sign of encouragement that says 'WC 5 km.' Dorpen have all uncouth names like Egg and Ill. This is a nasty Wald, inhabited by excessively hostile dwarves, trolls, etcetera. Even Castang was beginning to need a beer very badly indeed. How nice to discover the village and find a pub. Eminent French gastronomes, kind Mr. Gault and dear Mr. Millau, have been here, and have written on the door that this is one of the five hundred best pubs in Germany and what's more the food has 13–20. Vera made an enormous lunch. Castang also drank a great deal.

So then she had to drive. It is quite a short way to Regensburg. The rain has stopped. The sun is mopping up the mist. All is well. Castang studies brewery wagons. These, in Germany, are many. They have all an addiction to antique ornate red lettering on a white background, coats-of-arms, lengthy descriptions of their therapeutic virtues. One and all stem from pure Alpine rills: not a single one from water that has been twenty times through what the French call les voies urinaires. Guided by twin gothic spires Vera dived into the Old Town of Regensburg.

This was a mistake. One mustn't bring a car in here: even a tiny Alfa finds itself in gothic Gässe where one can't go forward, can't go backward, can't turn round. Like Strasbourg only much more so. One is obliged to dive into the bowels of the Parkhaus, thence to carry one's luggage by hand to hotels called the Alte Post and the Rode Hahn, with Biedermeier furniture but mercifully modern plumbing. Spirits below zero.

Terribly facetious all this; over-jaunty, Castang. He agrees. All my fault, he said ruefully. "The truth, I'm afraid, is that I hadn't taken any of this business seriously enough. I thought it would be downright impossible, or perhaps very easy. It looked like a holiday. They were paying me a generous fee, and expenses, for a line of enquiry nobody seemed to have thought of. You quite often find these, in police work. They look promising at first and then peter out. I didn't care either way, to my sorrow.

'Vera was jaunty too, poor girl. It was because she wasn't looking forward to the Czech Republic at all. You see, she knew what it would be like, and I didn't. She didn't want to come and I twisted her arm to make it easier for myself, having an interpreter along.

'I was reasoning, you see; fatal police habit. Negative capability, that's the thing. Oh, it's a concept of Vera's. A capacity for doubt, for not seeing, not understanding, without that stupid clutching at fact or logic.

'I learn. But boy, do I learn the hard way.'

Soothed by beer and medieval architecture he became less irritable.

"Why are there so many churches in places like this?"

"It is a people of profound simplicity, poor and hardworking and believing very strongly in God."

"Well so do I believe in God but without quite so many churches."

Archives were found, indeed, in a strongly archival, redolently ecclesiastical angle between two of them. And the answers to Castang's queries were very easy; no trouble at all.

"An SS Rest and Recup? Czech? A lake somewhere in the mountains. North, d'you think, or south? I mean up towards the Polish border—or down towards Austria?"

"Not too far from the Danube or so he thought."

"That will be the Lipno See. There was a village there, don't ask me what they call it in Czech though. Rather a complicated part of the world. Look, all along here is the Bayerische Wald, right? Chain of hills, quite high, good winter-sport. Well, if you were to go over the far side, which isn't as easy as it looks, that would be the Böhmische Wald, okay? This big See there in the hills."

The Seacoast of Bohemia, thought Castang madly. But never mind being Literary because Germans call anything a See, from a pond on up.

"No no, quite big, but sort of zigzag because of all these

damned hills. The local town they call now Ceske Budjewice but what we call it is Budweis. That's right; where the beer comes from. Know your chap's name? We can look him up."

"Nicolaas de Roodt, might not have been his name then."

"And in forty-three? Or maybe forty-four?"

"He was vague about the year but he knew it was summer. Normal I'd think, when you're on the Russian front."

"We'll try forty-three first. Sure, here we are. Post-operative treatment for bullet wounds, woo, he'd been badly shot up, must have had a terrific constitution. Tank captain, that sound right?"

"That's him."

So that old Klaas had told the truth. And if exact about this, wasn't it also probable that Ingrid would be exact, as well as true?

"Military area. Even now I don't think they'll let you in, anywhere round here, you'll have to go round by Pilsen, or else all the way down into Austria past Passau."

Never mind, he'd got it, and earned his Tafelspitz too.

"Where's the best place, for boiled beef and horseradish?"

'I'm a northerner,' remembered Castang. 'I don't belong in southern towns. Find them too hot, apart from all else. Hamburg or Glasgow, I'm at home. Copenhagen—St. Petersburg. But Beirut, even Marseille—no, d'you know what I mean? Out of my skin, my bones start feeling uneasy. Wouldn't have wanted to stay-behind-in-Casablanca . . . Vera's more of a southerner. Good, I love Barcelona too but she likes places like Istanbul which I don't feel I understand.

'These Mittel-Europa towns, which are hot like hell in summer and cold as charity in the wintertime, I'm in two minds. München says, it's yes and no. If I had to choose a German city to live in then it would be Berlin. These river-valley towns, be they Rhein or Donau, too humid. Regensburg. Or Strasbourg, all right to sit on a terrace and drink beer. But to work in . . .' He slept well though, in his repro-duction-Biedermeier bed at the Alte Post, even if woken at

the crack of dawn by an extraordinary racket in the Platz outside.

"Good God," he said to Vera, who is slow getting out of
bed. "There's a crazy outside, sitting by the fountain and
wearing a red hat. A rather sinister thing—he's beating on a
Tin Drum."

"Not a dwarf, I hope," said Vera, midway between Günter
Grass and Professor Tolkien. "That would be a bit much."

Still—a German breakfast. Castang claims that only in
Germany can you get a proper breakfast. The ghastly English
bacon-and-egg slowly simmered in lukewarm marge, the
limp-and-greasy French croissant, that over-blackened ratshit
coffee, no no, they may overdo the fruit and nut squirrelfood
(which Vera eats) but Germans are the only people who
know how to bake bread. So that greatly refreshed he points
the car towards the Czech Republic. A long way uphill over
this damned Wald, and it keeps saying 'Pilsen 150 km' but
the Alfa motor, beautifully engineered piece of Italian art,
breathes strongly, and even Vera . . . Yesterday she was convinced that she was in another world which did not move;
that the autobahn went in circles; that she had to get out and
pee in bushes; that these were horrible wet bushes. Today all
is well. She sings and it isn't Shirley Temple. 'South of the
Border, Down Mexico Way.'

No Rio Grande, but here *is* the border.

"If and when you come back this way," said the German
guard, "you might perhaps be very kind and put yourself on
the right side of the road." Chastened, Castang trundled on to
the Czechs, who looked at his passport, sneered, and said
'Out of Date.' Sagely, Vera said nothing.

"Oh good heavens." The bigger the bureaucrat the harder
they fall.

"Pull in to the side of the road." Oh dear, Vera is looking
highly sarcastic. They are ushered towards a nasty, smelly
sort of hut. There are two Czech officers with lieutenant's
stars. One is tall, fair, and has a sense of humour. The other
is blackavised, moustached, bureaucratic; no sense of humour whatever.

"I am guilty, Herr Kapitän," wailed Castang in a high soprano.

"Makes no odds. Zurück." Vera who has a healthy respect for the Czech Army keeps her mouth shut, despite 'But I only came on and sang' ('The Unlucky Family').

"Where are you going—Prag?"

"No—er—uh, Budweis, a small piece of business, maybe two days." The fair one sniggered, they looked at each other, the dark one shrugged his shoulders.

"Where you go out then—Passau? All right then, when they ask why no stamp in your pass you say nobody control you. You weren't here. You come in by Dresden. And now you fuck off quick. Vanish!"

We must present, from the back, an exceedingly self-conscious sight, thought Castang. Myself endeavouring to appear nonchalant; Vera with difficulty repressing giggles, but very strained, this merry laughter. Poor girl, at the sight of a Czech uniform fear crawls all the way down her back.

"Would you like to drive?" he asked. "He could just as easily have turned us back. A right nelly I'd have felt. And do."

This part of the land is black and unprepossessing. Even in spring it will be grim and muddy. Bits of the road are patched and pitted, in towns here and there cobblestoned. Large lumps of rusty machinery lie about. One could be in Lens or Douai, or a hundred such tough towns anywhere from Tyneside to Spanish Asturia, where coal is mined and iron forged, and a hardy, good-humoured, unmistakeably European people accepts that life is all work, poverty is endemic, and just like anywhere else the rich get richer while we have only one slogan: Hold On. We're further east so that the languages go a bit funny to our ears—PLZN how are you, sounds like Hebrew—but otherwise it's Valenciennes and you'd better remember that.

Those will be the Skoda works. A car as well turned out and as imaginatively engineered as anything from Fiat or Renault. The people look as well dressed, as well nourished as anywhere. Trams a bit antique, but any more so than they would in Lanark or Lisbon? Sure people are poor. And in Europe's heartland, on the streets of Paris and London, you will find them too, and aplenty. What is missing, here?

He had asked Vera to drive—she is doing so smoothly and competently—so that he can sharpen his wits, because here is where he must keep them about him; scratch the sensitivities free of rust, change the clogged old lubricating oil of bureaucratic habit. That, boy, is what you're here for. Like in the old days. You have been poor too. You have come home to cabbage and lace curtains and the noise of the children, and the racket of the radio through a thin party wall, and your one idea was to get your boots off, have your wife bring you a beer—if there is any.

In his own life, the missing element had been vulgarity, the gaudiness of furniture and decoration among people who have no taste beyond being cheerful. The bright crocheted cushion in the back of the car and the dancing dolly on the windscreen. And what's taste? He had it because his aunt had it? Vera has it and Czechs have it particularly, more even than in Spain or Italy? A junior police inspector in France was not at all well paid; they have been poor. Vera would rather an old oriental rug, secondhand and half worn out, to brand-new synthetic carpeting: their harmony on this sort of point had been a strong factor in their happiness. It would be the same, wouldn't it, if they had both wanted a doll in Andalusian costume to sit on a flounced divan cover.

Entertainment is missing. Drive through some tough mining town (never mind the south, think of Mons or Longwy; he wished he knew more of England, but there must be dozens such). There's a pub at every corner; shabby they might be but glowing, no, with companionship and a coal fire? If—here—things are as we knew them in 1950, wouldn't there be wood still to a bar counter, painted china beerpulls, some polished brass trelliswork and a lot of mirrors? Jesus—Pilsen—isn't this the most famous beer town in the world? In the remotest village of Holland you walk in and you ask for a pils. Is this what forty years of communism have done?

It was above all a puritanical form of government and fun seems to have been the element most rigorously excluded. There are grim little houses marked 'Bistrot' or 'Kaverna,' but they do not look at all forthcoming. Even more depressing are the sad notices saying 'Erotic Club.' What pinched housewives take their clothes off there to make the month's end a little less meagre? Some decidedly pasty girls, heavy-legged and bolster-breasted, will here display spangled underclothes and slack pale pink nipples, a bulge of thigh and peroxided pubic hair; it doesn't bear thinking of. He looks at Vera, beside him, frowning in concentration for the school-children swarming on the pavements and spilling into the roadway. Her bony bottom is like a frog's. Her shallow breasts have nourished two greedy great brats. Her belly is lined, she has saltcellars under her throat. And she is Czechly puritanical; she still puts on her nightdress before dragging her knickers off under it. But give her three glasses of champagne and she'll do a striptease to put you on the edge of your chair and to which the weary professionalism of the Crazy Horse has only suffocating boredom to offer. A very gifted people, Czechs.

Miracles also happen. Vera has to concentrate upon the road, to point the little Alfa with scrupulous exactitude. This is because in Western Europe even a winding country road will be policed—to use a Castang word: he means the white stripe down the middle and on each side, to keep you disciplined. The signs, as for a six-year-old in elementary-school, for bend and crossing, hump and railway line, slow and caution: like a good obedient child you learned them all off by heart before they'd give you your license and indeed throughout your entire life your Government expects you to attend elementary-school. You aren't there to Think; just to Conform: it's all very comforting and womblike. Here nobody says 'Soft Shoulders' since they all are; or 'No Lateral Markings' since there aren't any: there's just mud and you are supposed to be an adult in charge of a car.

Miracle is an overstatement; but of course: in the police world they are infrequent. Metaphorically at least he rubbed his eyes because—quite abruptly—the whole land changed: had they crossed an invisible frontier where there were no guards, passports, barriers, squalid huts or German-registered cars, and there wasn't even the shadow of a prostitute hanging about or even anyone anxious to change money? The road was no longer muddy; there was a white line down the middle and arrows saying you should hold to your near side; trim verges with painted pickets and cats' eyes.

"Am I imagining this?"

"No," said Vera.

Sun shone upon a rolling landscape, tilled and cherished by farmers who know their job and neither need nor want any telling what is or what isn't politically correct. And on the westerly horizon lay a shapely range of low mountain. One looked for a homely word; one had to make do with 'exquisite', however affected it might sound. Castang dropped all irritable fatigue: he felt his vision cleansed and refreshed.

Budweis: Castang calls it this since in Czech it's difficult to say. Not because he thinks the Austrian Empire still exists. It's a name known all over the world. This is the real one, and it's in Minneapolis that you must search for the illusion.

Castang will be much persecuted still, by his own illusions.

Chapter 7

They can both be forgiven; the day and the road had been too long, and both were more tired than they knew. The feeling that one is in a never-never land becomes strong, and acidly Castang began talking about 'Jamais-jamais pays'.

"They should have stayed in the Hapsburg Empire. Then we'd know where we stood." Yes, like the boxing manager who said after the fight 'We should have stood in bed.' The viewpoint is understandable. Austria, like Great Britain, has become very small, and Austrians like many British people have not grown accustomed to the idea that the Empire is no more. If, in the city of Wien, you search for the highway to Bratislava and the Slovak border (it is over the Marchfeld, the historic battlefield of Wagram) you will not find it. Frustrated, you begin to ask your way, and the Viennese look at you bemused. At last light dawns. "Oh—you mean Pressburg." Silesia too is packed with places once German, and now they all have Polish names. Eastern Europe is full of the dispossessed, and old habits die hard. Over all of this land lie shadows of darkness and tragedy, and Castang took long to learn the lessons.

Call it Budweis if you like it makes no difference. A southern baroque town with remnants of much beauty to it. The first lesson for Castang is to try and remember what German towns—many French and English towns—looked like in the 1950s. A lot of these old cities had been bombed. Solidly built, historic centres had a gaptoothed look but once the rubble had been tidied could be seen as recognisable and even more or less intact. Even at their worst—as in Warsaw—matters could be restored. But closely surrounding, and pressing in upon narrow historic streets, ugly and flimsy jerrybuilding was thrown up in haste, and since nothing lasts as long as the provisional, a great many hideous cardboard boxes were still there twenty years after, and a great many people had to live in them. Mostly now they have been replaced by prosperous modern buildings if still in very dubious taste, but not in the East.

So that in Budweis there is a lovely Altstadt, but it is ringed close about with municipal housing of the bleakest sort. Vera headed for the pretty group of spires and towers, parked the car by water with swans upon it, and they got out to stretch the leg, yawn and find one's bearings, wanting to get rid of car and cases, have a wash and be assured of an anchorage. "I'll ask," said the Czech-speaker, diving in to the greengrocers.

"Through here and then left along the big boulevard and there's a great big tower like a Holiday Inn but before that there's a smaller place done up fresh and one eats well there." They ranged up and down the boulevard three times: there was the big tower but of the 'nice place' . . . ? "Sure," said the man at the stall selling hot dogs, "just along, you can't miss it."

"Jamais-jamais pays," said Castang nastily. "Me for the tower; it doesn't look about to fall down and I want Food."

"Very odd," said Vera, much vexed. A surreal, not to say hysterical, evening followed. The tower was a joke. Western specification, not to say luxurious, but the execution distinctly communist. It's the commonplace of Eastern Europe, but Castang had not been here before, hadn't made the effort of imaginative adjustment, multiplied sarcasms. Soon, Vera was near crying.

She is a proud woman. She has stopped being ashamed of her Czechness and is the more proud of it in consequence, and touchy about it. She is sure that all the foreigners sit here guffawing and taking the piss. And of course Castang Is.

Some Czechs who have been many times among the Wessies have looked about them, taken lavish notes, said 'Good formula; we'll do it like that', and then Ossie workmen moved in and made a balls of it. Of Course the lavatory doesn't work and the bedroom mirror distorts like something in a funfair, and all the light switches have been put on crooked. But the window opens and it gives a lovely view; what more would one ask for? It's raining again and they're too tired to go out, descend to an impressive Restaurant. He gets Restored by local plonk called Frankovka, but the food goes on being comic, the veal medallion turns out pork and the waitress has a very tight miniskirt indeed in an odd crushed-velvet kind of material that his eye rests upon in a clinging manner offensive to his wife.

Anthony Powell remarks of his narrator that he is too young to understand how petty minor irritations can suddenly cumulate in an outburst of unreasoning red rage: he could have added that small humiliations convey the same consequence. Vera's laughter has been getting steadily more painful and Castang overdid facetious sarcasms. He offered to make love to her, which she wanted badly; she threw things, and howled.

I have made a very bad start, he told himself, in the watches of the night.

Breakfast was a great deal better, in a pretty arched room, white and decorated with green leaves. In classic communist style there were seven waiters and two waitresses, all smartly uniformed and all doing nothing whatever (since the service is help-oneself), but he was careful not to comment.

"I'll ask the girl about the Lipno See." This is a bit press-on after three cups of coffee.

"Isn't it a pity," very mildly; she is ashamed of outbursts, "not to look at the Altstadt? It's said to be worth the trouble."

"I quite agree," if anything over-conciliatory.

And outside Police Headquarters, "*That*'s the place to park the car."

It is not like Regensburg. Seventeenth-century arcades lead to a lovely big eighteenth-century square, there is lots of space and exuberant, flamboyant bohemian baroque; did them both no end of good. Vera bought champagne glasses; as an afterthought, sherry glasses, both extremely pretty, and they had lunch in the Hotel Svan which is also called the Silver Bells and is agreeably Hapsburg in style.

Police Headquarters are housed in quite a nice ochre-coloured building. Naturally, Castang could not resist opening the door to see what was inside, on the pretext of asking his way. It was pitch dark, decidedly dank and cobwebby, and no cop to be seen. Tja, the secret police must be some place else. Fine collection though of Skodas outside, from the very new, which only the police and blackmarketeers can afford, to the 1950 models much too well built to throw away.

The girl had been helpful about the Lipno See: he'd quite expected her to say she'd never heard of it. One took the Linz road, one branched off thus; there were three villages whose names she wrote down but sorry, she couldn't remember what order they came in; it's quite a big complicated See. Well-lunched and slightly drunk, the Alfa looking dirty and oddly hangdog—now we're off at last to do some real work.

"One drives up into the hills. Incidentally we can get out this way, if we want. Village called Whisky Bread—that's not what the Czechs call it—and a frontier crossing straight down to Linz if we want it."

"Do we want it? I thought we were looking for a woman called Ingrid; do you think there's any chance of finding her?"

"Complicated question. We might and we might not. We might find something else altogether. If the natives are hostile, that's what you've come along for. I'm ready now for any sort of surprise, either way. On the other hand, the Czech Republic is not conspicuous for the creature comforts."

"Are those what you want?" asked Vera humbly.

"I don't think I really know what I want," said Castang. "Look, there's the See." There was not much to be made out, and that much lost going again downhill, but the glimpse of a sheet of water and wooded headlands was reassuring; there really was a lake. Quite soon indeed they came to a village, hailed as one of the names written down by the hotel girl, but primitive, muddy and uninviting; farmyardy enough to be promptly named the Poop Dorp. Here too the road branched.

"Mm—try left." It climbed again, wound through pine forest. Scattered settlements appeared on the bluffs leading down to the lakeshore, and notices saying 'Hotel'. There were clumps of tiny holiday dwellings, like the wooden huts on garden allotments. In summer, plainly, there would be a large population but all was now closed, bleak and empty. The lake was large but in shape irregular, a jumble of capes, bays, inlets.

"This isn't getting us anywhere—but we'll just look at—is it a hotel? Looks more like a stable."

"Nonsense," said Vera. "But by the looks of it one of those Reserved for Party Members places."

"Nothing for us. Back to the poop dorp, and we'll try the other road."

This was almost instantly more promising since it followed the shore, ran out on to a long bridge crossing the lake at a bottleneck and the far shore was lower, dotted with chalets, little boats were beached and they crossed a railway line; this was evidently leading to a place of some size, and rounding a curve Castang let out a bark of satisfaction. There was a large, rambling village. Small factories gave local employment and even in winter there was an air of animation and some prosperity. At the centre larger buildings, of a pompous municipal sort, were grouped around a church and a little public garden, and here Castang parked. Down towards the shore were shops and a group of low concrete buildings of blockhouse aspect, distinctly communist in architecture and depressing in flavour, but bearing signs announcing lodging, refreshment, entertainment: a Nightclub so please you, and Gambling. All this to be sure looks miserable and ramshackle, but there was still ice on the lake. In summer it would be very different and even now a gleam of sun lent a sparkle to the scene. With an air of knowing what he's doing Castang marched towards a sombre building with notices outside the door; not maybe a Town Hall but certainly a centre of municipal administration. Vera followed, a bit dubious but ever Willing.

He has been in so many of these offices, in provincial France identical, in Spain or Portugal no different. In some small town in the highlands of Scotland the look and the smell would no doubt be exactly the same. The paint is always poop-colour, a muddy sort of ochre; there are dark green file cabinets with the look of nothing inside, but a great deal of paper in piles on tables, much of it browning at the edges. Little metal trees hold rubber stamps; the inkpads are always worn out, so that the Functionary must press hard and often before he visas your permit, and there are quite as many permits here as in France. The Func, here a neat, clean old man with a grey shirt buttoned at the collar and a day's silver stubble on his jaw, rests his behind upon a dubious-looking cushion; there is a tendency towards empty coffee-cups with a glazed varnish-like sediment within, as though they had been there a very long time, to worn-out linoleum and dusty windows, to the classic func atmosphere of lethargy, suspicion and every possible obstruction, and inevitably there is the air of the building itself having been designed for quite another purpose. A convent, probably, and nun-like activities of elementary-school or old-folks' home, and a fishy stuffy smell. Why else these peculiar gothic arches, these yellow pitchpine doors, these dank interminable passages, these battered firebuckets full of dirty sand and cigarette ends?

"Grüss Gott," said Castang cheerfully, loving all this and perfectly at home. Layer upon layer, here; further back are the tax-collectors; further still, the secret police.

They had a few words of German but Vera has to interpret, her 'literate' Czech and Slovak accent arousing as usual local distrust: Castang turning on lots of synthetic charm, like the classic baby, falsely-genial in-a-knitted-coat.

"I'm anxious to find the whereabouts of a lady who I'm pretty sure lived around here and perhaps still does, so that I'm hoping you can help me."

"Police?" said the old man politely; they are all still unerring at the identification, even after some years. "You've the necessary papers?"

"No no, it's nothing of any criminal nature. What we call an enquiry in the interest of the family—you'll have a similar nomenclature."

"To what purpose?"

"As you know they don't always tell us, but it's a safe guess there's money involved. Heritage perhaps? Long-lost relatives in the West. Last seen or heard-of in wartime, but now that the frontiers are open people try and regain contact. Your records ought to tell us. I've only been instructed to find an address and verify an identity. I realise of course this means a lot of tedious search so I hope you don't mind my trying to be cooperative." And Castang produces his trump card, a very simple one. He has experience. Six bottles of whisky had been stowed in the back of the Alfa.

They were intact too, if it had been a close squeak with the frontier guards who took a dislike to his passport. This one vanished with the speed municipal authorities can bring to such transactions. Not about to hold a party round the teatable. It brought about a thaw, though.

"You don't have much to go on. Ingrid, that's not such a common name here. But without a family name . . ."

"It struck me that it might be an assumed name. What I have though is a photo of her as a girl; would that be any use, think you?"

The official thought about it. "Wartime," he said sadly. Then he got an idea, went to the door, but no further in case they stole any valuable property, and bawled "Marta!"

Presently an old woman came in; one couldn't easily say what role she would play in the administration. A kind of janitor perhaps, emptying wastepaper baskets because she looked the sort of old woman who in France arranges chairs in churches; black dress of some shiny material, handknitted black cardigan, and man's shoes. The sharp look too; not going to miss anyone who lights a candle without putting a penny in the box. The man held out the photo.

"From a long time ago; perhaps when the Germans were here. You who know everyone—think about it, tell us whether you can recognise that face."

"Perhaps," said Castang slowly so that Vera could repeat, "when wounded soldiers were sent here to get fit again. A nurse maybe because the man who kept that photo was a soldier and he kept it through two years of war, and ever since . . . A mark," he added in an undertone, and Vera scrabbled in her bag.

Too late, Castang wondered whether that was wrong. Did that humiliate either woman? No no, because the old girl took a good look, as though about to spit on it for luck, and said, "Thank you, kind lady." In the Czech countryside, a mark is still a lot. She took another good look then, trying it with her glasses on and then at arm's length pushing them up, and gave a sudden brilliant smile. This turned into a broad cackle of laughter. There's no mistaking this nor faking it, thought Castang, who has seen a lot of people pretending not to recognise photos. There are clichés, of the 'recognition dawns' kind, there is a 'know this but can't quite bring it home,' but this was a 'no error I do'. He felt a flood of relief. Getting lucky again at last. Put his hand in his pocket, which he should have done earlier. This was a two-mark by the feel. Hell, a bottle of whiskey costs thirty ∴ . . The old woman was still laughing.

"I was young and pretty too. You wouldn't think it now, would you? Nix nurse. Liked the soldiers though, all right."

"Come on then, Marta, don't mess about," said the old man with a sharp authority that needed no translating.

"Is she still alive?" asked Castang, thinking tja—'they stay behind in Casablanca'. The old girl was still wiping her eyes on her sleeve.

"That's Frau Severing." Again, no translation needed: he's not beginning to understand Czech, but his wits are sharpening.

"Are you sure?" put in Vera, but he had heard the note of surprise, perhaps of consternation.

"Sure I'm sure. Isn't she my age?"

"All right, Marta. That will do," said the old man. And as Castang brought his hand out of his pocket "Marta! It would be as well, I think, not to talk about this." She went off highly delighted, and not only with the double tip.

The man held his hands up, dropped them on the table, a universal gesture of uncertainty, irresolution. He is wondering, thought Castang, whether to mention this to the police. Or is it a juicy scrap of village gossip? Or is it a moment for discretion? He was perhaps the secretary of the administration. He has influence, some power, no real authority. He was thinking too about the whiskey, which might 'get mentioned'. Not a Sweetener. Just a Way-Smoother.

"Well. That's a bit of a surprise. I should have seen that but there—I'm not old enough to have known her then.

"Well. There's no law against talking to people, and you say that's all you want. No police matter, you said. And you're sure of that? You see, Mrs. Severing is something of a—a notability, I think you might call it, around here. She was married—she's a widow now—to a man who was rather important in the Party, and I don't mean would be badly thought of since, or on that account, d'you follow me?" This was complicated and Vera took a moment disentangling it, but Castang was there already.

"I can promise you discretion, and there'll be no trouble—whatsoever."

"I'll come with you to the door. Oh she's around still, very much so. Is that your car? Follow the main road, keep along the shore, and about half a kilometre, up on the point, biggish house with green shutters. You're welcome. Yes, it's nice here in summer, pity it's still chilly. Spring comes late here, but very pretty when it does . . ." Bursting with curiosity, but what could one do?

Castang drove slowly, mumbling.

"Now wasn't that clever of me? Thing now, is to go on

being clever. Or one hopes lucky. Tiens, so Ingrid is a power in the land. I wonder what her real name is. And whether she's at home."

Jamais-jamais pays was never far away.

"The Seacoast of Bohemia," said Vera, looking at the lakeshore.

Chapter 8

A 'villa'. The stonework and the wood were beginning to weather but were recent enough still to look newish. It was quite big, with two stories generously measured and an attic, as well as a windowed basement. Tall gables, deep eaves, wood-pillared balconies along the whole length of the first floor, and on the lake- or south-facing side of the ground floor a large glassed conservatory built on. Not at all a country dacha. More like . . . Castang was astonished enough to stop the car while still on the road and stare, for several minutes . . . like houses he had seen in England, described to him as 'stockbrokers' tudor'. The style here had a Tyrolean look, such as you might expect of those rich little lakes within weekending distance of München or Salzburg. But—he did sums on his fingers—such houses were built, to these lavish specifications and with this rather vulgar ostentation, in the twenties when there was plenty of money about. This looked to be no more than twenty to twenty-five years old at most. That too would be the age of the hedges, protecting the garden from wind.

He went on looking, and then he thought he had an answer. If a small, ambitious boy had looked at a house like that in childhood, admiring this rather suburban grandeur, and had said to himself 'I'll have that, when I grow up'. Hadn't the man back there said 'a notable'? In local terms a big Party wheel? Then it would add up. Reaching an important position, with access to plenty of money, labour, material, then yes, he could have built a house like this; his Traumschloss, that he had dreamed of when small.

The tall gates, modern, but he admired the good wrought-iron work, Czechs know how to do it, were shut but a side-gate was on the latch. Well kept gravel, weeded; lawn, mowed; rosebeds and some magnolias, sheltered by the windbreaks; hm, thuya, should be yews but the fellow had been in a hurry to see his dream. The front door was on this side, the balcony supported by wooden pillars forming a porch. Nice, heavy, cherrywood door, brass knocker, a dolphin. He grinned at Vera. 'Elegant Southern Mansion.' An odd remote resemblance to Anita's house in Bruce, built at the turn of the century by a wealthy bourgeois manufacturer and no doubt an Exploiter of the People.

The door was opened by a scrawny little 'maid', a girl of fifteen only too glad, the guess was easy, to add even pitiful earnings to the family exchequer. Castang took his hat off; Vera asked formally "Is Madam Severing at home?" The child didn't know what to do, muttered something, left the door open, ran to get someone. A woman of forty appeared from the basement, broad-bosomed in a white apron. The cook, perhaps. A placid face but which looked distrustful. "Wait here, please. I'll see." A hall floor of black and white marble squares—very like Anita's.

"Madam's in the garden room, will you join her there?"— but Madam had already appeared, agog at this break in the monotony of winter days on the Lipno See.

"Who on earth can this be?" laughing heartily. Vera had been "rehearsed".

"We come from Belgium. We know an old friend, perhaps, who would be glad to have news of you."

"Strangers don't ask for news of me much nowadays," coquettish. "But I speak German, of course. English too if that suits you. A bit rusty, these days." Gust of laughter. Never mind the 'old friend'—it was her they'd come to see. "But come on in the garden room—this deserves a drink. Anna!" sharply to the little girl, "down to the cellar with you, the second bin on the right, with the black and gold labels, two of them, and three of the tall glasses, the good ones, properly on a nice tray." The child curtseyed; odd to see that, still. But they'd been told, hadn't they. Madam was a power in the land.

Castang had been looking. Birchwood furniture, and very good quality, with that pressed and stylised 'art déco' look of the thirties. Chair and table, commode and buffet, straight off the *Normandie*. Now coming back into fashion—this would be worth a lot now, in Paris!

Madam was fussing about, doing some hasty tidying. There were also pictures, mostly bad, violent oils, an obstreperous nude of the lady in her glory days; lavish, with green and violet shadows, the classic pose of the *maja desnuda*, a vulgar emphasis on breasts and pubis but perfectly recognisable: madam caught him peeking and went 'Ach' with a light laugh.

"No, the garden room will be nicer, it's in an awful mess but there's sun, today." But not before Castang-hawkeye had seen something, and known there was no mistake. An old poster, glassed, framed, cherished. Humphrey Bogart and Ingrid Bergman in *Casablanca*. They couldn't possibly have known that, in the Czech Protectorate of Bohemia in '43. It had been imagined, the romantic 'Ingrid', and with enough force to 'come true'.

Stranger things have happened.

Vera was loving the gardenroom, a fine conservatory highly enviable (thinking of her own house which has a little courtyard in the back but no orangery, alas).

Ingrid is still in a fluster but showing signs of coming to rest. A tall woman—we have now the observations of both Castang and Vera. Hitting seventy but in good shape; slim and straight, with fine fair hair, greyed but still a trifle reddish? In a chignon, but with hindsight yes, one could still see the young girl with 'her hair up'. Much lined, this thin skin, but 'good bones' which last well (like Vera's). Good expensive clothes (sage-green wool frock, one good gold brooch at the breast—an expensive bra). A resemblance to the 'other Ingrid'? A square strong jaw, a wide mobile mouth but set in

lines, accustomed to getting its own way. High Slav cheekbones and greeny-grey eyes much too small; Vera has these
looks but hers are big honest lamps. Power in a finely-
modelled forehead; determination in that strong, fierce,
highly-sensual mouth. Oh yes, had been a great beauty as a
girl. A colossal egoist, was that still. They'd come all this
way, just to see her; this 'old friend' didn't interest her at all.
Coquettish about the 'nude'!

"I could hardly pose like that now, could I? That was before I married." (Vera prudish, less out of puritanism than
because she's a better painter than that even with both hands
tied behind her back. Saying nowt, in consequence.) "Never
mind, time passes but we're still here. And what brings you
all this way?"

"Oh—tourism," said Castang but was interrupted by the
instructions given the little girl.

"Yes, that's nice, Anna, but you could perhaps have
thought of the ice-bucket. Never mind, it'll be cool enough
to drink. Perhaps Mr. Uh, you could open it for us. And what
were you saying when I so rudely interrupted?"

"Oh, I got given the names of four Czech villages. I don't
pronounce them right but in one of them I felt I had a chance
of finding you."

"Finding me!" delighted by the idea. "That's not difficult
in this lonely little hole. Not that I don't break out now and
again," with a roguish emphasis. "But didn't you say something about an old friend—now who could that be?"

Castang likes to make his effects theatrical (if, says Vera,
cheap). He was untwisting the wire, disentangling the foil.

"Klaus de Roodt." Pop! "The old freedom-fighter in person." 'Ingrid' who has herself a range of theatrical gestures
clasped her hands. A great beam spread across her face. Castang poured three glasses, handed her one, solemn as a butler, gave Vera hers, lifted his own and said, "Here's to Rest
and Recuperation."

She thinks, and quickly too. She took a careful, steady
drink, set the glass down and went off into a great peal of
laughter.

"Nicolaas! So he's still alive . . . and he remembers!"

"Remembers Ingrid," agreed Castang smiling. "What's your real name?"

"Wanda," with the mind far away, but then deciding that there was nothing that could compromise her now. "But what lovely memories you do bring back. 'Ingrid'—that was a fantasy of his. He was a most amusing man, and a delightful companion." She must have realised that this sounded false and stagey because she went on in a more natural voice. "These were all very innocent days. I was barely more than a child. We didn't think about anything like SS. We saw these boys simply as soldiers, who happened to have been wounded, and very handsome they were too. So there was some childish flirtation. And of course we all used to listen to the western radio, which naturally was strictly forbidden and that added a bit of spice. That's where 'Ingrid' came from."

She went across the room, to a grand piano. Rather a bourgeois feature of the environment, thought Castang, and likely enough nobody can play it. She lifted the lid, and standing picked out a sentimental little melody, in a major key and with one finger; sang, in a small soprano voice but still true—

"To You—my heart goes out Perfidia—For You were the love of my life—we too used to dance to that. How does it go on?—The—Stars—are echoing Perfidia . . ." Castang made a warning grimace at Vera, who had a haughty, revolted expression on her face at all this golden-syrup, decidedly "I *hated* Rebecca".

"But in between listening to Glenn Miller you found time to give him a baby." She looked up at the sardonic note, and the eyes blazed for a second. She snapped the lid down with a bang.

"Bogart and Ingrid dance to that in Paris—did Klaus tell you that?"

"But it's hardly a secret, is it? That was a thing which did tend to happen, especially in places where there were hand-

some soldiers recovering from wounds. Are those buildings
still there? Down by the shore?"

"Yes. Much changed now of course." She had controlled
herself, come back and picked up her glass, drunk from it.
"Give me some more, will you? You do seem to know a lot,
don't you? I suppose I may as well fill it in. No, I didn't
make a secret of it. I had that child and I brought him up.
And I stayed here. And later on when I married, my husband
was perfectly understanding about it. You had better top up
your wife's glass."

"Yes, tell us about your husband too."

She didn't seem to notice that he was questioning her like
any police official, and in her own home at that, and without
the slightest authority. She was still a bit flustered, suggested
Castang afterward. That I suddenly introduced the name of
old Klaas like that out of the blue put her off her stride
enough; or that anyhow was the general idea.

Don't even have to go that far, suggested Vera. Didn't you
notice she never even asked why you wanted to know, nor
what could possibly legitimise the enquiry. She's just an im-
possibly vain woman, and her own egotism made it perfectly
natural to her that one couldn't fail to be interested.

"Oh my husband," helping herself to a third glass and
quite comfortable again. "Well as you might have gathered
he was a government official in this part of the world, and indeed by far the most vigorous and intelligent for miles about.
And of course he built this house; he brought too a great deal
of energy and prosperity to the region, a lot of industry and
so forth to give local employment. Now of course it's all
going to be developed as a tourist resort. It's a pity he isn't
still here, he'd have loved the idea and been good at it. But
he died alack, around the time that ass Havel came to
power—oh of course I've nothing against Havel, he's a great
man in his way, but very rich you know, a real bourgeois,
they have immense property holdings." Something like envy
in that description?

"And the boy?" prompted Castang.

"He was very bright and we were very proud of him. As I

am still; he's become a famous man and we're very close." Realising perhaps that she had put a lot of emphasis into the three 'verys' she gave a light laugh. "He's in the movie industry and highly talented. Good heavens, now that we know old Klaas is still there, he really ought to go and look his father up—we never made any mystery of it you know, his father—I mean my husband—always said one should have these things in the open. We brought him up as our own but when he was old enough I told him, his real father was quite a romantic and picturesque individual. We felt sure he was dead by then of course. We never heard again. And I don't see that there's anything to be ashamed of either; it was a boy-and-girl affair typical of the times, and what did we know about the SS? I'm quite sure anyhow that Klaus never had anything to do with horrible happenings."

"I'd be very interested to meet your son," said Castang with much earnest zeal. "Where would I get in touch?" But that was a bit too crude: Ingrid's narrow eyes narrowed further.

"But I'm not sure I should be telling you all this. He might not altogether like it. People can be quite sensitive on such personal subjects. Of course I'd enjoy seeing Klaus again, we'd talk over old times and we'd find a lot to laugh about, they were tragic times of course and even now it hardly does to say so, but we had lots of fun. The Commandant you know was one of the old brigade and he too had been badly wounded in Russia, and all he wanted was an easy life; he used to natter on about discipline but he closed his eyes to quite a lot," with a few girlish giggles.

"Well this has been nice but I suppose we should be moving on."

"You seem to have come a step out of your way."

"Not really—we thought of heading over Passau way more or less and we were quite curious to see the Lipno See—there's quite a lot of building going forward, isn't there? I daresay it'll all be westernised in a year or so and you'll find yourselves in the humming hive."

"You must come back," suggested Wanda, with no move

towards the second bottle, "and see for yourselves. And then drop in, do, and remind me. And when you get back give my very best to Klaus. Bruxelles did you say it was?—he came from thereabouts I recall. Say he ought really to come and see for himself."

"I'll do that," said Castang, immensely hearty. And she came to the garden gate, polite about seeing them off the premises. Had a good look at the car. "Oh an Alfa—that's nice isn't it." Cheerful wave, as they drove away. "Nga," muttered Castang.

Chapter 9

"Whisky Bread," said Vera who had surrendered to this facetious nomenclature, "is up that way." Pointing to the path they had tried earlier; they'd stopped a moment in the Poop Dorp for consultations with the village shop. "She says there's a good road through the forest crossing over to Austria but a nasty long col downhill to Linz."

"The village will be ringing with our exploits," biting his finger. "If she thinks we've gone out through Passau, and is rid of us, so much the better. No, let's go to Prague. You promised to show me Prague. Something in the movie industry, that's where we'll get some info."

"All right," said Vera meekly. Now that she thought about it she wasn't averse to showing off. There, one would not feel ashamed or embarrassed—or no longer.

There was no hurry. It would be a good half-hour back to Budweis. He 'indulged in soliloquy'; Vera was used to this. One didn't know whether he was talking to her or to himself but it didn't much matter.

"Who do we know in the movie industry? Presumably East European. There's lots of it, mm, some a lot more talented than anything we ever get to see. All this shouldn't be too difficult. She might be greatly exaggerating his importance. He might turn out to be one of those credits which roll on interminably at the end; the Boom Man and the make-up girls—still it's a fairly restricted world. Mm, think we'd better go back through the town; don't think they run to a by-pass."

Castang is both a good and a bad driver. Bad because his mind is on other things and he does not always look where he's going: good because even now his reflexes are faster than most. He has the police habit of driving in the middle of the road; defends this by saying that in strange places one has to be ready to turn left or right, and that at the last moment. People put up road signs—helpfully, where you can't see them.

Certainly he was on the tram lines, and there might have been an excuse for a local, in a hurry, passing him on the right. Taxi-drivers, who have small use for strangers, always do. But was it a taxi? In any event it was unforgiveable to bear into the left when alongside him, forcing him out and straight into the path of the onrushing tram, which screeched at him.

He swerved right out to the left because there was nowhere else to go. This is after all a smallish, provincial, Czech town. The traffic is not intense. So that by the mercy of God there was nothing coming. In a Western town he would no doubt have been dead. One also thanks God for small mercies, while uttering a flood of police-or-barrack-room language.

"Fucking-*taxis*-sweet-jesus," plunging back again in front of the second tram clanging angrily at the Wessie maniac.

"Turn to your right," said Vera through clenched teeth. It was a main road and it said 'Prague' and one is thankful to get one's arse out of here entire. The town was trickling out into industrial suburb. The road widened and then narrowed. The traffic was speeding up. Castang speeded up. One wasn't in a hurry but one wasn't going to sit behind a row of 1950s Skodas neither, not all the way to Prague one wasn't.

"You might light me a cigarette, would you?" fiddling to adjust ventilators.

And so it was that neither of them really saw. The cigar-lighter had popped and Vera was bent over fishing it out. He had dropped his eye and hand to the heating control because this air coming in was hotter than he liked it. Banal situation, all round.

It was a largish, squarish thing. A delivery van? Maybe even a minibus, but so dingy and covered in dirt that one couldn't even tell the colour, let alone the number-plate. Czech though; no Wessie.

A simple enough manoeuvre. Castang was not really going fast; cruising. Ninety say, a hundred maybe; certainly no more. The van was fast though, fair flashed past him. Cut in, straight in front, braking because he saw the lights go on. So that Castang braked too, jabbing down his foot, with what seemed like every muscle he had.

It is a classic gesture of intimidation. The French, their vanities once bruised, have this nasty habit. La queue de poisson, and the flick of a powerful fish's tail describes it clearly. It is more to frighten you, and establish superiority, than anything else. If, of course, there's someone close behind you when you brake, you might well get crunched. While they flit away, laughing heartily.

Nothing dreadful happened. His reactions were quick, the tyres were nearly new, the road dry, the brakes in good shape, nobody on his tail, seat-belts fastened; just that our nerves are a little bit shaken already.

"Stop The Car," said Vera. She did not often adopt this tone of voice and when she did it was not the moment for a lot of arguing. "These people are trying to kill us," she said, quite levelly.

They were on a verge. Grass and mud, neither predominating. To the right, rather an unpleasant ditch. Left, traffic, trundling quite peaceably Prague-ward. A late afternoon in South Bohemia with spring beginning to colour a quiet, a pretty winter landscape. Large placid central-European clouds sailed, in no hurry. This skyscape also carries no hostile intent.

Castang had switched the motor out. He smoked the cigarette which Vera handed him. After thought, she lit one of her own. There was a soft tick of cooling metal. The motor's

ventilator started up in a fussy, nervous way, cut itself off
again.

"Yes," he said, looking for the ashtray. "That's intimidation. Furthermore, never two without three—maxim; my
grandfather," in a slightly ill-placed impulse to be facetious.

"And I am intimidated," said Vera. "This people—may I
say my countrymen?—are not normally given to this kind of
games."

"Oh I'm intimidated too. No mistaking that; those were
both on purpose. Has she been busy on the telephone? But
why would that be and the thing is, even if so, because that
could, you know, be nothing more than just normal anti-
Wessie irritation, don't think yourselves so almighty bloody
grand and don't start tramping on us. Sorry, lost track, do we
allow ourselves to feel intimidated?"

"I'm sorry," clearcut. "I'm not having either you or me or
even my new car bust up on account of vanities and fantasies
of whatever origin. I think I'd like to drive if you don't
mind." She is being extremely Crisp. "If I may say so you
were driving badly, which increases risks. I'm utterly unin-
terested in your bloodhound act. I'm not staying here. Prague
will simply be for another time because I'm not going there
with this hanging over me. We're barely ten kilometres out
of Budweis. I'm turning straight round and I'm hotfooting it
out of here, straight by the main road into Linz and I'll be
pleased when I'm over the border. I've no particular sympathy with Austrians but at least they're always late, which
proves some civilised instincts. I don't particularly want to
go to Linz, it's a town the Führer thought highly of, but we'll
find an autoroute there, takes us straight up to Passau, can't
be more than around a hundred and fifty kilometres, I don't
mind saying, I'll sleep a lot better when I'm back over the
border into Germany. I'm feeling altogether too Czech to
want to stay here any longer. So move over, d'you mind?"

Castang opened the window, threw out the cigarette end. It
is now quite a number of years since he has been married to
this Czech woman and he has learned one thing: her instincts

DALTON BOOKSELLER
STORE 4725 SEATTLE, WA (206) 364-5856

REG#03   BOOKSELLER#016
RECEIPT#   39326   01/01/97   1:02 PM

S 0446403717   SEACOAST OF BOHEMIA
                      1 @   5.99   5.99

SUBTOTAL   5.99
SALES TAX - 8.2%   .49
TOTAL   6.48
CASH PAYMENT   7.00
CHANGE   .52

    THANK YOU FOR SHOPPING AT B.DALTON!

are better than the reasoning powers he has sometimes felt vain of.

"I'm not going to quarrel. One thing is clear, that a little Alfa with Wessie number-plates is a sight too bloody conspicuous. Second thing clear, when they want you to feel intimidated, it's a sensible move to appear intimidated. Third, when I'm in Czechland and a Czech woman tells me to shake my ass I'll damwell listen." None of that is faked.

Reflections (in a passenger seat in a small Alfa).

Why am I so slow, so stupid, so null-and-void? Why am I not Humbert; observation of every squalid motel, restroom, gas-station and hot-dog-stand immeasurably sharpened by the presence of Lolita? Lyrical? Poetry? Marvellously memorable moments? True; my Vera, whatever she is, and hideously hardheaded; no Lolita her or is it she? And I'm just a dumm sausage pressed between two lumps of stodge; put all the onions and mustard and ketchup and Old Mother Riley's Hot Sauce you like I'm just a Lump. The Czechs couldn't care less about my passport as long as I'm leaving, and the Austrians are too lazy to look. Mm, that's Linz. Salud. This is an autoroute which Vera drives a sight faster than I'd trust myself to, and I feel so safe. Roll on Passau, and we'll think about it tomorrow.

What was it like, making love in a motel room to Lolita? Horrid; one was obsessed, and one loved her so much, and one felt so guilty and she hated it so, and it was underhand and squalid and one was miserable and all the lovely lyricism turns to ashes. Vera is like and unlike. This shallowness of breast and meagreness of bum and boniness of thigh is like and it is enrapturing and surely here in Passau—this is Germany; she will not feel fear. I will not feel guilt or anxiety or—yes and fear too.

No no, it was a piece of crude intimidation if it was anything at all. No more than that. Pure coincidence . . .

Vera does not like lakes. Especially she does not like lakes on or even near frontiers. She has vivid and unpleasant memories of a lake between Switzerland and Italy where he had had a very narrow scrape from assassination.

As for himself he has a knowledge which she shares, but his is unsaid and hers is unproved, of another lake (close enough by to make no difference) and a lakeside hotel where he had spent the night with a young, pretty Italian girl . . . this is unmentioned between them. Does that wound fester? No, but at moments like this the pain of old wounds returns, in the middle of the night, and he spent a disturbed night.

Breakfast was much better: they slept late, got up late, and there was a pleasant sensation of not going anywhere and not having to.

"Practically full circle," said Vera. It is only a hundred-odd kilometres further, back to Regensburg . . .

She too had ended by sleeping well. She had made up her mind to resist, to push back, to dismiss her nightmares. Alp-träume, the Germans call them. Horrors that come upon one in high places? Como; Lugano; those horrible lakes were in the Alpine region, one had only to lift the head and there the beastly Alps were. Would one see them, from Passau? On a clear day, no doubt. But now it is a sunny morning between yellow curtains with daffodils on the table, and she is look-ing out over a terrace upon the Donau. Isn't this the stretch of the Danube where the giant catfish are to be found?—hor-rible nightmare beasts . . . She drinks her coffee. She knows her man. She has got him out of Czechland and even out of Austria, but intimidated or not he has got hold of a thread, and his native tenacity will not allow him to let it go.

"What are you thinking?"

"That down there in Budweis Ingrid, or Ingrid's defunct husband, bless his bones, had a lot of friends, possibly for-mer Party luminaries, people well dug in and who do not wish their comforts disturbed. Very well. I won't disturb them. I'm going to circle round, get at Prague the other way. Take the road up toward Chemnitz, Dresden."

"Not in this car you aren't, it's too recognisable, and if it's noticed in Budweis it could also be conspicuous in Prague."

"I thought of that. This is all on Anita and she's had no ex-penses but these few hotel bills and a few litres of petrol. She can well afford a hired car. The comfortable anonymous black Mercedes, I rather think. A taxi, quoi?"

"You still won't get in; your passport's out of date."

"Damn, I'd forgotten that. I'll think of something. But it's a nice day, let's go to Dresden."

"Road I know well," said Vera, thinking back some years, to a moment when she had tried 'going home' and found it was no longer her home. "In through Teplice. Full of prostitutes."

"Is it?" said Castang. "Yes I seem vaguely to have heard."

It is a subject she has some sensitivity about. Since there is nothing whatever to be done about it, there is no point in sentimentalising. Simply that she has been herself a young, helpless Czech girl, with ideas of escaping to the West. Is that 'sentiment'? That bleak road past Dresden and over the Iron Mountains is the main Berlin highway. Thousands of Germans—rich Wessies—come this way for a weekend, for a bit of Fun. Life in Czechland is so cheap. The beer is so cheap. Yes and the girls are so cheap. The roadside is full of girls who can earn in a night more than their father, mother and brother combined could earn in a month. They only have to climb in a car with German plates. The Czech police look the other way. 'I was mortally ashamed the first time. But one soon gets used to it.' Vera thinks she would rather have starved and would have been quite ready to starve. But she hadn't been asked. Nothing had forced her. There have been wicked stories of girls brought over and set to work in the houses of Leipzig. Stories of girls drugged and even kidnapped, and brought further afield, to the bordels of Bruce and Antwerpen. Castang the former police officer shrugs. There are always these stories. True, now and then. The truth is more squalid. Few of them are more than passive freight, willing meat. As long as there are square meals every day and a pay-packet.

It is a longish way up and around, to Dresden, and they didn't reach it much before the early evening, and when they came to look for a hotel the tourist-board girl shook her head; there's never anything this late. Bed-and-breakfast in a private house, oh yes, we've plenty of those. She supplied a street-plan: I'll ring up and say you're coming. Vera's tastes run to the privacy of anonymity but Castang, a sociable soul, is quite content. A countrified Dresden, a place of fields and muddy roads, of pleasant humble houses standing in their own garden—and that garden full of daffodils.

"Things are not as bad as they were, for Ossies. Time was, not long ago either, my wife gathered those flowers, sat with a basket outside the Hauptbahnhof to sell them by the bunch. Believe me, every little helped."

It is a warm, comfortable house, a cosy livingroom. They had stopped to eat in the town, but yes, a bottle of beer is welcome. It was full of plants and flowers, and straightway Vera is deep with the woman. Castang looks with boredom at the television screen, asks the man 'what he does'.

"Sorry to say it but I'm a cop. Inspector on the municipal force, we don't get paid much. Not what you'd see on *Tatort*"—a familiar, long-standing German krimi-series on television.

"Well well well," says Castang, drinking beer; happily. His host begins to laugh. A thickset, strong-featured man of forty-odd. Pale heavy face like a ham, like Long John Silver, with small amused eyes. And well-well-well—"So it would be just the same in France? I've never been to France. My wife would like to take one of these bus tours to see Paris. They're quite cheap. Is that a good idea, would you say? I'd like to see, just once, the Seine and the Eiffel Tower, and the Notre-Dame and Montmartre; am I right? What would you advise?"

That's not complicated, says Castang. You come to us, right, in Brussels, and we'll fix you up. Plenty of buses from there and I'll give you a few addresses. And in exchange— I'm interested in Czechs, are you an authority or can you put me on to the Colleagues who are?

Long after Vera had gone to bed they sat comfortably conspiring . . .

* * *

If Anita had been going to worry about the expense-account being too cheap, she would now feel quite relieved at the length and number of telephone calls. Castang does know somebody in the movie industry, for the range and oddity of cops' acquaintanceships is impressive, at least superficially. It doesn't get him anywhere.

"Peer, did you say Peer?"

"Hard to tell when you've only word of mouth. Per maybe."

"Common name all over Scandinavia in one form or another. Be dozens of them. Should have thought it rare in eastern Europe."

"Yes, well, the informant is the kind of woman who doesn't know her fantasies from her realities. It might not be so at all."

"And Severing?"

"I only said perhaps Severing, that was her married name. Moderately impressive local Party chap, so might the name have given a boost at the beginnings, would one think?"

"Well we've got this enormous encyclopaedia, sort of *Who's Who,* lists absolutely everyone right down to Louis B. Mayer's Mum who used to make the double-chicken-consommé. De Roodt, did you say? Mm, Rot, Road, Rood, that's a broken reed. Tell you what, I can try the Film Library, they specialise in eastern Europe and even if it's Fred Karno's Army . . ."

"Call me back around lunchtime."

"You," menacingly, "are going to owe me a lunch."

"That's all right, I'm on expenses."

"Oh good, we'll make that a three-star."

When they got it they both burst out laughing because it is an old trick and one moreover that Castang has met before. The 'early Flemish' painter Rogier van der Weyden turns up in French galleries and art histories under the name of Roger de la Pasture: both mean 'Meadow' but you'd never guess until you were looking at the picture—or knew beforehand. It was an old Englishman in the Film Library who said

'There was a writer called Mrs. Henry de la Pasture, and her daughter went by the name of Delafield.'

"This guy calls himself Leroux. Don't know about your Per but his first name's Peter."

"Ticketyboo," said Castang, pleased. It fitted; the Per would be a fancy left over from the 'Ingrid' days.

"So if you were looking for a chap in Israel called David, you'd ask people called Jonathan?"

"You could always try."

His new German friends, amused by the idea of a Disguise, found no trouble in fixing him up with an identity card and a respectably anonymous police Opel, to be left in the garage all night with the doors open, to help get the smell out. But what could one go disguised as?

Another problem is Vera. Having refused, most obstinately, to re-enter the Czech Republic she now insists with equal obstinacy that she is accompanying the expedition.

"Look, it's not going to be dangerous," said Castang with a large, slightly sarcastic emphasis on the Dan. "It's likely to be very boring, and a probable fiasco."

"I don't care what it is. I take my share in whatever, risks on perils, boredoms or the Lost Heirs; I'm now going and that's flat."

This feminine presence, welcome when his mind was on tourism, is a professional embarrassment, but how to convey this with tact?

"The best bits of the movie, they say, are always those that got left on the cutting-room floor. It'll be very dull; why not take the Alfa and go to Leipzig or wherever there's a good concert on."

"I just haven't the least intention of doing so."

"It's not like down in the Indian country. Prague will be full of tourists because it always is, and I'll get by perfectly well on German or even English." It's of no use. What is one supposed to do, grow long muttonchop whiskers and say "I *forbid* it?" Rolf Steinmetz, their tactful German host, keeps a tactful silence.

"Your funeral," said Castang crossly; not the politest form

of phrasing and Frau Steinmetz said "More coffee?" over-animatedly.

Then there is the Disguise. It has to be simple, to be consistent with whatever might be known or guessed, and it has to be tasty bait to winkle out the good Herr Leroux, described in the book as 'metteur en scène' and he seems to have been assistant-director on a number of obscurish projects. One can't appear as the kind angel with a lot of money to give away, for some really original television work. Tell the truth, says Castang, or as near as makes no matter: Herr Steinmetz opines sagely with his bright, heavy head.

"Put in your own sugar," said Frau Steinmetz, "but you can't be a German cop, can you? No that sounds rude but even for a Wessie your accent's a bit too Frenchified."

"Alas yes, I have on occasion done the French-cop-on-a-mission but that was close to the border. I think money might be the answer. Something like this?—that my old man has won a million on the Lotto, and feeling himself nearer death than he is likely to agree in reality, is thinking of his romantically-engendered offspring, because his daughter is well-fixed, with plenty of the poppy. I think there's nothing like a lucky Lotto-ticket for bringing the long-lost heirs out of the woodwork."

"It doesn't sound at all convincing," said the two women together. "It wouldn't convince *me*," looking at each other and laughing.

"Doesn't matter," said Steinmetz, perfectly serious. "You can say anything, however silly, about money, they drink it in. I agree with Herr Castang. The Lotto numbers are prominent every week on our television, which everyone in Czechland watches." They are also, adds Castang, the theme of some pretty good publicity clips, such as any hard-up television genius would love to get a contract for.

"Oh yes," said Frau Steinmetz, "even I gamble the odd mark, because One Never Knows." Blushing at indulgent grins from the men while Vera keeps quiet; old priss. Doesn't gamble.

Chapter 10

Czech border guards gave them only the most perfunctory glance: Castang held up a card which could have said Heydrich for all they knew, and was waved on. Prostitutes are not apparent in the morning hours; need their sleep.

Vera found an expensive hotel, and Castang settled to another round of phone-calls. He must have struck oil in the end, because she came out of the bathroom in time for—"I don't think we should talk about this on the phone, Herr Leroux, because one never knows who may be listening," which as bait is not far short of a win on the Lotto. He stretched out comfortably on the bed, with his hands behind his head.

"We've got a dinner date," smiling. He didn't say 'I have'; he knew she wasn't going to let him out of her sight, here. There was nothing to be done about this. Since coming face to face with risk, the memories of Italy and his two close encounters there with death are too strong. Is it to be counted a great handicap, in these dealings? Yes, because he would be playing a part, and one she did not like. But also, oddly, No. In Italy they had come up against a man who did not hesitate to kill whoever got in his way. Castang had got nowhere with this man, and Vera tumbled him clear off his perch of arrogance. Castang astonished; not surprised though. Or less than the man.

She is happy to be here. Her hair is shiny; a glow on her skin.

"And where is it, your dinner date?"

"In the Malestrana—where is that?"

"We'll see it this afternoon. But you go by yourself, I think. I'd only be bored." A female reversal upon which one must not comment. "A lot of drinking, no doubt. But I've been on your back too much lately." She can indeed be annoyingly 'nanny'. There must have been a look of relief, a little. "Oh, I've my own resources, here," smiling. "Your police work . . ."

"He may not have the child at all. This entire scenario could be false from beginning to end. There's no real evidence."

"Oh, I think he has the child," in an uninflected voice, as though she were indifferent. "Let's go and be tourists."

They came out upon the quayside. A sunny afternoon in early spring. One looks across the river. One tries not to utter the usual clichés. One fails.

"This is the Moldau, is it? La la, la-la, la La?" Vera is immune to all such sentimentalisms.

"There was an extremely good ice-hockey player, name of Lala."

He does take rather a look sideways, to see if this is mockery. No. Just female.

"The Charles Bridge," piously averting her eyes from the souvenir-sellers, "and over there is the Malestrana. We'll have to climb. Bit steep, and lots of cobbles. And not quite spoilt yet."

"What about your leg?"

"When I'm here I don't feel my leg," pragmatically. Pragmatic sanctions; her head is full of half-remembered history. "Here is where they invented defenestration. Like sewing people into sacks and dropping them in the Seine, only more Pragmatic, very Czech."

"Does the word come from Prag?"

"Greek pragmatikos," says Vera in her best literary manner. "My philosophy is rather lacking; the doctrine by which the idea we have of a phenomenon or object is no more than

the sum of ideas we may process about the practical consequences of possible actions."

"Sounds exactly like a definition of police work."

"And isn't that exactly what's wrong with police work?
Leaves out the metaphysical elements."

And this of course is why it is good to have Vera around
when police work gets undertaken. Castang is a convention-
ally-trained cop; a bright conventional mind. Since this had
been in France, that strong theoretical formation, between
school and university a lot of 'philo' got packed in: he thinks
he does vaguely remember the name of William James. But
since meeting Vera he had had to learn to use his peripheral
vision. Dark side of the moon, quoi? Or a boiled egg has also
its metaphysical nature. And when he gets a little fanciful,
her pragmatic side comes in handy.

"Where's your restaurant?"

"I wrote it on a piece of paper," humbly.

"Mm, that's on our way . . . looks rather scruffy. Might be
nice inside."

A wonderful tourist afternoon, the more so for tourists
being thinner on the ground, the March sun deceptively
bright, the March east wind a skinning-knife here on the
heights where the clouds fly like banners. The spires and pin-
nacles huddle together and tilt vertiginously sideways. In this
thin clear air every rock and flower is new, just that moment
painted. One has climbed a thousand steps up from
madonna-level to the citadel seen in primitive Italian paint-
ings; acrobatic angels dash down upon one and wheel away
into the empyrean. A soldier in a helmet and hauberk rests
his spear against the wall, offers you a drink from his leather
bottle and it is a water clear and cold and more invigorating
than champagne. You are inside the picture and your vision
as clear, as brilliant as that of the man painting it. You could
be a saint or a prophet, even if you are just another money-
lender. You turn the corner of a courtyard and here is a full-
sized gothic cathedral; you rub your eyes since this is surely
a rarity even in the grandest of palaces: it will vanish again
and was perhaps an illusion. You totter over to the edge of a

terrace and peep between battlements and down there far away is Prague dim and blue and were you there? Will you be there again?

Castang lurched out between the tall gates into the square where there are small palaces belonging to fearful feudal nobles, or archbishops, or utterly ridiculous Ministries. Here there is a man in leather kneelers with a hammer, mending the patterns in the pavements. Castang picks up a cube of hard bluish stone and here is his reward.

After the Paris-Roubaix race (those harsh granite setts, made deliberately irregular so that oxen should not slip, though bicycles do, are now a national monument and may be destroyed no more) the valued prize for the most-combative rider is not a silver cup but a 'pavé': a sett.

A very great treasure, for the rider who has been blinded by the mud (or asphyxiated by the dust) of a Paris-Roubaix, who has slipped and fallen sideways, his bicycle above and below him on those atrocious cobbles, who has remounted torn from shoulder to knee, his blood trickling into his shirt and his socks; these grazes will heal on the morrow but this day stays with him his life long.

So that Castang weighs the little Praguer-pavé in his hand, and puts it in his pocket, because as he looks back across the square, Vera, a small figure, comes out through the gates to join him. He is footsore; she is not even limping.

A writer cannot treat a marriage, in a book. He—she—has perhaps a man-wife relation in the forefront of a narrative, but the most one can do is to stylise this in a few lines of dialogue. A joke or two? He can often see Vera in some short, crude phrase; the puddle in the soapdish and the toothpaste squeezed from the top and lavish lengths of lavatory paper, but that's not a marriage. Secrets given, and kept; pathetic vulnerable nakedness and richly, thickly, furred and padded formal clothing; a skinny, scrawny child on rough reddened knees with dirty fingernails; a noble standing figure, swathed and hieratic and impenetrable, a bronze hand raised to bless or to curse. A diplomatic treaty signed on a morocco blotter and passed with white-lipped freezing smile across the Louis

XV map-table; eye-gouging guerilla war in a muddy ditch: a
Rodin embrace in white marble and the slowest, tender dis-
solve. A child planted in a womb; and knickers scratched
down à la levrette across a kitchen table: Sienese madonnas
and lumpy grinning distorted Bosch vegetables: a portrait by
Giorgione, and another by Arcimboldo. She has crossed the
square and reaches him, smiling: he shows her his little cube
of stone and she understands it. A Czech graphic artist whose
tongue comes out between her lips and whose pencil makes a
magic springing line; a little meagre tight-skirted French
housewife bargaining in the market over a cucumber: a shot-
silk of generosity and avarice. They trudged tiredly down the
hill in silence arm-above and arm-below and he took all her
clothes off in a hotel bedroom.

Vera dressed, in a big ample skirt and a highnecked cashmere pullover; puts in 'pretty earrings'; she is going to a
Czech theatre, to a Czech play, spoken in Czech; he
wouldn't understand a word. She'll eat a bite in a café, before or after; she hasn't made her mind up. His trousers get
topped with a wool jacket, a silk scarf in the opening of a
sober shirt, all quite correct and anonymous and suitable. She
pulls the scarf and arranges it to suit her taste; wifely gesture,
a minute flick of irritation which he suppresses. She gives a
little affectionate wave on the doorstep and he walked off
back across the Charles Bridge. The sun had gone down and
the Moldau looked sullen; the souvenir stalls had mostly
packed up but the gargoyles still grinned at him. The
Malestrana was tuning up for the evening and cooking smells
came from doorways. Smells of steaks in shuttered ways?—
he gets his quotations from her and mostly gets them wrong.

A conventional sort of place, warm and stuffy and
crowded, lot of oak beams and check tablecloths, reeking of
schweine-schnitzel and schweine-braten and schwein in ke-
babs, too Germanic for his mood, and the alternatives are
duck and fish. Never mind, there's lots of lovely Czech beer
but he's going to stick to that rather tasty local-red-wine.

This man would certainly have caught his eye, held his attention even if it weren't the man he'd come to see; and in a

large room. Not a big man, nor impressive-looking, but
radio-active and would glow in the dark. The moment he
came in at the door, a stiff jerky walk, one shoulder higher
than the other (and in the street, Castang was to notice, he
swung only that arm, as though to keep it loose to grasp a
sword, keeping the shield-arm close to the body).

Thin and pale, a meagre hollow face. A word with the
waiter and he headed for the table with a big smile showing
bad teeth. Yes, there was something there of old Klaas' fero-
cious grin but not his massive build: Wanda too was a tall
woman but this was a man no bigger than Castang himself,
and he was at the bottom limit for a cop. And they were the
same age. Why had he thought of this man as young?—they
both dated from those confused days towards the end of the
war but this was the earlier of the two. And he knows his
parents, while I do not. We have more in common than was
expected. Castang got up. With the wide smile, a thin hand
was held out.

"Pierre Leroux." Voice indistinct; had he said Per, Peer?

The meagre look was in his clothes, smart but old and
verging on the shabby: a tobacco-brown suit, narrow and
well-cut but the seams whitening, as though he hadn't had
the money to renew it lately. And a good shirt resolutely
bleached against the yellowing of age. The bow tie was enviable though, a thick silk in brown and green stripes below a
prominent adam's apple and an angular shaved jaw. Only the
hair marked him as Ingrid's child, the pale basque-red going
dusty now and grey over the ears, and the high well-
modelled temples, and the small greenish eyes rather too
closely set. Yes, on study, the resemblance was close. The
smile was like his father, but what else?

Ears—Castang, cop. Vera will speak of a tall dark woman
with stiff movements (assistant in the local pharmacy) as
'that great black camel': it isn't meant as nasty, but to be
recognisable. Castang is trained 'to take a photograph' and
he remembers these large-lobed ears flat to the skull, from
the old man in Brussels.

"You've got a drink—think I'll join you in that. Thought

about food yet, have you?—the duck's good here. Fish?—
it's not bad either. Okay, that's settled. Bortsch is fair and
there's plenty of it. And I'll have hors d'oeuvres, what d'you
say in French, crudités. Prague ham, that's still always good.
And another of these," tapping the bottle with neat finger-
nails; the hand was long and fine, twitching aside the furred
sleeve in a renaissance portrait, ringed. Some vanity, thought
Castang. He spoke English, as though to make it known at
once that he belonged to the intelligentsia. Slight local accent, no more noticeable than Castang's own. The waiter
left, and he smiled and said, "You know, I'm still not at all
clear what this is about." The radio-activity was strong at
close quarters, a surge of nervous energy showing in clusters
of electric impulses near-visible, as though sparks might fly
from the knuckles. He took the bottle and poured himself a
glass, spilling a drop on the wooden table. This was not like
the sure neatness and precision of the big scarred craftsman's
hands which had struck Castang. Even when drunk Klaas
moved with hair's-breadth accuracy. Perhaps this chap has
had a few drinks already. Why so nervous, or is he always
like that? But there was also a warmth and easy friendliness,
nothing doggy but as though he had always this fund of
spontaneity. He is instantly likeable. Trustworthy would be
something else. "Nice to meet you, whatever." They clinked
glasses.

Would one attack? Or probe around edges?

"I met your mother."

"So she told me on the phone. Plays the lady of the manor
down there. What would I do in that hole?" He showed no
surprise at being found. "My father—I don't know him at all.
That's my fault, I suppose. But I don't see where you come
into the picture."

One pays out a little line.

"I do a bit of enquiry work—ex-police officer. The old
man wasn't too sure where to find you."

"She seemed a bit het-up." Yes, the 'accidents'—if that
was what they were. Italy a year ago had left Vera thin-
skinned, over-sensitive. Castang still felt it was probably no

more than xenophobia, and bad driving. There was no hard evidence to the contrary. But wait and see.

"Did you know?—you have a step-sister, in Brussels?"

"I really know very little about it. The old man was in the SS, wasn't he. Not a war criminal, but not very frequentable, and one would keep quiet about it. I suppose I felt a bit ashamed about this. I don't feel so now; a girlish escapade. What's to make a fuss about? Disgraceful? I suppose there'd be some people to think so, even now. I've never been much interested. She married a man who adopted me, acted as though he were my father. Fair enough. I liked him. We got on well."

Castang did think it 'fair enough'. What would I have done, he wondered. He has to put a little pressure upon his skepticism, upon the police side to his head. Was it all that uncomplicated? Is this man a little too over-glib?

"You have to remember," pouring out two glasses of wine, "these iron curtain years. He was a strong Party luminary, you know. Took a dim view of the West. He was also rather a skilful operator, in his quiet provincial way extremely able. Didn't do me any good, particularly. Of course, I'm very fond of Wanda. Daresay you noticed that under that girlish manner she's highly protective of her own position and comforts. Now that the frontiers are open she looks a little old-fashioned in her ways. Always was rather frightened that I might create scandals which would compromise her, doncha-know.

"I move in a different world. Our trouble always is short-age of capital, so that our eyes turn towards the West, a world alien to that Wanda has always moved in. Makes her suspicious.

"But to come back to what brings you here . . ."

"Mr. de Roodt is getting to be an old man. Like more who've lived a reckless sort of existence he's thinking about being prudent. Provident, say. Rather anxious to know more about you."

The man was eating his duck in a snatching way and gob-bling at the wine. Not very attractive. Still, there was something winning about him. Direct, certainly. He wiped his mouth and said, "How much money is there?"

"I'm not the notary. A fair bit, perhaps. Dealing there in antiques, skilful restorer. Quite a business—this will interest you—in theatrical artefacts, you want the jewelled cup for the emperor Nero to drink from, he's good at that."

"Sounds amusing."

"Highly so." And there at least he's doing old Klaas no injustice. "An old man starts thinking about his past? My instruction was to try and find you, identify you, no more. You might be well advised to make a little trip to Brussels. I've run my errand. He'd like me perhaps to know you a little better. When I get back he'll want a report—about you, your mode of life, your circumstances . . ."

Leroux was drinking a lot but his mind seemed pretty clear. One could see him thinking about all this. And why hesitate, unless there's a pretty large-scale snag?

"So I might stay a day," adds Castang, artless. "Get to see more of your lovely town. My wife came along for the ride—she's Czech, incidentally—she'd be glad to meet you."

"They make quite good pancakes here. Like to try some? She is? How did that happen?" There can be no harm in the truth, here.

"Good many years ago now. She was on the gymnastics team. Championships in western Europe, and she jumped ship. Not quite Rudolf Nureyev but there was a bit of a fuss at the time."

"Yes. Yes." The mind was spinning fast now. "There would be. That government was very Stalinist, worse than anything East German. Sounds interesting," not at all interested. "Of course I'd love to meet her, I'm a bit worried because there's rather a lot on the plate these coming days. Have to work something out. Have another bottle, shall we, to go with the pancakes? Tell me—I may as well say my father—got other children, has he?"

"Oh he got married, you know, I'm not up in the fine detail, daughter of some business family, lot of money but the wife died. There's a girl of this marriage whom I mentioned earlier, she'd be a bit younger than yourself." He was watching closely but the yellowish eyes stayed blank. "She seems to have inherited quite a bit on the mother's side and is herself married to a chap who's done well for himself in engineering. I couldn't say, but my impression would be that your father might take the view that she was pretty well fixed, so that if it boils down to the heritage question you could expect some measure of preference, I might put it—I repeat, I'm not a notary."

Castang had himself drunk a good deal. That's all right, in the way of business. This fellow is certainly plying me with drink in the hope of a loosened tongue, and aren't I doing much the same? I am, I suppose, gambling on my head being better than his.

"Rather a tragedy there, I seem to have heard. Man had a road accident, left him paraplegic, he's in a wheelchair. Only too frequent I'm afraid, the way traffic is in the West. And there was something about a child, died young I believe, they sound an unlucky family." The eyes were expressing a resolute lack of interest.

"Like some cognac with your coffee? We've always kept a taste for it here, even in the Stalinist time you could get good French stuff in places like this, if you were willing to pay, of course. No? Then we'll finish the bottle and move on. This is on me, by the way."

"No no," said Castang. "Your father wouldn't approve of that, gave me some expense money for an occasion of the sort, no question about it."

Leroux laughed. Perhaps relieved; by local estimation this would be quite an expensive place. He poured out the rest of the bottle, whose neck clinked on the glasses. Perhaps he was a bit stocious or perhaps it was the rather poor coordination Castang had noticed earlier. Both, probably: they'd both had quite a tankful.

"In these circumstances all right, I won't contest this. But now I've an idea, and here you'll be my guest, because I can fix it to be a bit of a freeby; like to take a peek at the Pouf?—

it's quite a classy one, and not many tourists get to hear about it."

Castang is both curious enough and unbuttoned enough, and indeed amused: all for taking a look at the bordel.

"Sure."

Must have been drunker than he thought. Reckless. No, not all that reckless.

"Don't want any of the girls. But ach, what, have some entertainment. Not sure I can be bothered. How far is this anyhow?"

"Round the corner, two minutes."

"Don't want to wake up with a hangover."

"No no, perfectly clean, I can promise."

"Not what worries me."

"You've been reading these spy stories. Get photographed through the peephole? Little spot of Stalinist blackmail, huh? None of that, Josephine, I know the management. This is the Poets' Society."

"What have you here then," paying the bill and lodging it carefully with the expense dockets, "that we can't find in Hamburg?"

"Don't be an ass, mate. The Chinese girls are for tourists, this is the real thing."

Nobody's drunk. There is no reeling or giggling or slipping on cobblestones. Nobody could say it was a disorderly house, either; it was quiet, grey, shuttered. Leroux knows his way about, has a word with a doorman, climbs dark stairs confidently; there's a dusty smell of old curtains and stale cigarsmoke and a door to warmth and light and Brazilian music, nice and soft; Castang had been in no mood to be deafened.

"Hallo, Maria."

Not like Hamburg and he was reminded of Budweis, and Austro-Hungarian Empires because of faded velvet and tarnished gilt, a fine Bohemian chandelier and lovely intricate polished parquet, dark wood cunningly inter-leaved with pale. No bar. Alcoves and comfortable seating and two girls dancing in the sort of samba-school costume that is equivalent to wearing nothing at all. He is after all going to enjoy himself because madam so plainly knows her business. Maria is tall and thin and much lined, taller still in a high-necked evening dress that covers her faded throat, but she has the remnants of fine looks and a slow, gentle smile.

"Would you like company? That's quite all right. You can always change your mind, later on. Call me, Peer, for anything your guest might wish."

"Only champagne or Chivas," apologised Leroux. "I can get fresh orange juice or something, later." The champagne was of respectable marque and even vintage, brought and carefully served by a pretty young girl in a lace apron, otherwise naked.

"This really is nice. Do by all means explain."

"It was a government subsidy in the old days; diplomats and whatever. We thought it worth keeping on as a real bit of the old Prague, sort of a syndicate; have to charge a lot of course. Americans love it. Not so many Russian Generals, nowadays, but tja, western investors, the embassies still naturally, Nato or the Treuhandanstalt, you name it, shit, I'm being indiscreet but coming out of Brussels, you'll understand." Another tall but pretty young woman in evening-dress crossed to one of the other alcoves half-curtained; there were sounds of enthusiasm. "The floor show's very good—there's a girl does a wonderful snake dance. Do publicise, but only in the right places, mm: I feel sure I can count on you."

"Wouldn't want to spoil it."

"Oh, Maria rules with a rod of iron, and of course if anyone got stroppy that bald-headed bugger downstairs does strongarm."

The champagne—excellent—played the principal role in events. Castang passed into that state—not unpleasant—where desire outruns performance, so that he could look with the keenest of—anyhow keen—interest at entertainment without lubricity. There was no vulgar movie or other electronic nudging; even the music wasn't a racket. The stately young woman was robbed of clothes in predictable but dignified fashion: the barmaid (hockey-playing uniform for northern tastes) was for rough play severely disciplined, a samba-dancer was seduced by another in a gaily liberated battle of flower-petals, and the snake-girl left one with a pleasant sense of ambiguity about the sex of pythons. Maria, costumed as a nun of austere demeanour, awoke novices to a sense of wordly responsibility, and a Hungarian hussar in thigh-high boots had a tiny ivory whip to persuade Frederick the Great's soldiers that horses, even ripely buttocked, are not suitable subjects for androgynous sexual desire. Castang even found himself dancing, oddly enough; when Vera wants to dance he is wooden and self-conscious.

The effect of champagne upon Leroux was literary, with musical leanings. Castang has heard of Janacek? No, forget about that boring old Moldau, and Smetana too: every damned opera season opens with the *Bartered Bride* to pull in the Wessies. Now leave aside *Jenufa,* a tolerably blood-boltered business, and likewise the *Cunning Little Vixen* (which Vera is fond of). There is lots more Janacek, and some of it—deservedly?—less known. Castang can't feel much enthusiasm for Monsieur Broucek, a fat, vulgar, petit-bourgeois Prague shopkeeper who gets pissed and fancies himself on the moon; says so. But if you wish to understand Czechs? All this is from a literary worthy called Svatopluk Cech, can he have heard that aright? Strong influence upon the whole generation typified by Vaclav Havel: quite so. Obligatory reading matter for any critique of Czech bourgeoisdom: admitted.

Virtuous, a scrap unsteady, watch those cobblestones, he made his way back to his hotel room; muddled a bit with Broucek, the *Affair Makropoulos,* quite a slice of cultural history and maybe more than he'd had appetite for, but now he has an idea who Leroux is. Peer Gynt. But Vera is asleep, the window is hygienically open, he must undress without a hideous noise and sort of slide into bed. Not too displeased with himself.

Chapter 11

"You were very late." A cold still voice, like the dawn air.

"True," he agreed, stretching. "One of those occasions where work seems excluded but you find yourself working in despite. Might prove useful," getting out of bed. Vera was already showered, in underclothes, drying her hair. "Did I wake you? I tried to make no noise."

"You weren't all that time in a restaurant."

"No," giggling. "Went on to the bordel." She switched off the dryer as though to hear better, went on brushing in the mechanical way in which she pushes the vacuum-cleaner; boring chore but necessary.

"The bordel. I see." He did not listen to this voice, had taken off pyjamas, was searching for clean underclothes while scratching in a male way, disagreeable but harmless.

"Things are clearer than they were. Friend Leroux has a professional interest in this business. It's a loose thread, and if one were to pull it——" He can't quite face a shower yet awhile. Perhaps after breakfast? Transferred attention to a shirt.

"I bet. And this interest you share?" He's hazy; large amount of plonk had been drunk.

"Amusing bordel too, former hideyhole for friends of the régime."

"Really. So that you felt impelled—quite professionally—to taste these delights." The warning note had begun to seep through as he took his trousers off the hanger; always meticulous about clothes. And this must be stopped, for Vera's particular definition of sexual moralities is narrow in concept, razor-edged in praxis.

"Do I have to explain? I'd no special wish to go there but he made rather a point of it and I'm keeping close to this fellow."

"So that naturally you tag along with the stimulating suggestion."

This is beginning to sting; one's hand has brushed a nettle.

"Look, I'll do my teeth," in no hurry to shave, either, "and if you're ready we'll go and have breakfast." Coffee seems the greatest immediate urgency.

"What's this army phrase you people use?—you gave your wick a dip." He is sorting through all the junk men have in their pockets. Irritability is gaining on him.

"Of course I did no such thing, there's no point in this, I drank a good deal, danced a bit, and that's the end of the story." It annoys him that enjoyment in dancing—he can't remember when he had last done so and the samba-girl had been near-professional in her footwork; glorious, even exhilarating—should be taken away. Can't these wretched women grasp that one doesn't have to take the girls into the back room? That (quite separate from the Leroux angle) one wouldn't, didn't, even want to. How does one put this in some short simple phrase, and not sound the total ninny?

"A pack of whores," said Vera to the hairbrush, "accommodating Monsieur." She wasn't there! How does one—familiar police problem—establish negative evidence? I-was-there and I can prove it, that's fine: I wasn't-but-I-can't never yet made any impression on a cop. You aren't to say that yes, the girls were accommodating as well as picturesque, that it was a comic occasion, that no, he didn't get closer to the charms; this idiotic concept of honour.

Castang's auntie brought him up left-wing: the ten commandments were socialist maxims and personal honour an important factor. He grew up with a piece of French history. Roger Salengro, Minister of the Interior in the Popular Front government of '36, killed himself. As a front-line soldier in the 14–18, he'd gone over the wire for a wounded comrade. The right-wing gutter press, then as it is now, accused him of desertion, and he felt his honour gone as surely as that of Katharina Blum. This in France has never been forgotten.

"Whores," said Vera flatly. "I smell them on you now. When you came in you were reeking of them." So what does one explain? That the police are used to whores? That they tend to smell of disinfectant? That they wear a lot of perfume in consequence? That he'd been too lazy to take a shower? That if he had he'd have been accused of effacing tell-tale traces? Women turn everything back to front. In his cop time, when whores were bread-and-butter, she had taken his world (squalid enough lord knows) for granted. Why should there be an uproar at a moment of—nostalgic?—reminiscence? Unfair!

She is examining him through the looking-glass, in which he sees her face with contempt written on it. This hurts.

"I can't let you out of sight for a moment, can I?" Out of sight! Like a small child . . . "When we were working in Paris you were in bed with Carlotta Salès." It's true, but love-of-god, this episode, never mentioned since, is ten years old and honour while bruised had not been lost. "Last year in Italy you leapt into that great village-beauty whose name I forget." Worse because true, and because she has used the cutting colloquialism 'dorfs-schöne' to underline her contempt. The accusation had never been made. He could only have met it with 'stout denial' if it had!

But how crude, this amalgam; this rubbishly mix of suspicion, supposition. How unjust towards a basically honest girl who had been under heavy strain and fighting her own corruption. To himself a stab in the back; he'd been none too secure, and had come near paying with his own skin. Women can be extremely coarse but Vera—this is revolting. She'll be calling for the death penalty next. He got angry.

"A typical village outlook. Peasant, and now elderly bigot." Said he, and slammed out of the door.

Take your time; have a proper breakfast; go take a shower, shave; you've work to do. You lost your temper there and re-

gret it already, but it might not be unsalutory. She ought to
know, after all these years. That the police officer is a professional schizophrenic. They have to be, because when at work
they have to be professionally unshockable. He has seen vile
things. He has known children locked in cupboards, starved
and beaten, tortured to death. There is nothing particularly
striking about Auschwitz. Is something worse because it is
on a bigger scale? There is no vileness that the human race
does not, cannot encompass. No idiocy greater than the sentiment of 'God cannot exist since He would never allow such
things.'

So that a lot of policemen, brutalised, take their brutish-
ness home with them, and when their wives walk out they lie
there on the unmade bed like pigs and drink from the bottle.
Others try for an extra sensitivity or delicacy in their homes;
or why stay alive? This isn't sentimentalising: it's survival.

Vera did not appear at the breakfast table. Tja, she's being
Czech. When one thinks about it, she is disturbed. This dig-
ging about, in her delectable city, pokes uncomfortably close
to her roots. Even with this tiny garden fork; proper police
work would be a pick-and-shovel. Such as I no longer possess, have no right to use. Give her time to settle down.

He came upstairs and fumbled with the hotel key: a middle-aged chambermaid with an armful of sheets passed along
the passage, smiled and said 'Good morning' and he gave
her a big jolly wink.

The room was silent, neat. The beds were stripped. Vera's
clothes, suitcase—herself—had disappeared. A piece of hotel
writing-paper lay on the dressing-table. Her neat, legible,
good-schoolgirl handwriting. 'I am leaving.' Short, unsweet.
There seems to be a lot in these three words. Hm, one of the
nice things about shock is anaesthesia. You were going to
have a shower, and shave. You had better do so; you'll feel
more comfortable. Stendhal's words come to mind (they
often do). A man should do something more with his life
than give himself the trouble of being born.

Tja, close on fifty years of a pretty pisspot existence. So
subtract the last twenty-five, which contain the only woman

you've ever really had time for, and what is left? I am, for it has never been taken away, a Divisional Commissaire of the PJ. A highish rank, for that's a Chief Superintendent; in the US, a Captain. Within the Community of Europe I am a counsellor; it's not a diplomatic rank and doesn't fall within the Nomenklatura, but I'm thought a man, fairly long-headed, whose opinion on a legal matter would be worth consideration. I am also the father of two now grown-up daughters and I had thought to have made a fairly good job of that. And what else am I?

A murderer.

I know, and so does any working cop, how very easy it is to kill people. Motive?—och, motives lie around aplenty in anybody's life; you can take your choice, afterwards. It is Physically so easy. Yoh, take a woman by the neck, it will break. Not much muscular force needed; it's a small spasm. And then she is no longer there. Like now. You'd walk downstairs and tell the manager to call the police. They'd be polite, call an interpreter, ring the embassy, they'll send a consul (cross, but calm; it's a commonplace sort of job, why am I alliterating?). Like a cup of coffee? We'll get the doctor—no, not for her: just to run you over for state-of-mind. Killed your wife?—well, we've all been through that. One does or one doesn't, and which side of the frontier are you on?

Castang gave an open-handed slap to the tiles of the shower compartment. Not too hard, boy; it might fall down. He shaved, with care, and a new blade; he doesn't like electric razors. It is rare for him to nick himself; does happen sometimes. Don't let it happen today because it is important to show a good face today and the hands are trembling, just a scrap. One does have thoughts about suicide, now and then, but not this way. Not here, either; not fair to the chambermaid.

Dressed? Good. Light a cigarette. Check your pockets. Key of police-car. Key of Alfa, back in Dresden. Rubbish, rather a lot, but money, likewise credit card, likewise various documents establishing your identity, your Reason for Existing. A small suitcase to pack, and a plastic bag for dirty underclothes. One pays one's bill, extracts the scruffy police-Opel, drives along the road saying Germany. The hell with Czechs and the hell with Peer Gynt. Back in Bruxelles, it will be a very large, bare, empty house. But worry about that when you get there. It's a long way, back to when you were in your early twenties. First stop, Berlin.

He is a nobody here; a stranger, a foreigner. He has been here only as a tourist, knows no one, nothing. Traffic is intense, autos plunge at him from every angle, he is tired and flustered, takes the wrong turning two or three times, does what he should have in the first place; park the car and find your bearings, stupe. He is in a quiet, residential street of old houses. There are trees, the young green of spring come to Berlin; it's nice here. Leafy. "When lilacs last in the dooryard bloomed": he doesn't know how it goes on and it doesn't matter. One line is enough, when that is a good one. Buy a map, imbecile, these shops aren't shut yet. Good god, I'm in Charlottenburg, which is just about the opposite to what I intended. But not far away there will be little hotel-pension places; there will be a pub. Get these ragged edges unruffled. Beer; a phone.

The phone rings a long time and he is about to put it down when a voice says suddenly "Emma, yes?" Instinctively he speaks in French. She doesn't sound at all surprised. Not even particularly pleased. But she's a polite girl.

"Oh it's you. Are you calling from home? You're in Berlin?" But 'save the explanations'. "Mm, better come up here, I suppose."

"Thought we could eat a bite together."

"Yes, that's possible. I've quite a lot of work, but since you're here. No, not the car, stupid, that's too complicated, take the S-Bahn. Ring the bell, the name's on the door. Okay, see you." Not a high level of enthusiasm! But she's his daughter, as well as Vera's.

Away the hell-and-gone, in the Kreuzberg. But beloved, rattly, enchanting S-Bahn, as delightful as the Underground is horrible. Wonderful evening light. What a beautiful city this is.

Odd girl, Emma. Lydia had always been the confident one; brash, a noisy-Nelly. Adventurous; setting sail for New York. And now she was there, prudent, wary. Letters did not convey detail, but there were torments, plagues, sensitivities about virginity. She had always been 'his girl'; she looks like him, talks like him. He did not worry, she's quite hard-headed. Girl of nineteen, learning to come to terms with herself. Gets bashed about but she'll shake down. Bright; too apt to jump into things without thinking. Well yes, he does worry. But to what end? What's the point?

Emma was a year and a half younger; barely eighteen, quiet and withdrawn, her mother's child; secretive, private, rarely uttering. A plodder, and lived in the shadow of the quick, slapdash sister. Musical, thoughtful a round face, nice and rather plain.

Gravely in error, all this. Passed her exams with better marks than Lydia had; came to him last autumn, and with unmoveable obstinacy announced that she wanted to leave home, wanted to go to Germany (speaks good German, much better than his), Won't Budge. Vera, unexpectedly, supported her. There'd been a considerable row. Castang—of course—ended by giving in, ran around pulling every string he could think of, found her a student place in Berlin. She'd always been protected and sheltered: she must find some nice girls to share lodgings with and he will make her a generous if not extravagant allowance, damn it, he has plenty of money nowadays. Primly, she had reported that Pa was in every sense obeyed, that she was very serious, working hard, and saved to go to concerts in the Vierte Galerie: Berlin is a marvellous Musik-Stadt. This is all very good for Castang's conscience and he feels proud of his little daughter. It is an odd reversal of the roles. Well now he has come, to see for himself; virtuously.

Another old house, tall and tatty but solid 1890s: one is always surprised at how much is left. Rows of bells, some sort of accountancy on street level and a 'Rechtsanwalt' on the

mezzanine; six floors of apartments, two to a landing and
'Castang-Weber' at the top: Castang approves of this sober
and economical 'sous les toits' living but hopes the girls are
not huddled in some freezing and squalid attic. Interphone:
Emma's voice quacks, "Sorry, lots of stairs." The entrance is
marble but that only goes as far as the lawyer. As one would
expect; the rest is a narrow spiral of creaky bare boards and
landing windows one can't see out of. But clean; that's a
great plus point. At the very top there is fresh white paint and
green plants and Emma with her door open; cool and unex-
cited. "Hallo Pa." But a nice warm kiss. Her brown hair has
grown out a lot, is a clean chestnutty colour. She is taller,
and a lot thinner. The room is mansarded, not a lot of light
but freshly painted, bright, airy. There is a quite hideous carpeting on the floor but nearly new. There is no squalor.

"Well, sit. D'you want a beer?" There is a low, much-
worn sofa which will be difficult to get out of. There is a sur-
prising large kitchen. "Can I pee?" There is a perfectly good
bathroom: in all of Europe 'only Germans understand bath-
rooms'. This is unexpectedly grand. How clever of these
children, to be so well organised. Who or what is Mademoi-
selle Weber? Emma is getting a beer out of the fridge when
all is explained: a big tall boy walks in (where from? the
bedroom?) and says "Hi" in a quiet and friendly fashion, sits
on another old sofa opposite (Biedermeier, threadbare velvet,
how the hell did they get that up the stairs), stretches out
much-broken jeans with a lot of hairy leg showing through,
smiles, utters no further. Emma brings the beer, in a pub
glass saying 'Beck'. Bremen beer, he knows it well, it's very
good.

"Did you want one, John?"

'If there's one going." Soft deep voice. Not a spotty-boy.
Lot of rippling-muscle, a big swimmer's chest in the tight T-
shirt.

"John?"

"People have these complicated names. Karl-Uwe-
Friedrich. I'm just Johannes."

"And John is simpler still," said Emma affectionately.

"I'd like to ask you both out."

"But you haven't seen your daughter in quite a while. I understand." There is some desultory talk. Schools, studies, rents, distances. Castang admires the kitchen. Yes, all secondhand, but all in good condition. He avoids looking at the bedroom but she's not in the least self-conscious.

"It's only two mattresses on the floor. Is it warm out or do I need a coat?"

"What's the pub like?"

"Just a pub. It's eatable."

"Enjoy yourselves," said John peaceably.

"He'll open a can," said Emma on the stairs.

Food is thought about, dealt with.

"Have a speak, if I may. Don't get to see it often; treat, rather." Castang 'sits back'; proud of his pretty daughter.

"Where's Ma?"

"I'm not quite sure, to tell the truth. Prague—maybe."

"I see. Or do I?"

"You do." He is not sure how to deal with this poised girl.

"You better tell me." Yes, he has to.

"We were in Prague. Chap I'm anxious to get to know better—business. We had dinner, got a bit pissed, went on to the Pouf."

"And did you . . . ?"

"No, but she thought I did." Suddenly there is the need for the clean breast. "You remember last year? In Italy? Before Lyddy left. Then, yes. An accident, but I'm not making excuses for it. She didn't know but she guessed. you know how uncanny her instincts are."

"And now you're very unhappy." Putting her knife and fork together. "That was good, must say." She's only eighteen; a healthy appetite. He lit a cigar.

"I'm perfectly miserable."

"I was rather nervous of telling her, about me, I mean. Got a fag for me, have you? No, I don't, much, they're so dear, here, and John's so mean with his. But she went to bed with you, didn't she—when you first met?"

"She did indeed."

"Get me another beer, will you? I don't want coffee. I understand her very well. And you, too. You're a guter Mensch, but a schlechter Musikant, and she's a good artist. Did you think I didn't know about all this? And stupid Lyddy, always making this hideous fuss about who she is or she isn't going to bed with. She's Ma's daughter, all right. Do you know, why I wanted to come to Germany? Only they understand, about the guilt, all that hideous guilt for the Nazi time. What am I? Am I French? We have done things every bit as bad, and we weren't told about them at school. So have the Americans, the Brits—and the Czechs. Here, in Berlin, we know all about this. I know about guilt. I know about you, you were a cop, and sometimes you've been a dirty bastard. And about Ma. Thought herself a little Czech whore who broke your career up because of ducking out away from the Party. Goddamn Stasi. Probably more of them there than there are here in Germany. Leave them alone, don't worry about them. If you bring Ma to a place like Prague, you must bloody well expect to pay the consequences."

"You're giving me good advice." Yes, and I'm feeling humbled.

"I know who I am," surprisingly gently. "You, you don't. You were an abandoned child and you don't know whether you were French or English or what. You became a cop with a lot of vague muddled ideologies, and it was a lousy job and you fudged and cheated and stretched but you tried to be a good human being and still do, and you succeed, most of the time. You're surprised! Haven't Lyddy and I talked about this, often! Ma—the little Czech peasant, and her father a good straight man, the best kind of communist you find, but she found out she was an artist and she had to make a statement about that, and it's given her endless grief and guilt. Give me a fag, no, give me the packet, fuck all these prigs who kill people and sit wailing about being cruel to the butterflies. So I'm half Czech and half some other bloody thing and now I'm German and I'm giving my body to a German, does that upset you?"

"No. I thought it would have but it doesn't. I saw you still as my little daughter, and the Tampax packet in the bathroom was a little bit of a shock." Emma burst out laughing.

"I do see. You were Good, d'you know that? You've always been true to my mother, and she to you, she couldn't be anything else and that's why she's now so upset. You brought us up, Lyddy and me, with faith and love and truth, and total security, and that's why now I'm able to live, and I'm grateful."

"Have you more advice, for me?"

"Just go back, and say you're sorry."

"I don't even know where she is."

"Good God, man, you're a cop, aren't you? Use your loaf," coarsely.

"What d'you need, as a present for your new flat?"

"A washing machine," said Emma.

Chapter 12

"Oh, Mr. Castang," said the reception-girl. "The key . . . oh, it's not there. Madam must be upstairs." Worse than bright; arch. Of course they all knew he'd had a flaming row with his wife and doubtless the chambermaid's amused tale had lost nothing in the telling. He cleared his throat and said "I don't know the number." Putting out more flags—had Vera gone out and got drunk?—meant a much better and larger room. It was good—no doubt—not to have some ghastly woman in the administration querying his expense notes. 'What on earth is this item for petrol to Berlin and back?' He knocked at the door. 'Come in' in Czech is the same as in any language. That the voice saying it should be the same: that counts.

Sitting at the dressing table, Vera was painting her finger-nails. She looked up and said "I was expecting you last night really." She wouldn't have 'rushed into his arms' anyhow; not her style. He bent over and kissed her hair. "Mind my paint."

"I stopped overnight in Dresden. Yes, this's a much better room. Oh good—two ashtrays."

"I made rather a to-do, about that shower dripping all night, drove me bats. Having to keep the bathroom door shut, meant it got so stuffy. It all made me hypernervous." He sat, in the sort of stiff little armchair one finds nowhere else, lit a small cigar.

"Emma sends her love."

"Ah yes, you were in Berlin."

"The hot news there is she has a regular boyfriend and they're living together." This was a slight provocation, perhaps a tiny revenge; Vera took it well.

"What a good idea. Nearly dry," looking at her nails. "I hope he's suitable."

"Seems nice. Not a skinhead. Name of Johannes. Music student. German, to be sure."

"Ossie or Wessie?"

"Do you know, I didn't ask; does it matter?"

"No."

"Berliner by the sound. Perhaps what the French call an 'Aussi'."

"Would you like me to get undressed?"

"Yes but I'd like a brief verbal report first. Police officer, you remember."

"There was a man in the paper the other day, talking about François Truffaut, who had that extraordinary mania for Alfred Hitchcock, all that idiotic suspense stuff. So why, and this man said oh, it was because they shared this extraordinary Jewish-Christian sense of Guilt. Are there other senses of guilt, one wonders?"

"The French are utterly idiotic, little lycée girls of twelve being solemnly taught in class how to pull a French letter on to a boy's cock. They must try to get rid of every sense of guilt, and of responsibility too while they're at it."

"Yes, talking of little girls of twelve I think I've got this boy of Anita's for you."

Castang nearly fell off his chair.

"Calms the ardour, I should think," she went on (she has certainly never tried) "but what worries me is getting it on is bad enough but getting it off must be infinitely worse, is that the boy's job or the girl's?" Impatient as Castang is, yes, one must ask such things. Isn't this one of the differences between a crime story and a Hitchcock movie?—Grace Kelly struggling with a French letter? The mirror cracked from side to side. Weren't there moments when the pipe was disgusting and the coffee tasted vile and Sherlock Holmes said 'I don't know, I can't think this morning, don't ask me, I didn't notice; shit, there are no clean needles left, and by the way, Watson, you're much too extravagant with the toothpaste'?

"Is there anything in the mini-bar beside beer and phony champagne—what I need is vodka." What *has* Vera done? She thinks in terms of moral-immoral, but not of legal-illegal.

"You had dinner with Peer Gynt. Yes, that's interesting, but how do you get the child back? Is he just going to say oh, sorry, and that will do the trick?" Wrenching the door open fit to break it, this is quite an expensive hotel, there are all those sweet little miniatures Graham Greene thought of playing chess with.

"Don't be so silly," said Vera. "Those things are madly dear; phone down and tell them to send a bottle and be sure for once it's cold, I can do with some too." Castang was trying very hard to be patient with this female inability to come to the point. She had already picked the phone up and was talking to it in incisive Czech words. "They do nothing unless you crack the whip a bit, these communist habits are hard to shake off but stamp a bit and it's 'Sofort Herr Oberst'; where was I, yes I kept thinking 'What's in the child's mind?' Haven't you any fags?" sounding exactly like Emma. Women, he's not going to feel any more guilt. Nor humiliations. But some new anxieties. There might be a knock at the door, and it isn't a waiter with a nice cold vodka bottle but it's the State Police: they are still there and plenty of them. And then there *is* a knock on the door and Vera says Pronto or whatever it is in Czech and his imagination has run away with him. Vera signs the check (that was fast!) and he's opening the bottle: this is needed.

"He suddenly got the idea of phoning his mother to say 'I'm all right.' He knows his mother. He was kidnapped but not drugged or forced, he must have been told something completely, overwhelmingly convincing and came along, what—willingly, happily? This must be your man, Peer Gynt, must have that particular talent, that his stories are utterly convincing, to himself first and foremost, or they wouldn't work on others. All right, a child of eight; who knows what wonderful tales of witches and goblins were poured in on him? Does one ever know how vivid a child's imagination is and how this can become a total satisfying reality? But now, these years later. What does the child know? What does it think? What fantasies has it constructed, to fit the world in which it finds itself? Thank you," accepting the glass, "that's just what I need."

"Stop a moment," said Castang. "I've no legal grip, no legal proof. My idea was to trick the man out of here, no matter where, Dresden, Bruxelles, anywhere I could land on him, twist his arm, tell him to restore this child or he'd be facing a kidnapping charge. I don't even know if it's an extraditable offence nor whether a western government has any treaty with these former Ost-Bloc countries—where does one stand legally, and how d'you pin the bugger down?"

"I thought of all this," said Vera, not listening. "To bring the child across here, to have papers stating whatever, guardianship, no, he must have claimed he was the child's father to get away with it here all these years—he must have got some faked-up papers. And where would he get them? Ingrid, don't you think? As we learned, Ingrid's man was high up in the Party, and had some strings to pull with the government here in Prague. To get official certificates, official stamps on them—don't you think? And those would all still be good, accepted by the government today."

"Yes, I do think. They can't denounce every piece of paper issued under the old régime."

"But why not go and see the woman? His wife."

"You did?"

"Not all that difficult. It isn't just a tourist town, is it? People live here, work here. I wondered what was behind all that movie talk. Well I can tell you—nothing very grand."

"He had plenty of money to push about; that's quite an expensive restaurant." Reference to the bordel might be tactless.

"People who have some sort of black market activity had better not be too obvious about it. Don't want to attract the attention of a whole army of spies and sneaks," shrewdly enough.

"Go on," said Castang, much impressed.

One wouldn't oneself want to attract the attention of spies and sneaks. Unless things have greatly changed—and there is still a great deal that hasn't—Vera felt fairly confident. She has been frequenting the police for many years and knows how they behave. In earlier years, indeed, she had been friends with the younger men and women in her husband's brigade, and police are the same everywhere you go. In uniform, that is something else again, but plain clothes are no different from her own and she is not extravagant in appearance. Her jeans and German raincoat are anonymous, her shoes and umbrella workmanlike. She left her bag behind. There is no need for the air of petty authority, impatient, even bullying; she has noticed that if you act, simply, as though you possess authority, very few people question it. She didn't know what sort of card or medal Stapo people produced if challenged. Her own French resident's identity card looks impressive, has an official stamp across her photograph, would at a pinch give her some immunity if real authority should cross her path. She isn't doing anything illegal. This is an acquaintance of her husband and she's only asking. Thus rehearsed and trembling a bit, but boldfaced, she went out and took the tram. She looks no more and no less Czech than the people in it. She has known, and even seen her own man do this on half a dozen occasions. 'You want information, ask for it, in the tone of authority."

This kind of apartment block is recognisable, had been like this even in her time: a type of housing that bit more privileged than ordinary working quarters. This one got given as a middle-rank state servant. Something clerical in ministries; a superior schoolteacher; head-of-échelon in a public service; police officers! Nothing grand, and even pretty cramped. But nicely situated near a park, and even the washing hung out on little balconies bespeaks functiondom. She found the bellpush and pressed it; no answer; woman out

working; went in search of a janitor; every concierge or fur-
nacestoker is the lowest level of police informer.

"That's right, chap with sort of reddish hair, bit dotty.
Don't quite know what he does, arts-something, irregular
hours. Wife though, that's easy, librarian or something in the
university, documentation service, you'd catch her there, no
doubt."

"No time," said Vera severely. "When does she get back?"

"Quite early, round four, got a little boy, gets out of school
soon after, what's it for, then?"

"Never you mind."

"Sorry—anything I can do to help." He's old; the old are
the downtrodden. They don't have any hopes from these
changes people call democratic. The rich get richer and the
poor get poorer is all we know.

"Describe," snappish.

"Her or him? Nice chap, laughs a lot, always a joke. She's
quiet, pretty woman, dark hair, shoulder-length, sort of
ringlets—nice figure."

"Never mind your lecheries, man. Car, or takes the tram?"

"Tram. Whitish face, these sharp eyebrows, bit taller than
you. Red corduroy trousers is what she wears, dark jacket,
carries a briefcase."

"Thaddle do." Try now a few neighbours. Old ones is
what we want, widows on small pensions. She pushed a few
bells before striking oil.

"Nice woman, friendly, passes the time of day. Nice little
boy, well-mannered, not like some. Skips and jumps, talks to
itself, you know—imaginative."

"Stick to her."

"Nothing much. I don't like him, he puts on this big act
like he's something important, I don't reckon much on those
ones, easy come and easy go, know what I mean? I can make
you a cup of coffee if you'd like it. But she's respectable,
regular job, always on time, and polite, you know. Stays at
home. Some, you know, out all hours, second job they call
that, mutton-hawkers is what my husband used to call them,
pardon the expression but these girls nowadays, no shame

and no patriotism neither, I've always been true-blue, and you make a note of that, I co-operate."

"Good. So she's home, round four?"

"Does her shopping, be nearer five, but if you want a character reference ask the greengrocer, I've been going there these thirty years, he'll tell you, I'm in good standing, always have been, not one to go out shouting and waving flags, what I say is we were a sight better off when we knew where we stood: what has it brought us, everything now costs the earth and it's the crafty ones profit, now he's crafty, as the wind blows so I set my jacket . . ."

A disgusting old woman? No no; Vera corrected herself. On a state pension, and worrying about prices going up. All the older ones have spent these forty years under the metal stamp and what can the change mean to them? Bewilderment, fear, envy. Insecurity. They can't understand, and hanker for the good old days. They no longer have the Stalinist authority which always backed them, and look helplessly on at 'the crafty ones', the sly, the risk-takers.

But go and have some lunch. Where is Henri? But I don't care, I'm going through with it now, this job, screw myself up to the taking of risks.

She was back at four, hovered. Nobody looked at her or asked what she was doing—it was very possible that the old woman had spread a word about: Stapo agent! They'd be watching, behind the lace curtains; they'd have her 'well photographed.'

And here she comes! Exactly as described, there can be no mistaking the dark hair, wavy, rather pretty, the 'whitish face', the red corduroy trousers. A quick nervous walk, something irregular about it, not very well coordinated, or 'how late I'm getting'. She rushed in looking neither right nor left, setting the shopping bag down to fumble with her keys, dropping the briefcase while she hunted in her pockets. Anxious—Vera thought that she knew a good deal about the things that make a woman anxious. Disappeared like a mouse bolting into its hole. Give her a moment to take her coat off, but I'm about, my girl, to make you more anxious.

Vera rang at the door; it opened almost at once. A pretty woman, the eyebrows were set in a lovely curve, but the dark eyes had a neurotic sort of glare. "Yes? What is it?"

"I'm from the police." A statement true in its way. "I've come to talk to you about Maurice." The clichés are accurate. The eyes switched from side to side: is anyone looking, listening?

Yes she did look hunted. But perhaps she often looked hunted. The thing was that she didn't stop to query Vera's right to come ringing at the door. Supposing I had been at home; I wouldn't have shut the door because I'd never have opened it! In Western countries one opens the door to nobody! Man or woman. You'd say—fairly politely—'D'you mind showing me your authority' and you'd look at that with a good deal of care, keeping the door on the chain because it's too damned easy to say 'I'm the gas' or 'we're conducting a survey'. A very foolish thing to open your door, even to a woman. And here—"You'd better come in then." And now I'm in, you're not getting rid of me so easily! Yes, I'm frightened of the police too. But I'm married to one. I counted on this, to be honest.

"My man's away. He's in Dresden." That's a little pathetic. 'My man goes to and fro, and to foreign places, which means I'm not just a total nobody.'

"I think we'd better sit down," said Vera, "talk quietly." It's a small flat; government issue. A narrow hallway full of housekeeping leads to a largish livingroom which is so packed there's hardly room to sit. Shelves of books overhang, threaten to topple over on to tables full of paper, video equipment, photo-stills, two television sets and a video recorder, piles and piles of manuscript, typescript, printouts, the 'personal computer', cassette and—it spills on to the floor, how does she ever do any dusting?

"Sorry about this—this is his workroom. He's a movie director. We're beginning now to get organised but all these years you know, one had to work at home and there was never any room."

"I understand," said Vera. "But I'll come straight to the

point. Nowadays, you know, we co-operate, with the western police."

"I don't see at all what this has to do with anything. What's all this about?" Keeping her end up.

"That this is not your son. And he knows his mother."

"But we've, we've legal rights. Peer is his father."

"No more his father than I am."

"How can you possibly know that?"

"Because his mother is Peer's sister."

"But he has no sisters—his mother—"

"Wanda, yes, we know about Wanda. His father got married, shortly after the war."

"Oh my God."

"So that this is now an Interpol affair."

"But we have all the legal papers to confirm—"

"Acquired under the former régime and upon false premises."

"These certificates are recognised by the court."

"Discovering that it had been misled, the court would reverse itself."

"You're telling me all this, but I need to hear what a lawyer has to say."

"I don't think you know very much about lawyers, nor about the State."

"I don't understand. And Peer isn't here—I don't know what you're trying to do, are you claiming you can try to take the boy away?"

"Certainly the State can take the boy away," feeling that this was rather thin ice, "but I don't wish to put undue pressure on you—how far are you aware of some of your husband's activities?" Fear gave the woman courage.

"That's easy to say when he's not here to defend—no, to explain himself. I'm sure there isn't anything illegal."

"Suggestions have been made," said Vera carefully, for might she be sawing off the branch she was sitting on? "that the Prosecutor might consider putting before the court." She has picked up, in her day, fragments of police jargon. "He might be prepared to—" close an eye? No. "—To leave things in abeyance if the boy is returned to his rightful parents with no further ado."

"God, what has he been up to now?" And since Vera doesn't know and isn't too confident about inventing—

"That doesn't come within my instructions." The woman is twisting her hands nervously.

"I wish he were here—God, there's the boy now." A cheerful ting-ting at the door, some banging and bumping in the passageway. A very ordinary-looking twelve-year-old, ungainly in this crowded room that was overfull of furniture, slapdash rather than awkward. Nowhere here to put his feet, no space for big energetic gestures. Nice-looking boy, wavy fair hair, a Czech pallor in the face, features rather small for a well-developed sturdy body and long limbs. Grinned, said "Hi," didn't know what to do next and collapsed into a chair looking at his feet. The woman was paralysed and Vera saw an opening.

"Maurice." They might have changed his name but he hadn't forgotten his own. He looked up, startled. "Do you remember your mother's phone number?" He got paler still. "You can say it in Czech. And in French too since you learned it by heart." He didn't speak. She wondered about the secret world of his imagination and who inhabited it. Masked men with rayguns? Tennis players or footballers? People who invented wonderful machines which can bore the earth, fly the skies, swoop upon and zap relentlessly—the who? The little yellow horde? Crooked wicked old Jews? Nazis in black uniforms banging the table and shouting 'Schweinhund'? Vera had brought up two girls, doesn't know much about boys.

"If you like, I can take you home. Would you like to go home?"

Vera doesn't care about the woman. Perfectly reasonable decent woman but she must have known about the kidnapping, she must have colluded, and if it comes home to her, too bad. She doesn't care about the man. She's had the luck to find him away, running no doubt after some daft scheme or dirty little fiddle such as Henri had vaguely adumbrated.

He's away and his wife doesn't know where he is, so that
this now is her chance. The boy was looking at her with
enormous eyes; who is this biddy and how does she know
even one of my secrets? She can't kidnap the boy. But if he
is irresolute she can be in tune, perhaps, with a dream.

"I can get you on a plane. Tomorrow." Hoping she can fix
that, but why not? She feels Powerful. "That would be rather
nice. A good surprise for your parents when we get off the
plane in Brussels. Rather a good surprise for you too. You've
had quite an adventure. You'll be able to tell the other boys,
that you lived here, you learned Czech, you know all about
it. You were kidnapped when you were little, it's rather a
grand story." The woman is looking at her with despair in
her face and Vera turned on her. "Don't be sorry for yourself. You knew, at least afterwards, that it must be wrong.
We're not talking legality here, we're talking morality. You
thought it would never catch up, but it does. Now you get his
things together and tell the school whatever you like; he's
going back to his parents. There'll be things he wants, as
well as his clothes. And don't look so downcast, be grateful
it's no worse."

"When can we go?" in a boy's voice which squeaks when
about to break.

"I'll have to book the plane," smiling at him. "Amsterdam
perhaps or Köln if I can't get a direct flight. Home for supper." Yes, he wanted that; he'd have such a lot to tell, even
unembellished by imagination.

Castang said, "Oh, heilig herrgott" at this moment, while
also looking at the bottle, which was more than half-empty.

"If you have objections," said Vera in a silky sort of voice,
"now is the time to state them since," looking at her watch,
"I don't have such a great deal of time, I've a plane to catch
so that while your arrival might be opportune do keep it
brief."

"It wouldn't be brief, it would be nearly as long as the
State Attorney's requisition against you in court, you've
made corned beef and cabbage of about half the penal code

and my arse will be in jail for aiding and abetting, you mean to say you left the two of them there overnight and now you're going to pick the child up and dump it on a plane while this woman—and I—stand there fluttering the hand-kerchief?"

"That's it exactly," immune to these primitive sarcasms. "I thought it out. What else would you suggest I should have done, bring the child here? Leaving her alone just rubs in the helplessness. What can she do? I told her, naturally, that flight or evasion would mean defiance and she'd be in worse trouble than ever. The boy wants to go home and told her she wouldn't stop him."

"And if Leroux comes storming in and makes a huge out-cry."

"I don't think he'd have the nerve, honest, even if he knew, but she doesn't know where he is."

"She may have done exactly as she threatened and phoned a lawyer."

"Seemed to me a risk I had to take. But how did the man get hold of the child in Bruce? Waylaying, kidnapping with some sort of specious tale, he must have had false papers al-ready prepared to cross frontiers with. Listening to the boy talk, no lawyer will want to get involved. I've got to get packed. Listen, what about you—are you bringing that car back?"

"No, I'm sick of travelling for a day or two. I think too I'd better stay here awhile, to see how friend Leroux takes this. I'd rather like to see his face when he hears how he's been diddled." Castang has had time to think.

She had her mind made up, and it is futile to try to stop this kind of woman in that case. He admired the plan any-way; simple, bold and outrageous, just what he'd have liked himself—his own muddled brains had been dimly revolving around court orders, with the suggestion that the Belgian government might be pleased by neighbourly goodfellow-ship in this small matter, from Czech counterparts. Diplo-matic channels, quoi.

What he had not said to Vera was that this woman, finding

herself with no grounds for any complaint in official circles, might turn for support to Wanda: he was still not totally convinced that the two near-accidents with the car were coincidence, but apart from knowing a few louts in her own corner she might have pals in the administration. One never quite knew what an old cow of this type might think up, and whether she might go beyond a crude gesture of intimidation.

Blithe as a bird Vera got into a taxi. He wasn't going to follow her! Probably she would notice, and certainly she would be raging. But he didn't feel too happy about the airport check. All he said was: "Look, give me a phone-call from Bruce, when you get in. It'll be a fine surprise for Anita. I don't think she need have any worries, but she should tell her lawyers; they'd want to mend fences discreetly, with the Foreign Ministry having a quiet word with the Czechs. See you in a day or two no doubt—I'll have to go back through Dresden because of the car. No point is there in saying Take Care?"

"You've said it all three times already," snappish because nervous.

Would that woman want to go out to the airport? Not if she had any sense. He'd rather like to know what she looked like. Never mind, he had her address.

Out at the airport he hung about, on tenterhooks a little more than a little. What were they, these tenterhooks, and how do they come to be synonymous with nervous churnings? Add the ghastly depression which hangs about any airport, the miasma of tension, fear, irrational terrors; now Wilbur, just bear in mind I've told you, huh?—that thing of yours will never leave the ground. Castang has no fears of flying, Freudian or other. He doesn't mind the plane, it's the terminal that gets him down. It's here that vertigo and boredom combine (having a stiff drink, at inflated prices, at the airport bar). There's always enough of that aimless crowd milling about to preserve anonymity. One can see across the barrier. Vera is a competent woman, checks her reservation (not overbooked this early in the tourist season) and luggage—the boy hasn't much: excited, flying is still a treat at twelve years old: slings two shoulder bags through the scanner tunnel. He can just glimpse the passport check beyond: military uniforms. Vera laughing and joking in Czech—she is content when speaking her own language. They are through, and lost to sight in the vile little limbo where one waits for flights to be called. The boy would be restless and roam around the duty-free shop. Vera might buy a souvenir.

And Castang now has a sediment of emotion, enough to think of the woman left behind. She had no children of her own. She had had four years in which to love this child, to think of it as her own.

There is a law in France, and a bad one, which holds that the ties of blood take precedence over those of love. It can happen that a woman who has adopted a child at birth may see that child torn from her, by the order of a judge, and returned to the mother who had abandoned it. He has had to enforce that.

In no way is this situation comparable. But he can feel the pain of a woman alone, in a flat that is too full, and is empty.

He went up to the gallery overlooking the runways, for the flight has been final-called, in a gabble of four languages, a garble of tin loudspeakers. He watches the fat metal blob lumbering off, manoeuvring clumsily, waiting for permission to leave—the moment which never fails to impress him, when the monster hurtles. You feel like a soldier of Alexander. They had seen everything, but not elephants charging. His neck bristles now, when the pilot puts his foot down and the big tin stupe goes straight up into the sky.

Great holes up there in the ozone layer. And down here it's spring and that means too much ozone, and high pollen levels, they'll start shouting at us about our hayfever and our asthma, our bronchitis and our emphysema. But up there—empyrean.

Only for an hour. Next stop Schiphol; laborious, dirty, nerve-wracking and even dangerous. But just for this bare hour Vera is up there swanning. He must stay here at earth level, and plod.

Chapter 13

Feelings of content—no, of self-satisfaction, were paling before Castang left the airport.

For a moment there, euphoria; in the words of a more than usually imbecile beer advertisement.

> 'Sail Away!
> Dream your dreams.
> You can always make your F e e l i n g s
> Come True!'

No no no, that plane *wouldn't* crash. Within an hour or two, Vera, underplaying the scene, would decant a happy small boy, for this was all to him a delightful adventure, into the arms of a very happy Anita; it was to be hoped that she wouldn't overplay either, since boys on the threshold of adolescence feel embarrassment among the acutest and most painful of emotions. But these are sensible people; they understand suffering and they understand self-control. Monsieur Rogier would know how not to ask too many questions.

He'd think his money well spent too, and this would be rather nice, and would definitely run to a new rather than a secondhand washing machine for his daughter Emma.

Why then does this euphoria seem to be petering away so suddenly? Because we have scotched the snake, not killed it? But this is not one of those action-packed thrillers. Vera is safe in the tin-and-plastic bosom of KLM: that may sound denigrating but those people are serious as well as Dutch, and it's as safe as you can get. If anyone is vulnerable it's Castang himself, here in delectable Prague, strolling around the old quarter and fancying an Urquell.

I'm rather dubious about the Ur Quell. The 'original source,' said to go very deep. Let's hope it does indeed go very deep, because Pilsen anywhere near the surface is pretty high on pollution levels.

Why am I hanging around here? Do some thinking. Is there any thinking still needed, about Monsieur Pierre or Pierrot, Per or Peer Leroux? His thinking about 'Peer Gynt' was sound as far as it went. It had been a help that he himself, born around the same time and, one suspected, in circumstances not much different, understood that the man should say 'Who is Peer Gynt?' and have crises about the meaning of this identity. A bright and a sensitive boy with a fundamental instability of character, feeble and indecisive; that idiotic kidnapping fits the pattern, and leave the rest to psychiatry. In the event (extremely unlikely) that a criminal charge was made and pushed through, and brought before a court, a judge would ask for a psychiatric report straight off, and the result would go far towards a verdict of guilty-but-with-diminished-responsibilities.

Now that the child was gone, Peer Gynt would lose interest. He would be busy already with other glowing grandiose schemes for becoming rich and powerful and making a fool of the world. He'd hardly even show himself disconcerted by the checkmating of this particular fantasy. It had never been 'real'.

The wife would be more interesting. Himself he hadn't even seen her, and Vera had seen so little. Was she no more than a poor thing, patient and passive, and unable to bear her own child? He felt pity, but inevitably, not very much. One would say 'Poor Ada', and Vera had. 'I bleed for her, but one can't hesitate.' But what new and doubtless wonderful trick would Peer Gynt be thinking up now?

Castang knew, suddenly, what was bothering him. The bordel. He had been frivolous, even odious about this; now takes it seriously. Mate, don't just sit here supping beer among the dreaming spires. Piece together what you've got.

The 'movie' cover does have some reality, from Vera's evidence about the flat, as well as the one or two minor credits the Film-Library people had shrugged over, but it's pitifully little and will never make Peer rich. But within his own fantasy-magnificence yes, he is capable of real crime, a lot less debatable than the child-stealing, because anyone to whom other people are never quite real has a strong criminal potential. You have to look at where the putative starts to merge into the actual.

Going on about prostitutes; that's something of a bee in Vera's bonnet. Be fair, in the bonnet of any woman with a strong sense of personal honour.

His new friend Mr. Steinmetz had said, "We haven't been taking all this girl stuff very seriously, and now we're wondering whether perhaps we should. Always the same story—too much else to worry about."

Nobody says there isn't a big traffic in girls, and it's getting steadily more organised. Sensational weeklies (sex sells more copies) start yattering about a Mafia. For the Bundesrepublik it's just part of the very worrying refugee problem. What are you to do, build a bloody great electric fence across the whole damned enormous eastern frontier? Contrary to the Constitution, mate; haven't we had enough of Walls, and barbed wire, and police states? You are touching our basic nerve here. This indeed is what Lyndon called slipping your hand up our trouser leg. You can put it crudely: we don't like it.

Jugoslav, Roumanian, Hungarian or Russian girls are an embarrassment the Federal Republic would prefer not to talk about.

Of course in France if something nasty is contrary to the Constitution you'll have a flock of politicians yelling 'Then change the Law.' Germany is not like this.

We signed a treaty with the Czechs. We owe them, because of what happened in Munich in 1938. As an Englishman of the time put it

"Dear Czechoslovakia

We don't think they'll attack yer,

But don't think we're going to back ya."

Germany has to pay now for that. It goes deeper than Richard von Weiszäcker showing politeness to Havel.

The Federal Republic does not want its police forces to gain undue influence, power, or publicity, and especially it doesn't want to know about Czech girls who are poor and see prostitution as a quick penny, while there are far too many good German citizens anxious to aid, abet, and get-in-there.

It is rather probable that Peer Gynt, said by his wife to be 'in Dresden' although plainly she doesn't know, and is accustomed (poor wretch) to being told anything that might come into his head, is now finding that girls can make one a lot richer a lot quicker than little pisspot movie jobs. One wants to get OUT of that abject little apartment block. Poor Ada! One isn't really supposed to take the 'Solveig' figure seriously, is one? Isn't she mythical, the unattainable ideal? Perhaps poor Ada takes her literally.

Now your other piece of evidence, which is Wanda-Ingrid. Have you given enough thought to her?

She's still an active and vigorous woman (and she has an embittered, failed, frustrated son). Is she content to sit there in her tiny backwater on the seacoast of Bohemia and play the lady of the manor? You'll give me leave to doubt that.

Her man as we learned was a local figure of some prominence, with good Party connections, and there's every reason to suppose she's kept a lot of that going. A business woman too, a pusher and an organiser. Those frontier posts down to Linz—ways in and out for Austrians with money to spend. Why had he had a near miss, twice, from road accidents? Not perhaps efforts to cause personal injury, but bashing the car is as good a way as any of saying "Mind your own business." Vera's instinct had been quicker than his own.

It's possible, Castang, that you might be in some danger here.

Perhaps they haven't added the different elements together as yet. Let's see how that might go.

Suppose that Ada, made distraught by Vera's threats and unable to reach Peer, had got on to Wanda; she has a good local grapevine but would it stretch to Prague?

Ada has not seen him at all, but only Vera. While Peer has not seen Vera, and has said nothing of meeting me to Ada, or she'd not have taken Vera for a real police agent, and been so intimidated. I spoke to him of Bruce, though, and of old Klaas, and he'll put it all together quick enough. While Wanda has seen the two of us, and didn't like it. The moment Peer hears of Vera's antics, it might not be a car accident that would come to mind. He could well have friends nastier than himself.

Where the hell is Peer? Said to be in Dresden, and that sounds like the truth. Oh yes, it begins to become interesting.

Castang does have a bit of cover. The idea of the Alfa beginning to look conspicuous was sound; the accident of his passport being out of date was lucky. He has a German identity card, phony but covered by friend-Steinmetz, and a borrowed car. This should be enough to get him out of here. But he had better waste no more time.

Driving north, on this now-familiar Dresden road, he is thinking only in generalities. The Czech-German friendship treaty has made passage here a commonplace. Nobody looks at cars with a German registration, and that's what most of them are. Floods, though, swarming in from Poland and Russia and Roumania, not to speak of all these new countries—what's Moldavia? Czechland is a staging post for these hordes; Bosnians, Ruthenians and Gypsies; they've pretty permeable frontiers, one may guess, to anyone able to pay the standard bribery rates for papers establishing some German blood, which would allow them to settle and be maintained in Germany. Castang, as one of the Community's experts (criminal law has proved an elastic concept) has had something to do—and also much ado—with the Schengen agreement: the idea of free movement within the Community coupled with a tight exterior barrier. A lot of worries this had caused, about the Rights of Man, and about Police States. Well well, lucky old England to be thus handily surrounded by Channels and a North Sea. (Come to that, lucky old Swedes and even Danes; nothing like lots of water for keeping out the Wogs.)

Within Germany, there is also a tremendous traffic in stolen cars. These are headed out, eastwards, where the market for them flourishes. A Minister of the Interior, in some despair, thought that perhaps a great big wall might be nice, to cover the whole immense eastern frontier. What about all that barbed wire left behind from DDR days? Hundreds of lovely guard towers. Electronically tripped alarm fences. Mine fields!

He stopped in Teplice, with the idea of a pee and a cup of coffee; getting rid of unwanted small change. A small town, bright with municipal flowerbeds, determined to look clean and welcoming.

Because here is where people cough: beyond is the passage of the Ore Mountains, the strange, sinister shapes of the Erzgebirge whose iron and lignite have turned half of eastern Europe into a sterile wilderness. Your expectation of life, here, is not great. And the girls, here? Pretty but pale, and you'd be worrying about their lungs. There were none hanging about with meaningful looks. But perhaps, nowadays, they're rather more professionally organised. The side of the road is damp, perfunctory, uncomfortable.

The Czech frontier post here was elaborate, but they didn't even look at him. We don't bother much now; it's something for the Germans to worry about. Everyone has the right to make a little money, okay? We have little; Germans have lots. There would be some eye-closing: What prostitutes?

At the German post beyond, the barrier was down. They'll come out with the dog now and then, let it sniff well round. But Castang knows his policemen. There is the Absence of Zeal principle, well established. When a queue starts to form, the Dai-Shoni syndrome. ("What about the women?" "Foock the women." "But have we got the Time?")

But today there was no crowd. That's all right. If Herr Peterhansel, a good German citizen, is on his way back from a weekend in Prague, and there's some nice Czech girl sitting next him, then who are we to ask all these questions? Her papers are regular and no doubt Herr P. pays his taxes, has no criminal record; he looks respectable and his car is roadworthy.

Peer Gynt could come carting past here with a truck full of movie extras. That's right, we're filming this week in Berlin, for the Funkausstellung.

Supply your girls with passable papers and you're in business. Who can tell she's Russian when half the Aussiedler don't even speak German, but you see we had this German granny whom Stalin decided would feel happier in Tadjikistan?

Dai didn't bother saluting, held his hand out for the card, looked at it, looked at the back, looked at it upside-down. "Auto papers. Mm. Just a moment, Herr Peterhansel. Bore the cards off into his hut. Shoni walked round the car, strolling, bending over to look at things, came back, leaned on the door-latch in a friendly way. "Rather a lot of mud. Number-plate a bit obscured. Lamps, too. You could do with a good wash; might see to that, would you? Not sure I'm happy with your exhaust-emission neether." Pronounced Saxon accent. "Got your roadworthiness certificate up to date? Not seen that, have I?" Another car came, drew in behind them. Dai came back, smiling pleasantly, looked at this, and said "Tell you what, why don't you pull over there to the side . . . Kill the motor." Beckoning Castang out, relaxed, nowise unpleasant. "Like to have a word, inside?" Shoni leaned in at the little ticket window and pressed the button to let the next car go through.

Damn.

Castang is not worried. He's in no hurry. Maybe there's a bit of explaining to do. This might be just a thought tricky; he doesn't want to compromise his friend Mr. Steinmetz.

In the warmed, bright interior Dai put the papers on the table behind him, leaned his bottom against it and said gently, "I don't know but what we mightn't have a wee problem here, Herr Dingus, because you see this vehicle is signalled as missing, query stolen, so we'd like to establish your title to ownership, d'ye follow me?" Tja, he hadn't seen Shoni giving Dai a nod. They have of course their code.

"Maybe I'd better have a word with your officer."

"I'm here. You can have the word with me." A foot had been put wrong, stupidly, unnecessarily, and the chap had bristled. Ensuing explanations made things worse. What to the Czechs had merely sounded funny here sounded fraudulent.

"Uh, the car belongs to the Dresden police," turning out pockets in the hope of some convincing evidence. He has still his "medal" identifying him as a senior PJ officer. It is better suppressed. For if put on the Bundesgrenzschutz computer that would create waves in Paris which he does not, but definitely, wish to hear nor see.

"That sounds like your bad luck, mate. If as you claim it was lent you, how come it's not accounted for?" Castang who knows all about police vehicles being unaccountably diverted for private purposes is cursing the earnest dunderhead who got cross about 'not properly signed-out.'

"Look, keep it off the official rails, that's your interest as well as mine." It is possible that an unfussed tone might have won the day against the fact that if you pinch a car, that's common form, but pinching a police car is cheeky, and will get hammered. At this moment Dai was distracted by a noisy irruption of two or three people through the back door, where the road leads back to Czechland. And in the forefront was Peer Gynt, all jovial bonhomie and a peculiar parti-coloured coat; what was that then? Some sort of goddam piebald ponyskin? This looked both funny-peculiar and funny-haha, but Castang was unimpressed by the first and unamused by the second. A line in facetious jester's speech had been adopted to go with it.

"Ho, mighty Viceroy, behold us then, returned from far-flung climes, having dispensed strange dreams to your noble folk—no opium I'm sorry to say. Wending our way homeward bearing gifts, not quite as many as one would wish."

He caught sight of Castang then and stopped short; the mouth was open already but it opened further. "Oho. And Aha. Quelle horrible surprise! Or is that what one calls a co-incidence, then? Now one comes to think of it, not altogether unexpected."

"You know the gentleman," said the policeman, interest quickening: the clown act he had seen before. Monsieur Leroux seemed a familiar figure hereabouts. Castang's mind registered the circumstance.

"Know him? I know of him. What I know I don't like. A nasty, sneaky sort of little man. I would bid you beware, o great king, and especially of strangers bearing gifts. I would fain have speech of this worm my own self, having indeed some unfinished business." This volubility was a bit much for the police officer.

"You wouldn't mind waiting outside then, a second, while we finish our own business." The troop withdrew ostenta-tiously, Leroux with his nose in the air and loud sniffs. "Dai" waited for Castang to speak; when he didn't, said dryly, "Curious."

"I agree."

"We were beginning to get to know a bit about you. It's not quite enough. Here are your papers, Herr Castang-Peter-hansel, and as you tell me, you're just going down the road to return their property to the Dresden Police. Your business with Czechs doesn't particularly interest me," showing his teeth in a nice white Colgate grin but unamused, "you can sort that out with them. Now if you'll give me a reference in Dresden I can take seriously, that would go some way to re-store my confidence." There was nothing else for it.

"Steinmetz, Kripo."

"Less bad." He walked over to the glassed partition of the inner office, where a uniformed girl was typing. "Get me Steinmetz in the Praesidium and if he's off duty have them patch it to his house, his car or whatever because he's wanted for a verification."

Outside, a diesel motor started noisily. That would be Peer Gynt on his way. He can't do anything here, thought Castang, and that is just as well. But he'd got the news! And that's of interest—Ada didn't know where he was but plainly someone did. Wanda is likely if not certain. He had sounded drunk, which is unsurprising. Or is it only standard exuberance at a place where he's known? He must shuttle here, fairly often.

Dai was in the inner office now, standing talking on the phone, but keeping quite a beady eye on Castang's appearance and demeanour. Laughing a little. Well, Steinmetz has authority enough to clear himself with these border people, and if he's cross about my indiscretions, too bad. Should have kept a closer eye on his motor-pool sergeant, and I'll tell him so. I just might have something to pay him back with, for his trouble.

Dai came back and gave another of his mirthless smiles.

"All right, Mister Castang, you're vouched for. We'd be pleased if you didn't try that gag, another time; we'd rather prefer you to get your own passport up to date and use that. You can trundle on down the hill—and just see that the car goes back where it belongs Okay? And I don't owe you any apologies either."

Outside, it had got dark. A cloudy night. It had been raining, and would rain again. This was pleasant; the sour smell, betimes shrilly acrid, of this part of the world had given way to the comforting scent of spring foliage by night, when the trees soak up carbon dioxide and breathe out oxygen, and one does not see the damage caused by sulphurs, and just as well because one doesn't want to know.

It is a longish way still, down to Dresden. The city lies in the Elbe valley, and here we've crossed the col, and must wind through the little country road of the Saxon-Switzerland, a slightly pathetic holiday area of little villages, country auberge and wooden chalet; not terribly inviting, but in the DDR time had no doubt been a very agreeable change from the grim old townscapes jagged from war damage and simple downright neglect. Pretty similar when one came to think of it to the fairly joyless delights of Party rest-and-recreation places on the Lipno See. All still the seacoast of

Bohemia. Anything can happen here, but is it real? Is it only taking place inside the imagination? Stories of lost children miraculously restored—if you are having breakfast with Shakespeare the grittiest landscape will start to shimmer. (What did he have for breakfast? No coffee, and even the bread pretty dubious unless one knew an honest miller, traditionally a great rarity. Soup perhaps, like the French peasant of only two generations back. Beer? For the most part, bit of rusty bacon, bit of rancid butter.)

It didn't sound encouraging but in this company who knew what might not happen? Wouldn't it still be better than even the most palatial breakfast on the terrace of the Palace Hotel, overlooking the most glorious of broad white clean and beautiful Atlantic beaches—at La Baule, at Royan, at Biarritz, but in the Unimaginative company of Walther Ulbricht?

Behind Castang's car (the more unimaginative sort of Opel Rekord) there's the bluntish silhouette, recognisable from round headlights and upright profile, of the old-model Volkswagen minibus. A solid affair; hundreds of thousands of them still on the road. Castang went cold suddenly. He had heard again in his head the characteristic sound of that motor starting. Pulling away. Now had that been a forward gear, or a reverse? All at once there wasn't enough traffic on this road. Not enough villages either.

This chilly sensation; don't believe people, police officers or otherwise, who tell you they do not feel fear: even the very young ones. The SAS, which stakes out IRA arms dumps in the middle of the night, are élite troops brought to an exceptionally high level of physical training and psychological preparation, and they're scared shitless. Castang is at a low level of both. The PJ officer is frightened exactly because experienced enough to know that people like Peer Gynt are unpredictable, and violence comes naturally to them.

Castang felt for a gun and there wasn't any gun. His was at home, 'war souvenir'; antique (bluing much worn) .38 calibre revolver; simple, reliable weapon; the good-old-firm of

S & W. He'd never needed nor wanted anything else. His last year in the PJ, he'd been drinking coffee with a colleague who'd said 'You still carting about that old thing?' and hitched out his own nine-millimetre FN Browning. Twenty shots in that magazine; now that's a gun. Castang had jeered. "Might as well have a Kalashnikov. Fire all twenty before you know they're gone and still hit nothing." He'd been trained the old way: you need no more than two, 'the double tap'.

Yes and now he didn't have any.

The minibus passed him in a rush, clipped across his bow and the brake-lights glared on. Castang stopped; he didn't have any other choices. He got out because it's better to be out than in. Locking the doors won't help; there are three men and two of them big. On a road like this at night nobody even glances at a stranded car. With or without men round it.

"Just something to remember us by," a light, mocking voice.

"Better not kill him, he's an ex-cop." He got a paralysing smash on the kneecap. He fell down because there was nowhere else to go. Hedgehog position; try and protect your face and your balls. "A few more good ones." This word 'few' needs defining. " 'n' now kick him in the ditch 'n let's hope the bastard catches pneumonia—hear me?—you won't be so quick to meddle, again." A last kick and a nasty one in the face. They picked him up by the shoes and the collar. "Maybe there's nettles," said one, laughing. They left the car; it would attract no attention.

He didn't lose consciousness. At least, he thought he didn't. He couldn't get up, though. Pain banishes fear, but then you have to cope with the pain. He hoped he did cope; not the first time. No yelling though; hurts too much.

Steinmetz found him. It wasn't quite clear just how broad a hint the border guard had given: it never would be clear how much that guard guessed or put together. People like that will draw attention to some things and close their eyes to others. That's the way the world goes: as long as you have your own ass covered. The message was garbled but enough, said Steinmetz, to make him think he ought to go out and look. Car by the side of the road—well of course, since it was one of ours . . .

Damages bill, neither light nor really heavy. Badly swollen knee, nothing much for that but rest. Extensive bruising, ditto unless you start pissing blood and one hopes not. Bone bruises, some of this is damned painful and goes on being so. The teeth, well, the dentist says if you get kicked in the mouth an Italian shoe is preferable to skinheads with big boots. A nice little bridge, true, rather an expensive item, does your private insurance complement the Krankenkasse?

Steinmetz, who was blaming himself a good deal, brought Castang to his own home. Hospitals will only make you a great deal iller than you already were. The police doctor said he didn't *think* there'd be any Lasting damage, and Castang by then had thought of one of Vera's 'Evelyn-Waugh' jokes—'You may be breathing arsenical smoke this very minute; watch your urine in three days' time.'

Ring Vera. "Sorry, yes, my mouth's a bit funny." Vera said she'd come. "No need. Frau Steinmetz is a nurse, and she's a Good German Woman, understands the uses of herbs. Don't budge, but I want you to take precautions . . . Tell Mr. Suarez it was a car accident." ('Oh dear,' said Mr. Suarez. 'He is unlucky, isn't he,' with the memory of the year before in Italy; cracked ribs 'falling off a ladder' and a badly cut hand, which healed but it was touch-and-go there with the tendons awhile.)

"Won't be long," said Castang brightly, knowing it might be longer than the ten days of his rough estimate. Never mind; herbs, liniments, water therapy; a good nurse with a big kind German bosom.

Chapter 14

Despite arsenical smoke—'when the wind's the wrong direction Dresden has every other kind so why not that too?'—a good nurse, a lot of paddling in warm water and a nice girl physiotherapist—'No Massage!' screamed Castang but, 'No no no, you don't understand yet'—he was up and about and even quite bright (good, Vera was getting extremely restless) in less than five. Mr. Steinmetz, feeling vindictive, had been doing homework. Not just the Bundesgrenzschutz, but the Bundesverfassungsschutz. Well, strictly speaking, that means we're protecting the Constitution, and the trouble with the German Constitution is that to make up for the Nazi times of evil memory it's a lot more liberal and civilised than anyone else's constitution, and we don't like the idea of changing it.

"All nice and mobile," remarked Frau Steinmetz in no spirit of self-congratulation. Castang poured himself out coffee, buttered lovely-smelling black bread, arranged the little wooden board that is a proper part of a German breakfast, agreed.

"I congratulate myself. I still pity myself. Why is it always me? Dilapidated. In decrepitude. Those are two interesting words." He was teaching her French. "Dé-crépi; the plaster falls off the house, leaving bare stones, tatty brickwork, this is me." But despite the gaptooth grin and the mottled green leg (cheese with sage in it) he was on parade; took the tram in to "the office". Steinmetz was studying the big wall map, that huge sagging eastern frontier.

"Need several army corps to plug that gap. No more nice Oder-Neisse line. I don't *want* Silesia back."

"Give me a fortnight and I'll be on the Vistula," agreed Castang, borrowing someone's cigarettes. "Is that Hitler or was it Napoleon?"

"No point anyhow in stopping people on the border. One would like to know where they went then. I've done some work on this and without a lot of result. I don't bring it home to anywhere round here. Course, we've lots of Czech girls already . . . as I've told you several times, the hierarchy is not much interested. Lorry-load of drugs out of Turkey, there'd be some kudos for us in that."

"Stopping a thirty-ton truck and reducing it to small component parts," agreed Castang.

"They went on through, and where to?" The two stared again at the wall map, this time at western Germany. "It's sort of large."

"We do of course have people in Bruce getting worked up about this flesh traffic, but if I were to tell them—you know the story of the two page-boys in the Ritz? One said 'General de Gaulle's over there' and the other said 'Give me news, not history.' "

"Wait for them to cross the border with a fresh load."

"Hm yes, that minibus; ask where they're going and it's a cheap holiday in Paris—bringing their own food."

"No but following them."

"Who, me, in my all-too-recognisable little silver Alfa? Not to mention that they might go the other way, through from Austria up to Passau," thinking again about Wanda. "But I've got to go home anyhow, I've at least done the job I set out to do, and the holidays are now over. But would it be possible, supposing one did mark them at a border crossing, to stick a direction-finder under the minibus?"

"Wouldn't interest our people much. Too many different police authorities concerned. Those things need recalibrating every couple of hundred kilometres: federal affair, not for

Länder. All we know is suppositions anyhow; we've no leverage. Bundeskriminalamt calls it trivial and a waste of time."

"Supposing I could raise some interest, perhaps some finance, out of the Community?" Steinmetz looked dubious and well he might.

"You could try."

Vera was glad to see him back. The cheese was fading back towards ordinary cheddar.

"But oh your poor teeth. Dentist's appointment quick; you need crowning or capping, what is it?"

"Madly dear," said Castang gloomily. "Muster all one's insurance companies and they'll all say we haven't read the small print." But oddly enough, Mr. Suarez got quite fierce and Spanish about the small happening.

"Let me get this clear. Over there among Czechs you got on the path of some people selling girls to bordels? You will insist on meddling with things which are no earthly business of ours. I do realise that you're an ex-police officer and that reminds me, Paris is quarrelling again over who's to pay what proportion of your pension. You were moved by your sense of civic responsibilities, we could do with a bit more of that. I noticed some people breaking into the house of my neighbours and I rang the police and I got no thanks for it; everybody leaving their cars in no-parking areas, tous des cochons, m'entends-tu? Cochons, Schlamperei and Schweinerei y puercoprocedimiento, you hear me?" in a most unusual display of disapproval. "I'm not having my people beaten up by petty gangsters—yes yes, your dentist, I'm aware, now you get over there to those people in the Quartier Leopold and tell them I'm having a word with their chef about this."

"I suppose it might work in a sort of arseways fashion," said the gentleman in the Quartier Leopold, but without enthusiasm. "The Germans have so much on their plate they don't want to know about girls. It's only the tiniest drop in that gigantic immigrant problem. They make an Abstraction

of it; all part of that interminable debate about the Abtrei-
bung: is this new clause permitting abortions of German
women unconstitutional?

"Furthermore no German co-operation means no money
here and no money here means no Mitarbeit; the daily Catch-
22 and bread-and-butter of every one of us, forever up
against a National Interest.

"All we do anyhow is sit here and collect ever more statistics; we've no funds for this sort of operation. Tell you what,
try Strasbourg."

This is exactly like the man in Dickens who went to the
Circumlocution Office and said he wanted to know. 'Tell
you what, try Mr. Jenkins in Room Three-oh-two—he'll be
most interested.'

The Community's police-co-ordination unit in Strasbourg
is known to Castang. He used to be in on some of these do-
ings in their early days; had once indeed been a delegate to a
conference in Munich, as the only senior officer Paris could
find who could speak a bit of German, not the sort one learns
in phrasebooks but at least he wouldn't appear ridiculous.
There he had made friends, like Geoffrey Dawson (long
since resigned from the CID in protest against little lapses
from virtue like faking evidence against suspects), or
Colonel—now a General and rather grand—Roberto Bona-
corsi. He'd learned, a year or so ago in Italy, that a sturdy
ally in the Carabinieri is a very good thing to have when also
a strong admirer of Vera's.

These channels still existed, but were badly silted up. A
Criminal Commissaire out of Karlsruhe; that sounds like the
Ku Klux Klan but is called Horst Schröder and listens pa-
tiently, sympathetically.

"Find me girls being shipped to Buenos Aires and I can
get you Unesco, Unicef and the whole damned World Health
Organisation, together with their Japanese chiefs and colossal Swiss bank accounts. Girls being shipped to Karlsruhe,
be they Czech or Russian, they've got to come from somewhere. Customers like the exotic flavour. Leila from Odessa

gets it up quicker than die Christl off the farm, from back-woods-Beyern."

"More desirable," agreed Castang, "in both senses."

"The moral angle—but what's fashionable? Sex is pop; this comforting belief that all the girls like nothing better, so why not Czechs? You've heard the joke about the fishing boats; that Bruce decreed they shouldn't be allowed beyond five kilometres off shore without a stock of minimum two hundred rubbers in the cabin."

"Boy, my wife would go to town on you!"

"So does mine—and does that bring us any further?"

Castang and his wife were asked to dinner, by Arnold Rogier. This was rather a formal occasion, because thanks had to be paid formally. A bonus handed over, so that to make all this less stiff there was a lot to eat and to drink. Just the four of them and at the start it took a lot of effort; until everyone gets a bit unbuttoned and even this serious, and perhaps rather humourless pair lose the crippling sense of having to be grateful about the recovery of the pride and joy, the one and only, the Blessing. Nice little boy, thought Castang, who had never seen him before. Present and much so before dinner, highly exuberant in fact, allowed a glass of champagne 'to drink your guests' health'; greeting Vera as an old friend and fascinated by Castang as a Deliverance figure: cops *ought* to be like this, swooping in from the sky to rescue people. The reality, Castang feared, would be a terrible letdown.

"Have you got a gun?—I mean are you wearing it?"

"No. I never do, now. Didn't much then, to tell you the truth; cops only wear them on television, they're very uncomfortable and very rarely of any use. Carrying it is bullshit and you can tell your friends I said so."

"The other day there was a man on the autoroute doing two hundred and fifty, in a Porsche I expect. They got him though."

"Coming back from the races no doubt; thought himself on the circuit at Spa—you do get these ones with fantasies sometimes."

"What's the fastest you've ever done?"

"Not me, mate, my driver, he's the professional, that's what he's there for. I had my eyes Tight Shut. Don't look at me like that. Cops get frightened too, you know."

"Even Clint Eastwood?"

"Especially Clint Eastwood," rightly supposing this to be a fictional toughy.

"That's a nice boy," after he had been banished.

"Won't last," said Arnold resignedly. "Right now he's nice, it's as though the whole episode had been unreal, imaginary, left no mark. There'll be a return of the pendulum, is what I fear. Who knows what nightmares lie in wait? Hidden defence mechanisms of every nasty sort, aggressions—fugues? I want to go as easy as I can on the psycho-analysis stuff; don't want to encourage him to think himself abnormal. Child of that age—other day in France—carrying a gun, in school so please you—shot another boy bigger and stronger than himself. People blame the schools and it's the parents who're at fault."

"That I'm sure is a wise attitude, let him think it's all part of the day's work, children will accept the unlikeliest situations without question until somebody starts to make a fuss."

"Don't want him thinking himself a glamour figure."

Vera and Anita got into an animated discussion on this very point, so that the two men were left for a while to one another.

"This chap for instance—total fantasist, in fact I see him as Peer Gynt, turns everything into dreams of power and success and I don't think the kidnap was anything much beyond a dotty notion of I-can-do-anything; course, I'm only a police-psychologist, an analyst would doubtless find a lot more. He thought he had a big career in movies and now he's shipping girls across the border to German bordels. I don't much like this, the slavery element bothers me, but nobody's interested or prepared to put money and effort into stopping it."

"Fact of life, Castang, just the same in big companies such as my own, they'll give a huge sum to phony philanthropies or a bogus artist and behind it is nothing but naked cynicism:

it's the immediate promotional financial advantage or it's nothing at all."

One could look at Rogier and think, Oh dear. The hollows in the cheeks and temples, the ears and nose which stuck out: at bad moments he could look haggard to the point of dissolution. When Castang saw him first he looked tired to death, and resigned to it; the refusal to give in worn surely thin. Look again now and one was struck by the energy in the eyes, in the muscles of the throat and shoulders.

"You think of me perhaps as—within the company—an important and a privileged figure? So I am; I'm skilled and I'm an inventor, a thing much prized. Being a cripple, or having been long years with this firm, making a lot of money for them too, prestige advancements, stealing a march on the competition, stuff like that; this has no importance to myself and it's important to remember, I have none to them. I'm cossetted; and I'm very well paid. And if they, as is at any given moment likely, were to seek a fusion to make themselves still bigger, find themselves with another research branch containing younger men, they could and they would sack me tomorrow. Unjustifiable drag on the balance-sheet. As it is—come up with something new every year or—A la trappe, Mère Ubu."

"Whereas this dim, functionary world of mine—we live wrapped in cotton wool. Clinging on, for our pensions. If we get anything done at all it's by accident. You—you live on the dangerous edge of things. I'm astonished to find myself feeling envious." Rogier only laughed, and signalled for some more wine.

For this 'little'—almost a 'family' party they hadn't bothered getting the maid in. It was 'Monsieur Jean' in a white jacket who padded about, opening bottles, clearing plates away; Anita had done the cooking herself. Odd character, and Castang's eye rested on him for a moment, recalling that he had felt curious, even suspicious, as to what went on behind that impassive face. Nurse, even a sort of governess, personal valet, intimate and privileged attendant, he seemed perfectly content to play the parlourmaid. Very little in this

house escaped him; you could say nothing. When he went
out to get the cheese Castang put the question to Arnold,
who laughed, short and abrupt.

"I've learned not to ask. He's there, luckily for ourselves,
and that's about all there is to it. He does go away from time
to time, as though to remind himself—and me—that he must
have another life, and that he has the right to lead it. He'll
come, ask formally whether I can spare him for a week; it's
never longer. Of course I say yes at once and without hesitation, it's good for us all not to be over-dependent. One of
these moments is probably about due. Now that the boy is
back—to whom he was always most attached without ever
showing it—but one must never ask," as the cheese appeared.

"You were talking about 'Peer Gynt' "—Anita had turned
back towards him, feeling herself discourteous, while Rogier
with as easy a movement concentrated on being polite to
Vera (they would get on well together)—"I'm interested, because horrible as all this was, criminal and quite mad, and it
must have been a dreadful responsibility to you to determine
which, I still feel him as my brother, in a confused fashion,
and I feel sad and sorry, and I wonder so much about it all,
and would you be in favour I wonder of putting out some
sort of feeler, attempting to mend fences?"

"I don't feel able to form an opinion," said Castang. "I
only met the man once." He had never mentioned the being
beaten-up. "That was superficial; he was putting on the
charm, of which he has a great deal."

"Maurice liked him in odd ways and felt—still feels—
much affection for his wife, who is childless, poor woman—
but if that's a little bit of the motivation there's so much else
I can't grasp."

"I can't and I won't. He's a bit your brother, and you're a
bit his sister and if he felt hatred for you he feels love too. I
don't know, I think he may have come in secret to find out
what he could of the lost parentage, and he looked at you,
and suddenly got swamped in a complicated fantasy, which

he doesn't distinguish from realities. I don't suppose there's much you can do."

"Yes, that is pretty well the opinion of the lawyers. Arnold has laid down that he doesn't want to press criminal charges, but there's quite a lot of diplomatic mouthing going on behind the scenes. There's one person who is really rancorous about this whole business—is it really closed? Can it ever be closed? That is my father; 'Old Klaas'. And that of course is understandable. He's always felt that whatever he did in those unhappy times keeps on coming back to haunt him. That he can never be entirely free of it. Shame, and guilt, and regret: I mean one does something so small, for a man at least, trivial in wartime, and it's irrecoverable, it comes back, it casts the long shadow over six lives—the seventh my own child. What is this Ingrid like?—you've met her, you must tell me."

"No," said Castang. "Better not." Anita looked at him steadily and then dropped her eyes.

"Very likely you're right ... I made a cake," she said to the table generally, "but I fear it's a bit of a flop. Maurice will eat it, he eats anything."

"So do I," said Vera. Anita laughed.

"Very well, and Arnold, d'you think we could have some cognac or something? I feel I'd rather like one."

A force that through a green fuse drives a—no no, not quite right. There are though plants, modest, humble, that will lift, split, large heavy stones and pop up, jauntily, into the sunlight. Uh, dandelions and things.

Castang with the telephone tucked in the collarbone put his feet on the desk. He had always wanted to do this. Like American Presidents. A Monarch-of-all-I-survey act. Expansive. Devil may care. It was not really all that comfortable and he couldn't reach the little cigar tin. Never mind.

Who had struck the match that lit this fuse? Mr. Schröder is explaining down the telephone at some length and with much false modesty that it's him. There's perhaps a better chance that Mr. Suarez, somewhere ...

"Won't say we went quite as far as Havel but we did find some Czechs who did finally agree that this wasn't doing the image much good. Stumbling-block up there in Bonn, exactly as I expected, Germany's black reputation, pull the feather-bed over all this. Trembling terribly lest *Spiegel* start yet another scandal; the Motzki syndrome applies."

Light dawns. *Motzki* is a satirical television programme which caused much upheaval: he's a Berliner of coarse mind and with a perfectly foul tongue who ascribes all the evils of the world to Easterners, Turks, Wogs, Niggers; every one of whom is living the life of Riley at his expense, and all due to the grovelling pusillanimity of those Arseholes in Bonn. He is quite repulsive and often very funny. The trouble is that there are lots of Germans who don't find him in the least funny because secretly they agree and don't dare say so out loud, but—Saxons! Hang one on every tree and there'll still be too many: uneasy when Motzki shouts it at the top of his voice . . .

This minibus Castang has been on about, it's heading through Germany, and it's being traced. There are some police officers who are co-ordinating this job and will Castang note their names please, for information, for co-operation, and—and so forth? Herr Wirtz, Herr Bogner, Liebetrau and Sitruk. He himself is not immediately concerned. They're heading up north you see; their destination is Denmark.

Castang couldn't remember Motzki's first name, if he has one, but amuses himself fitting names to these worthies. Christoph, Gerhard, Holger and Ernst-Georg. Sound men all. Gloating, he went to see Mr. Suarez.

"Denmark," he said pointedly—"*that's* interesting." But Herr Chef knew all about it already and needed no persuading; still cross about Castang's teeth.

"Danes—they don't like the Schengen space, don't like the Maastricht agreements, don't like anything much. See what they make of this! Well, perhaps now's your chance to do us some good, and perhaps a little useful work. You have after all some personal enthusiasm to go on."

He's going to get some official footing! Expensive though

Denmark is, and Mr. Suarez is mean about expenses. Of course Castang says nothing about Vera. Denmark is fearfully dear, but what about that generous payment made over by Monsieur Rogier? Suarez is searching for a piece of paper.

"I have an official introduction for you, a Commissaire—er—Dahlgren."

What he didn't know was that Vera, in some excitement and innocently indiscreet, which she seldom is, let the fact drop in conversation with Anita Rogier; a woman who had been much impressed by Vera's bold stroke in recapturing her child. They were 'drinking coffee together' but Vera hadn't thought it of any particular importance.

Chapter 15

The man's name was not Dahlgren but plain Dahl.

"It's a common name," indifferently. "There are only three pages of us in the phone book."

"Only three?" said Castang, laughing.

"You be grateful it isn't Christiansen—ten and a half pages of them, and once I wanted someone called Kai, looked him up and there were forty-seven of them; oh yes and thirty-four more called Karen."

This one's Max, and he looks Danish and he looks like a cop. Big, broad, pale, smooth, nicely shaved and a bit over-aftershaved. Big white carnivorous teeth and a nice smile, but can get nasty if vexed. Slow and thorough?—these are clichés; can also get speedy when the need arises. Calm certainly but beware of worn-out words like 'placid'. Danes mostly *look* placid, yes, and cops mostly make a professional thing of not getting excited.

There are also Colleagues. One called Frost—"there are only two columns of us"—one called Hvid (he's not quite sure of the spelling) and one with the good old Danish name of Kauffman. They're all nice, all welcoming in a reserved sort of Danish way, and they all speak excellent English. Max is not quite altogether happy about Vera being here. Sure, here we're extremely feminist; nowhere more so. The place, Präsidium or whatever the police here call it, simply swarms with tall tough girls slim-bottomed in tight trousers, but lookit, Castang's official standing is one thing, Vera's isn't. 'Anyhow this chap knows you and can maybe recognise *you:* we want you both kept in the background: very. But keep the atmosphere light.'

"Don't look up the Jensens—you'd get awfully tired."

Copenhagen—apart from being dear—is an extremely nice town.

They'd walked from the hotel: that special smell of hotel rooms and in particular, corridors (here, a hint of curry powder—why?) that is common to every country he has known but he has never before been on the streets of a northern capital. Amsterdam or Hamburg are only northerly, and they belong to the mainland. Certainly not London, though it doesn't: the flavour of London, so individual and overwhelming, is to him delightfully musty, a deep cellar of the Museum full of damp books and mice: the sea-girt imperial grandeur, so splendidly indifferent to any aesthetic consideration, is orgulously irrelevant to the present purpose. Copenhagen, all broad straight boulevards lined with solid buildings of the late nineteenth century, ornate with Haussmanesque pretension, Italianate stucco and iron balconies, will still be quite at home in the coming century. He snuffed the air, strode pavements so that Vera had ado to keep up; enjoyed himself.

The immense respectability of Denmark: the grip of Calvinism still makes itself felt. A dignified, self-disciplined people—though the traffic is not: cars scream along the street as reckless as in Rome. Scarcely any police presence, and even around the station no junkies, clochards, whores or hooligans are to be seen. He is captivated by these women, tall, free-moving, eccentrically dressed and so perfectly at ease in their skins, their floating draperies, so commanding upon those wonderful intricate bicycles.

He scoured along, until Vera said humbly "I'm out of breath. Are you in a hurry?"

"Who, me?"

"These policemen aren't waiting for you?"

"They'll keep."

"Can we sit and eat herring?"

"Want some lunch anyhow, won't we?"

"There's a nice-looking terrace, and it says Brasserie."

In the sharp, spring sunlight, acid as a green apple—but when spring comes, Danes move resolutely out of doors—Castang ordered a bottle of white wine. He won't do that again, after he sees the price. But now is now, a moment of perfect happiness. While the girl (plain and magnificent) is away assembling her herring, he sits imperially, he studies his own, his 'Andean and sweet Rita', her hair blown everywhere by wind. What is this woman with whom he lives, with whom he loves? She is the soul, not yet perhaps totally liberated but ascending, of whom Thomas Vaughan wrote (and Mrs. Erdleigh spoke), ascending, looking at the sunset towards the west wind, and hearing secret harmonies. He does not understand her—is it certain that she fully understands herself?—but that does not matter. She understands love, and occasionally, as now, he is aware that he begins to have an inkling. Begins too to learn about time—Time that is intolerant

> Of the brave and innocent
> And indifferent in a week

To a beautiful physique—that time Auden was talking about 'which will pardon Paul Claudel' and which surely also pardons Auden, but of which she is free. She tasted her wine (he was already on his second glass), decided to go to the lavatory, and do something to her hair: that's all right, the herring won't get cold.

He thought about Peer Gynt; not at all liberated, prisoner of time; prisoner of every other damn thing one could think of. Should one be feeling sorry for him? Perhaps but that's not enough. Castang no longer feels vengeful. Nothing got broken but the teeth, a bit, (the insurance has paid that and they now look better than they did); the bruises have healed and so has vanity. Yes, one is sorry for an adolescence harmed, certainly distorted by an accident of birth—but so was his own. Sorry for someone who found himself Czech in that bad Stalinist time—but so were all the others, and so was Vera. Sorry about that awful mother? And a great many people have awful mothers.

One had to have Law. One loathed Law, that pompous, inefficient and so partial mimicry of justice. But if one learned anything in the thirty years of police work, always a failure because forever trying to escape Law, it was that law had to be. People would not impose it upon themselves; it had to be imposed from without, by constraint and where needful by force and even by violence. Moses presumably was a wise man; a shaman, certainly. Faced with all those Jews, since forever a tedious and turbulent Volk, he'd had to invent going up the mountain and coming back with stone tablets; a fine piece of theatre with which to impress an anarchic mob of howling individualists. One must have had those ten commandments a long time before Moses' day; they were natural laws, for they'd been the base for every codification then or since, and one disregarded them today to the peril of the world.

But Castang is trying to remember another of Vera's poets, something Chinese and antique. It is not enough to despise the world. Not enough to live life as though riches and power were nothings. They are not. But to grasp, feel the world grow great in the grasp is not enough either. The secret is to grasp and then let go. Peer Gynt has an inefficient grasp, and can't let go. Too bad for him.

Vera came back from the lav, looked at the bottle and said indignantly "You've had more than your fair share." Since the herring had come he ordered another bottle—woe, woe, when they came to leave.

But by then, Castang was determined that he would see Peer Gynt well hammered. A pacific and immensely civilised people, these Danes. But they would know how.

"Procuring young women for immoral purposes, that's a grave criminal charge," said Mr. Dahl.

"Can't we get something a bit tougher than that?"

"Yes, well, living on the earnings of prostitution, we can

probably establish that. False declarations to the border police at Puttgarden, that's intent to defraud."

"We'd like something quite nasty to happen to him."

"Why?" asked Dahl mildly.

"Charge of malicious wounding, in Germany, and we
haven't really the evidence to make it stick."

"Courts in Denmark are fairly liberal in outlook. Judges
mostly slow to award severe prison sentences. I get your
point of course," showing his own teeth, which are white and
even, textbook teeth, "you mean you'd like to see the Polizei
give'm a good workout. We wouldn't get away with it.
Judge would take a dim view. Opposite effect to that intended," breaking a cigarette in half and then deciding to do
without. "Don't want to sound sanctimonious but this isn't
France. You'd get the automatic backing of your Minister,
while I might well catch a mark of official disapproval."

"Don't get me wrong," said Castang. "I've admiration, respect, I'll say envy too; I thought just as you do. This brings
out the worst in me; I've been behind desks for too long."

"And don't get me wrong; you've what, sixty million-odd
of Poles and Corsicans, the Sénégalais and the Maghrébins,
to hold inside the net and call it France: how many kilometres of frontier do you have? You've still got five million
peasants living in the thirteenth century and when you get
into Paris you're in Chinatown. We live in a different world;
the thing is, we don't want to see it diluted. Stick around a
day or so while we sort this out and I hope the flavour ap-
peals to you."

"You live in a different century," said Castang, "and I
don't see much chance of us catching up. The idea we're trying to pursue in Brussels is that the small countries of the
Community should civilise the big ones. Your enigma is how
to make that happen without cutting yourselves off too
much—the dilution you speak of."

"We'll try," said Dahl. "You find us small, provincial and
very self-satisfied. We'll try to do some police work. It has
been known here too that people needed calming after arrest,
and sometimes it's been known that people fell into the type-

writer while being interrogated. First thing is to find these people, observe them, isolate them, get the proofs to satisfy a court. We do know how to do that. You be tourists," smiling at Vera, "and you come back maybe in forty-eight hours and I might have some news for you." Mr. Dahl hadn't quite known what to make of Vera. She'd been very ladylike, and he wasn't sure he was gentlemanly enough.

"He's highly proper," she said, outside. "They're all a bit over-bland."

"On the face of it," remarked Castang. "Tougher than they look. Not all house plants and high prices. The blandness will be deceptive—disregard the bleeding little mermaids."

The afternoon was spent exploring the theory. Castang's hat kept blowing off at draughty street corners. Exasperated, he bought a Hamburg Schippers-cap with elegant braided cord and a high peak, at which she sniggered. While his face injuries were healing he had grown a short beard, depressed to find it coming out greyer than he'd expected: he still had this. The combination, said Vera giggling, looked like Admiral Scheer. Could be a bit of a disguise, he thought, momentarily less frivolous. We're in the centre of a relatively small town. And who knows, there might be unexpected meetings. One felt a bit more secure this way. And Vera is unknown to these gentry.

It's a most attractive city. In Vera's summing up: 'This would be an agreeable town to live in, don't you think?' Yes, he did think.

The place suffers, initially, from that mawkish Hans Andersen image. Just as tourists think that the odious little Manneken-Pis somehow symbolises Bruxellois self-content, they will also imagine that the frightful little mermaid (put, mercifully, well out of sight) illustrates a Danish sentimentality which is far from according with realities. This happens in a number of places. There are people who think the English will be like Winston Churchill. Or, suggested Vera, that Czechs will be Kafka. 'They want it to be somebody; who will you suggest? Kierkegaard? Baroness Blixen?'

But one place which does live up to tourist expectation—

goes indeed well beyond it—is the Tivoli Garden, and when
Vera suggested eating there that evening ('Good God, it says
there are twenty-eight restaurants') Castang agreed readily.
It's right in the centre of the town, and there's a high wall
round it, and this whets the curiosity. Look at all those people pouring in. Those aren't tourists; those are locals. One
goes in the evening because then the children have been put
to bed. Well, some have. And then it's all lit up.

Astounding; and there's no way this could be thought a
trivial pleasure-ground, for the design is perfect, and unique.
Like that of a very good picture? wonders Vera. Since the
landscaping is so well composed and controlled that within
this tiny compass every step brings its new astonishment?
Or, since it is pure pleasure, the Ballet, in Diaghilev's hey-
day? *Le Coq d'Or* and *Le Tricorne; Scheherezade* and *The
Good-humoured Ladies:* Nijinsky and Massine, and
Lopokhova as well as Karsavina. Nothing is missing, the
costuming or the setting, the dancing or the music. All married in the harmony of sheer delight, and Vera would get up
on her points if she knew how, to throw a grande jetée.

Of course it's vulgar; why wouldn't it be—wasn't it designed for the volk? The word becomes meaningless; one has
only to recall the crude inanities of the mouse-empire, and
this in comparison will be found in a taste as dryly classical
as the Pantheon.

They ate, lavishly, and drank much beer, and watched ac-
robats and jugglers and musicians, and the million coloured
lights in the trees, and the staggering masses of flowers. And
Castang cannot believe his eyes or ears since this crowd does
not throw rubbish, picks no quarrels, is not sick in the lake,
and watches the fireworks in a homely, an innocent—a gentle—enjoyment.

Yes, there are moments, and so pitifully few because there
are hardly any Parisiens left remaining, when the fourteenth
of July is a clear night, on which old men and women will
stand up together to dance, smiling timidly at each other; and
when a young girl will cross to an old, bent granny to say
'Dance with me'; for there are young girls and grannies still.

But Belleville is no more. The speculators have torn it down, and save this one short, sad moment when the music plays 'Le Temps des Cerises' there is nothing but the ghost of Casque d'Or. The granny—she has always her shopping bag because you never know what you may find—can she still speak Yiddish, or Russian? Or has she too forgotten how?

Castang is saved from his moment of the black pit by his kindly amiably drunk wife, for they have worked step-by-step over to the fairground end of the garden. The rattle overhead, and the colossal screams of girls on the steep curves—Vera is insisting that she wants to ride on the roller-coaster. Which is called the Odin Express and is quite small and harmless, but lethal enough to give a Divisional Commissaire the galloping vertigos. "I'll probably be sick," he says, laughing.

"You're frightened," says Vera giggling evilly. So that of course he climbs in to the shallow wooden cart.

The young man on the platform strolls along the line to make sure that everyone is sitting, because of people drunk or foolhardy enough to act-the-zouave; he works the safety bar which pins one's lower half. Castang takes Vera firmly round the waist, grits his teeth and shuts his eyes: hell, it only lasts two minutes. Indeed he is delighted, since she screams in a full-throated soprano to rival any teenager. I wish I had the girls here, thinks Castang. Lydia, a powerful screamer, would not be content with less than three goes. Emma—who never screams—would have been likelier to set her jaw and refuse pointblank; but she has changed. Now she takes risks and looks them in the face. Not like me—you sad coward, but you do not balance on railings, you do not skip airily along high narrow walls. As your wife did, in her gymnast Czech childhood.

He opened his eyes; he had not been sick. The train stopped and people got out, lighting cigarettes and laughing to show that they could be gay dogs too. And among those laughing faces was one he knew because it had also been laughing the last time he saw it, when the foot belonging to it launched a kick on the kneecap he could still feel.

So that he is glad that he is a prudent chap. Very far back now are the days when he had been a fit and enthusiastic young street cop with a belief in physical exercise—Jesus, he had boxed at welterweight and even been quite a fair parallel-bars performer. Didn't get dizzy then. Had even once done the act of the eleven boys balanced on one motorbike . . . Vera clutches his arm, electric with enjoyment. And he's glad of this little grizzly naval beard! And of his cap. It has a broad band with a pattern of oak-leaves, like a French general's képi. But they are not gold; they're just brown, and they do not attract attention. He may have been seen but he wouldn't be recognised. In a crowd it's the forehead which identifies and the way the hair grows.

He has turned back into cop, and smartish, but he's not going to try anything here. Things are not in his favour. It would be no great matter to do the footstep-dogging in this crowd which eddies, saunters, stops to gaze and has no eyes for others, relaxed and astroll on one of the first fine evenings of the northern spring. But even the simple technique the police call grasshopping (the verb is in the new *Shorter Oxford,* its use ascribed to John Fowles, but he did not invent it) is impossible with Vera on his arm, and he will not allow himself to spoil the innocence of her recaptured childhood.

A fine evening—a navy-blue blazer. Likely enough to be raining again by tomorrow, so that is not of much use. One will know again that particular set of the shoulders, that rolling lurching walk, cocky and confident. A girl is with him. Not, probably, one of 'the girls'. One of the locals, more likely. ('Nurses!' said Dahl disgustedly. All Western countries are short of nurses; a hard and often hellish job of long hours and poor pay; physically demanding and above all heavy with responsibility. No wonder that French and German girls rarely feel drawn to this. A vocation is needed. So that we've been advertising for Czech girls, hard workers, used to tough conditions. "Nurses—that's all we needed; I'll give them some nursing to do . . .") What would we do without our Arab and Turkish girls? La grosse Polonaise to drive the tractor? And now big-Czech-Magda, to lift me when I cannot walk. Her French is hesitant but her hands are safe, she empties the pot and her face laughs, and my day will laugh too, with her.

They might well stay here carousing until three in the morning, but in any case I'm not even going to try. Stay with them long enough to mark them—one doesn't have to draw an M in chalk on the blue blazer. As in the Fritz Lang film.

They hadn't left, and that's something. Denmark wouldn't be an easy place to leave, said Mr. Dahl, and he sounded confident.

Chapter 16

It was raining at breakfast and Vera was a little disappointed; she wanted to see the Castle of Elsinore, 'but I'd like it to be a nice day.'

"That reminds me, have to make a phone call." Mr. Dahl was in his office.

"I saw the two heavies last night. Not my friend Mister Leroux, but he won't be far away. In the Tivoli Garden, couldn't tag them but you'll like to know they're on the spot."

"I know already," dampeningly. "Found the minibus. But I'm not ready to move yet. Need to lay my hands on these girls. And you—you're where?"

"My wife likes to look at pictures when it's raining."

"Come to lunch—pub just down the road." And rang off.

This is a nice gallery, says Vera with a professional glance around. One isn't coming here to be drowned in the Caraccis and the Caravaggios. "It's the local people who interest me—how they look at Denmark." Right, if it's tedious old Bartolommeo Whosit you're after, you look in the Louvre—and Castang has; his time in Fine Art Fraud hadn't been altogether a waste. You don't come here to look at especially famous pictures; simply at good ones, of which they've plenty, well hung and highly visible. Fine Netherlands collection, lots of fine—everything you don't find in the Louvre, and would be too tired to look at if you did. Policemen don't look enough at pictures, more's the pity: no time, they say. Did Mr. Dahl come here, and Mr. Frost? Very likely, for they are highly civilised people.

Vera is best left alone in places like this: she gets into corners and broods, mutters, walks backwards, goes into trances. Castang should look more carefully at these Danish pictures, and doesn't: he is 'distrait', finds quiet rooms to sit. Cross the legs, elbow on the knee, cup the palm and put the chin in it. Like the Rodin man, Thinking. But it's true—picture galleries are also good places for this sort of activity.

Castang was looking at Danish seascapes; cloudy, misty. A tremendous storm has blown up. A catastrophe out there, for several figures are making animated movements: they would launch the life-boat if they could, but the atmosphere is of despair; the sea is too high. They would lose their own lives, and save no others: they are onlookers, and impotent.

He is not really seeing this. In the eye of the mind is another landscape, one of which he is very fond, and when he was a working cop, with a PJ 'antenna' under his command, in Picardy, he drove out often to look at it, though it was not strictly in his district. The black land, and the black pyramids. Behind the black hills is a narrow strip of clear white light against which the pit-head towers (the lifts are stilled and the wheels do not turn) stand out stark and beautiful. Above, filling the whole immense sky, the magnificent rain-laden cloudscape of the coal country of Lens, Loos, Valenciennes. Yes, and beyond—the Borinage of Belgium. His own area lies more south—the chalk hills of the Somme, of Far Wood and Beaumont Hamel, the land where General Haig thought little of killing fifty thousand boys in a day. That interests him, but not very much, no more really than the sentimentalities of Zola, of *Germinal*. One got killed down the mine, by a gas explosion, by the collapse of a gallery; one got killed on the surface, stumbling up the steep hill carrying fifty kilos of useless junk, facing the machine-guns or running away, they got you just the same. That was the law. There is no justice; poetic or plain, natural or put into codes of Equity; there is only the Law, and he—Castang—there to administer, to enforce, and no damned thinking about it.

When they are young, the idealists talk a lot about the law. They remark that one can avoid it, that you need only not to be found out, and that this is the justification for nearly everyone. One can flout the law, and this proves how little it means; it's only a set of rules for those who happen to get caught. But the Idealist knows that behind all the rubbish of regimented text, and also behind the trickery of legal loophole and bribed official, there is the natural law of right and wrong. Disregard this and you will get rich, but you are a hypocrite, and worthless in the eye of every honest man. Castang has been through all this. Every police officer of any experience, say a year, very well, say two, knows it by heart and doesn't think about it, because behind this is a law much older, the Law that killed the soldiers of the Somme, and the miners of Loos. This one says that the world, inexorably, punishes the good and rewards the bad. So that you must leave this world; detach yourself from it. The easy way is to die; the soldier on the hill, the miner below ground. There are other ways. Your daily work; do it: if the mine, go down it, and if the rifle, carry it: that has been his choice because the alternative, to look on and make no sound, is not permissible.

And if you are given orders which you must disobey you do that too. You will mostly get away with this, and even earn some sort of respect: there were also SS men who said no. You may well get sacked and that will be your bad luck. Once in a while you might get yourself shot, an idea that you had better learn to live with: your wife has. Living, which is sometimes better than merely drawing breath, is done in Tangentopolis, admirable Italian label for a world of disconcerting rebounds and never quite the same twice running. The spheres are shiny with grease and do they interlock or do they just touch? Are they even spheres though this is what they look like? A picture gallery is a good place, and not ignoble, because these things hanging on the wall are man's effort and struggle against baseness. "Oh, There you are," said Vera's voice. As though he had been hiding.

Chapter 17

Three kinds of herring, and lessons in the local beer; temptations to join in the local pastime of small cold glasses of schnapps in between, not quite as terrifying as the Hamburg version but will have you on your ear just the same; the Danish police, bland and smiling, presenting unreadable, tangential surfaces, seems pickled against ill-effects.

"We've got this quite nicely set up," said Dahl. Big and smiling and leisurely, the rounded contours of this broad pale face like a ham—salted but not smoked—'Max' is more unreadable than most and Castang, hearing a rather pretty mousetrap described, is going to make damn sure he isn't the cheese. "They won't even see you," Max went on in a voice of immense sincerity. "Frosty knows the place. He takes girls there before working his evil will on them."

A mousetrap is one of the oldest police techniques existing, and a piece of jargon nigh-universal. Dumas says it dates back to the seventeenth century at least, and it is probable from long before that. The principle is extremely simple: a house thought suspect is quietly invested. You then let anyone in who cares to come, but getting out again is another matter.

The traduced Mr. Frost, who wears glasses and looks like the more earnest kind of student, is being polite to Vera. A literary conversation.

"I was interested about Peer Gynt. He's a very Nordic figure. I find myself muddled in the last act."

"My thinking changes," Castang was saying to Dahl. "True; Leroux had me beaten up. But not before I'd worked a few dirty tricks myself. That's police work, you'd say. But strictly speaking, this wasn't."

"Isn't he dead?" It was worrying Frost. "Wasn't he killed in the storm coming home?"

"Don't see that it makes any difference," said Dahl. "There's too much of a good pinch, and I'll give it to the press."

"And what about Solveig?" Vera was saying. "Old woman there sitting spinning all those years; ridiculous."

"Law's there to be upheld." Inspector Dahl with his mouth full of cheese. "You're personally involved: I'm not."

"But Solveig's real. She doesn't just exist in his imagination."

"Everything else does," objected Frost. "Leave some cheese for me."

"He kidnapped a child," said Castang, "and that's how I came up against him. Nothing to do with these phony nurses. I'll tell you about it."

"You mean she has to be real since all the rest is imagined? What about Ingrid whom he carries off and rapes?" Castang wonders whether he has dipped overmuch into the schnapps. Solveig is real all right; sitting here at the table.

"I've booked for the four of us," Dahl was explaining. "Expensive—but the administration pays the bill. I'll get some stick for that if it doesn't work but it's worth trying. Little trap of a restaurant—a greasy sod this, glib with his tongue. You'll see for yourself. I think he's the organiser this end, might own the house where they put the girls. Like to catch the bugger on a big stack of undeclared income and pinch him on the tax fraud."

Mr. Frost is still uncertain whether Peer Gynt shouldn't have to answer to a few serious charges under the criminal code.

"The stage director," suggested Vera, "has to decide if the whole home-coming piece isn't just a vision."

"This stage director," said Dahl, guffawing, "is going to make sure this particular last act isn't any vision."

It wasn't easily found; among the peculiarities of the old inner city is that of buildings remade and street-numbers gone cockeyed; a struggle with geography, and a struggle with—what would he call this? Conscience? Dahl's notion is normal police procedure. Castang has taken part in such actions on many occasions, thought out and directed more than one: he should be perfectly happy. And this time, isn't it a little too close to a personal vengeance? If he were still a working police officer there would be no hesitation. In present circumstances, isn't he a little too much the finger? It is not altogether a role he enjoys.

A one-way street, no better than an alleyway. A crooked old house which would be dark behind small windows. On the ground floor a homely little café, and only initiates would notice the scruffy little hand-lettered notice in the doorway, telling one that the restaurant was 'Through and up the stairs.' Yes, a good setting for a mousetrap. He took his hands out of his pockets and shrugged. He had a clear mandate from Mr. Suarez, and that is where he gets his orders. Rancorous feelings are just a state of mind.

Nerves: this ailment, before action, is highly contagious and nearly everyone suffers, because the only known immunity is to have no imagination at all. Even among policemen that is not as common as one might suppose, and only three out of the four were police officers. The symptoms were never better described than by the young men, of every army involved between 1914 and '18, for whom the phrase 'going over the top' was invented. In English it's called 'getting the wind up' since the characteristic symptom is the need to yawn constantly, not to speak of hiccups, belching—Castang hopes to heaven that nobody will fart, for they are in a highly confined space.

He doesn't like this at all; he has been part of an entrapment team on a few occasions and while one admits that this place (as described by Mr. Frost who has been here before) is good for pinning people down since it is all extremely narrow and the only way out is a steep little flight of stairs, the arresting-officers have no room either.

Max, for all the massive, stolid look, is a-twitter for wondering what might go wrong. Frost had made careful plans, chosen this particular table, worked it all out with log-tables because he's that kind of chap. One has to remind oneself that 'Whatever can go wrong, invariably will.'

"You aren't carrying, I hope."

"Good God no," said Castang. "What, in Denmark! Are you?"

"We do—occasionally—even in Denmark . . ."

Vera is not happy a bit. She doesn't like *any* entrapment-device, still less being—however passive, however marginal—part of one. Of her own masquerading as a Stapo agent, her own entrapment of that poor wretched Ada, she is now thoroughly ashamed—goes hot and cold just thinking about it.

Also she hates all this whispering. When the head-thief came with his menus, greasy and voluble, in Danish for Dahl, who in his business-man's suit is supposed to be the host, and in English for the tourists, she had muttered 'Pederast' in Czech (nobody understands Czech). Castang aimed a kick under the table, before she remembered that those people down two steps and across a narrow service passage do understand, because that's what they *are*. Luckily it was a mutter; luckily all the tables are in alcoves and enclosed by wooden partitions—but Un-luckily there is no language left to communicate in: Monsieur Leroux, not visible but a presence much felt, is said to be pretty fluent in French as well as German and English. Castang can patter Spanish but she can't. She is smoking too much. They all are. They are all drinking too much. This white wine (Spanish, highly recommended by the Patron) is dry, drinkable, if ridiculously expensive; and we are punishing it.

Mr. Frost was ostensibly the calmest of the four since he had perfect faith in his plan. But he is trying very hard not to fart, because he is sitting opposite Vera.

"Why must we be here at all?" Vera has asked on the way.

"If these people are coming to dinner why can't the Danes just round them up?"

"Max wants me there for a formal identification. He's looking to make this watertight for the prosecutor. If afterward I do him a written statement that yes, these are the people who beat me up by the road to Dresden, then I won't be called on to come again to give evidence in court. But for that to work I have to be here."

"But I don't, and I wish I hadn't come." Poor Dahl, who had planned to reward them with a good dinner.

The three villains are having a grand dinner, to celebrate their successful deal, and maybe this is on-the-house, for the thief is garrulous and lipsmacking with everyone but especially at this table (the best; there are only eight all told). He is talking German, so that we are all listening with bated-breath, except that we aren't bating it successfully (Mr. Frost has gone to the men's room to get rid of wind).

"A fish like this," hands a good eighty centimetres apart, "and if it isn't straight out of the sea you throw it straight at me, okay?" Oh, gales of merriment. ("Liar," muttered Dahl. "It will be plaice.") "And then a steak, I personally promise hung for twenty-eight days and you eat it with a spoon." There was an exchange in Czech, but too low for Vera to catch.

This men's room is the key to the operation: it is at the end of the service passage, and one passes the table in question. On the way there is another table for two, but this is occupied by a young couple, and they are greatly wrapped up in one another. Next to the men's room on the blank wall are coat hangers. Castang has had to surrender, unwillingly, his cap. "Oh what a beauty," cried the putative-pederast. "We'll take the *greatest* care of it."

They have eaten their own food, every mouthful of it sand, and the thief has passed by, all grins of self-congratulation with four little glasses of Calvados. "For that's our speciality, you know, this is Le Trou Normand," merrier than ever.

It is time. Dahl got up first for the trip to the lav. Castang would give him exactly two minutes before following. Frost, whose job was to close off the passage, got himself, his legs, and his gun nice and loose. Vera stays where she is, looking to see if there's a glass left in the latest of several bottles. She's not going to get any pudding, which will be as well for her digestion.

Leroux was sitting at the outside of the table with his back to them, leaning forward round-shouldered, propped on his elbows, a post-prandial haze. Castang glanced to see that Dahl was ready, and gave the table a hard shove, to pin the two big louts on the bench behind it by the waist. In this position you can't stand up and the only way you're getting a gun is out of your open mouth.

"Hallo Pierrot," he said affectionately.

Max held his gun low, tucked in front of his hip, aiming it into the space between the two astonished faces.

"We'll have no disturbances while I'm taking the three of you into custody." Leroux, freed of the table, was getting slowly to his feet.

There were a number of tiny distractions. The two at the next table were goggling; the man said something in Danish. A protest perhaps at unseemly events in public? Something about telling people their rights, or "Shouldn't you identify yourselves?" The low comedy was provided by Mr. Frost, who was taking in the scene a little too gleefully (Look how well I thought that out) and slipped on the step, coming to earth ungracefully and trying to keep his gun out of his eye.

One didn't expect it—least of all from Leroux—that remarkable agility of the drunk. As he came upright he headbutted Castang in the ribs, without enough leverage to be painful but with force enough to entangle our-hero in the coatrack. Dahl, with the two Czechs still gazing at him like one o'clock struck, concentrated on keeping them that way. "Put your hands in front of you and put them together." Mr. Frost was still recovering from making a fool of himself. Castang, flustered, was fighting somebody's raincoat.

We counted, afterwards. There are fourteen steps to that stairway from the street level; they're both steep and narrow, for it's an old house and was never designed for the present use.

Frost who was best placed to see (clutching the banister at the top to regain balance) swore that Leroux took it in two bounds like a goddamn-fleeing-kangaroo. It takes a drunk, said Dahl sorrowfully, but never mind, he-can't-get-out-of-Denmark, and we've got these two beauties here, haven't we, loveys. Castang went down the stairs, carefully. There'd been some fracas down there, a couple of people pushed abruptly and a few beers upset. In the street nothing was to be seen but a man loitering who seemed to Castang vaguely familiar, one of Dahl's minions no doubt. Policemen are the same everywhere. 'Well, chief, we hadn't had instructions about that.' Peer Gynt was long gone.

"Where were those two clowns who were supposed to be outside the door then? Still sitting in their wagon at the corner, I suppose." Max gave short shrift to the loudly-protesting owner. This was in Danish but readily understandable as "I want you in my office nice and early tomorrow morning and there'll be a lot of questions, and now shut up." Castang did not enquire whether the two oafs would spend the night handcuffed to the radiator in the basement; that would have been tactless. They were both armed, and that's enough for a nice cool-off overnight in any country, and you be grateful it's not the Turkish police, who wouldn't be tender.

He has no real abiding interest. Vera is tired, and unhappy, and soggy with drink, and finds the whole thing utterly hateful; far too close a reminder of a past she has long put in limbo where it belongs. Nothing there but to put her into a taxi and bring her home. It was a lousy dinner too, perfectly ordinary Spanish plonk and they were asking two hundred kroner a bottle.

"Well we didn't pay for it," wondering who the man in the street reminded him of. Leroux was loose and he doesn't care. He will have to go to Dahl's office in the morning to make his formal written deposition, worded—a talent police officers must possess—to be proof against the most sceptical of judicial authorities and every bloodyminded chicanery that could be thought up by some young hotshot of a defence lawyer. And after that he wants to take the next train out of here. He has done his bit to persuade the bureaucrats that yes, we do try to put a few dints in the eastern-European Mafias, but really he'd like to get down to some peaceful paperwork: it begins to look quite fresh again, piling up on the desk in Brussels calling 'Castang, don't neglect me; show Loyalty.'

Chapter 18

Vera at breakfast was a lot more buoyant than he felt. Whatever else, that white wine had brought about a good night's sleep.

"I can't help feeling I've *seen* Copenhagen. A very nice town, but too full of policemen." Vera butters bread, wrinkles her nose at Danish sausage (it isn't very good), puts salt on it instead. "But this is like spending a weekend in Paris and thinking you've seen France. I haven't seen Denmark at all. At the very least I want to see Kronborg and Frederiksborg which sounds enchanting and we need only take a bus. Even if Suarez does refuse the expense account I don't care, we've lots of lovely money from kind Monsieur Rogier and I'm damned if I'll just slink away because of these awful policemen . . ." This as he realises well is the wife-stubborn, the female-contrariwise, and to seek, to strive, to find and not to yield is its motto, so don't start warfare over this rather-inferior hotel coffee.

A thunderbolt hit him. He got up to gain some time. He carried his cup for more coffee he didn't want; he looked to see if he had one of his little cigars. Left upstairs, but faithful old Gitane-filter will have to do instead.

"Vera, had you mentioned at all the fact that we were going to be here in Copenhagen?" Some people are liars, and everyone tells lies. She is expert enough at those two classical police techniques, the 'suppressio veri' and the 'suggestio falsi' (they sound so much better when dignified by legal

Latin). She can and does lie like a lawyer, but not when an
appeal to responsibility is at stake. There are female sorts of
truth too. 'I didn't forget it: it was driven out of my mind'
are two different concepts.

"I don't feel sure, now. Might I have mentioned it perhaps
to Anita?" Castang went upstairs, where he would find a
small cigar, a toothbrush, a telephone, a lavatory, 'the note-
book'—not necessarily in that order. Looked at his watch
and punched a Brussels number. Got the cleaning woman.

"Good morning, is Madame around?"

"I think she just came in—ne quittez pas." And breath-
less—

"Sorry—I just got back from driving Arnold to the office."

"Ah. So your man, I can't remember his name, the valet,
the butler—"

"Oh, Monsieur Jean—he's taken a few days off. He does
sometimes—one can't refuse, you know."

"No, that's all I wanted to know."

"It wasn't something about Maurice?" at once a little
edgy.

"Not unless you've noticed something untoward."

"I suppose it's just a little peculiar, but no one seems to
have seen anything of my father these last couple of days."

Castang can also take liberties with the truth, and said
"Can't see anything to worry about there," and lay for a moment on an unmade bed, to digest all this. What exactly was
one to tell Vera? And what about Max Dahl? This is a city of
half a million people. The old town itself . . . Monsieur Jean;
now there's a chap who is good at melting-unperceived-into-
backgrounds, and his eyes are as sharp as his ears. But that
big-boned old man with his distinctive looks . . . And we say
'Oh, by the way' in that elaborately casual manner meaning
not in the least by-the-way, but very much to the point. Vera
had been indiscreet. And so no doubt has Anita. We have
been walking round the town quite openly, confident that
this middle-aged tourist couple makes an adequate disguise.
Old Klaas has never seen Vera. But 'Monsieur Jean', now
that's quite a little gimlet.

De we presume that neither of them knew or would recognise Leroux? The method has been to follow me, since I do know him, and I meet local policemen too.

Any more deductions? Since that little man was in the street last night it's safe to suppose that he does know now. Since Leroux made off at a dead run, he couldn't track the target any further. But the old man—what are we to make of that? A link between those two must be accepted. One recalls that 'Jean' was said to be, stronger than 'fond of', devoted to the little boy. Old Klaas's much cherished grandson; the only one he has.

Whatever else, we have to go see Dahl this morning. And two detectives are better than one. Might those two have a fairish guess by now as to where the elusive Peer is to be found? Vera came out of the bathroom and said, "Raining again."

The adjustment and polishing of police prose, to be suitable for judicial consummation, took up an hour or so.

"You'll be going home soon?" said Max a bit over casually.

"Yes. Pity it's raining. My wife would like to see the castles. Might hang on an extra day for Kronborg and Frederiksborg."

"Well worth the visit. And—by the way—you can leave friend Leroux safely to us—we'll get him. Rather odd where he can have got to, since he didn't go back to the hotel where those three clowns were staying. But now he's without resources he'll drop off the branch quick enough. Can't get off the island. Matter of hours," so throwaway that Castang knows he must have a lead.

You—you have been a PJ officer for years. Come now, put yourself into Dahl's shoes. What would you do? And what would Leroux do?

"Be a detective," he said to Vera. They were having lunch, comfortable in a big glassed-in brasserie, sitting by the window. Rain trickled down this but nobody in Copenhagen lets that detail worry them. People milled on the pavement outside, waiting to cross the road when the lights changed. A soft spring rain, good for cows, for fields, for the sources of drinking-water and for brewing beer. People here like it, hardly even bother with umbrellas save to protect some bourgeois woman's over-elaborate hairstyle. And did this spark an idea in Vera's mind?

"Wouldn't he do as you did, and try to disguise himself?"

"It would have to be better than mine."

"He's quite small-boned." Yes, unlike his father. "And Danish women are tall," said Vera, watching the street.

"As a woman, you mean? The idea just occurred to me too. It's possible, certainly, but to leave the country you'd need a passport and"—but another idea struck: I am fertile in them this morning. This was good-quality red bourgogne they were drinking and suddenly it is worth the price. "The Czechs have confiscated those girls' identity papers and I wonder whether Dahl has recovered them."

"That's a pretty dubious thought," said Vera, all commonsense, "they'll be paying particular attention to Czech passports at all the borders. Sly little Peer wouldn't risk it."

"What other choices has he got? He can buy some women's clothes—he's probably got plenty of money. They sold—quite literally—those girls, to that greasy little restaurant keeper; one's glad that Dahl got him anyway, hold him on the pimping charge and launch a horrible great enquiry into his tax declarations—but this is beside the point: half the women passing are in jeans and an anorak and the thing is the hair—to alter his looks at all he'd have to buy a wig ... *That's* what Dahl has done," banging the table and just escaping an upset glass. "Came to me a bit belated but that's what I'd do. Have a few chaps scour round the hairdressers—beauty shops; where else would they sell wigs? Can't be all that many." But Vera has objections.

"It would look very odd. A man in Printemps or the Samaritaine, buying undies for the girlfriend, that would pass without comment. But if a woman wants a wig she buys it for herself and tries it on."

"I do see," he admitted. "There are the shoes, too, they are the other giveaway. Do you recall Hitchcock's woman in *The Lady Vanishes*?—she's dressed as a nun but she's wearing high heels. Short of looking like a transvestite, which would be remembered, he's got to find a woman, and where? You don't pick that up in the street, do you? You could perhaps bribe a prostitute but that's only in spy stories. Dahl won't bother with a detail like this, he'll tell his people to ask—what wigs have you sold today and in what style? While we ask—who could the buyer be?" Not Monsieur Jean! Does Leroux realise there are others after him?

They looked at each other, and both spoke together.

"Ingrid," said Castang. "Wanda," said Vera.

Chapter 19

Anywhere north of Paris, on a rainy evening in spring, night falls early. But at midday the light has a shimmer of hard brightness and the rain adds blackness to the blacks, colours become more vivid; the reflections bounce and dazzle.

"Look out of the window," said Vera. "No—where I'm looking—I mean in my direction." The other detective craning backwards over his shoulder, seeing nothing, being told he is too late.

"No—the other side, stupe."

"How can I look if you don't tell me where." The police use an observer-jargon. Twelve o'clock, high. Even if Vera knew it this is difficult for a person sitting facing one.

Nerves are strung tight and the edginess adds to the imprecision. The violins are not in tune and false notes squawk, screech. Between this couple, sudden quarrels are even more violent and meaningless.

"I've told you often enough; be more precise. Silly bitch."

"And I've told you; should have ought to marry a Spanish woman who scrubs her bottom twice a day and cleans her teeth after every meal, and keeps her wits about her." Grammar fails her when angry, as well as logic.

"What's that got to do with anything?" exasperated. "What did you see, anyhow? Or thought you saw?"

"I'm no longer sure and I'm not going to say."

"Balls of the Virgin," a metaphysical sort of expletive which sounds better in Catalan. How is one to explain that what painters see, metaphysically, is not at all what the police sees or thinks it sees? Knowing her, it is possible that the reference to Spanish women throws light upon the metaphysical inclinations of Spanish painters, but one can't be sure. What Vera thought she saw, through the rain on the windows, was two oldish men, one small and the other tall, but this has no narrative value because by the time Castang got it right they were gone. Faced with this sort of thing the novelist uses his privilege to make a time-shift and write the afterthinking. As—at the end of the day—Castang said to Dahl "One lives life forward, but it's only looking backward that one understands anything."

A pompous platitude but 'the end of the day' was by now well into the following morning and two police officers were looking back over the mistakes they have made: being experienced, polite about the other's fumbling stupidity.

It is also interesting to observe the parallel development of two police minds: Dahl guided by logic. Castang by other considerations but he has digested these by now.

"Remember," said Max a little reproachfully, "I knew nothing about this woman."

"Knew nothing myself until too late," apologetic. "Came to infer—some tortuous climbing back up ladders. Felt sure then she was there—both my wife and I would recognise her. But where would she be? Any of a hundred or more hotels. I reasoned that they would try for a night train. Where else can you give your passports to the conductor, and the guards don't compare with the physical presence since they're all asleep in bunks? A risk, but one they had to take." Dahl nodded; it had been his own logic.

"Neither of us knew anything about the two men. I saw the one—I still only know him as Jean—outside the restaurant, thought I knew the face but took him for one of your men. Was the old man there too? Must have been him who tracked Leroux back to that hotel. Jean was watching me, reckoning on my contacts with you to guide them in the right direction.

"To the old man it must have been a hotel like any other.

"But a tough old boy and hadn't forgotten things he'd learned fifty years before—like how to stake out a position. And when he saw the woman he'd know her."

"How come?" asked Dahl. They were both grainy-eyed and very tired. One kept forgetting the earlier part of the story.

"Fifty years ago she was his girl . . . and our man Leroux was his son . . . after all this time, I don't know; a face gets blurred with age. But the little mannerisms and movements—a way of walking perhaps. Outside our experience. We're neither of us seventy years old. But he loved her, you see. Knew her only for a few months, but this wasn't a passing kiss-up."

"I do see," and Dahl meant it.

"I wasn't there," Castang went on, "and I've had to reconstruct. That she went out, bought clothes, a wig, whatever, and she could do that without attracting attention. She could make the booking—trains wouldn't be crowded this time of year. The boys and girls with backpacks don't make sleeper reservations; they're too dear. I looked it up in a travel bureau—half that train goes to Zürich and the other half through to Munich, so I thought—that's it. I reckoned if I staked out the station I'd see them. It would be easy to phone you—but you'd reached the same conclusion."

"Sure," said Dahl. "Much as you did. Police minds think alike. They'd never risk the airport or the roads. Copenhagen's on an island."

To be sure. At airports one is scrutinised under bright lights. Elsewhere there are ferries, and these are easily watched. The dénouement to a story should be high-romantic, a setting for *Tosca,* or anti-romantic and a squalid alleyway. Neither suits the character of this town, a sober place, built and maintained by a sober, self-denying people. People like Dahl. Of course there is a strongly metaphysical side to Denmark—perceivable for instance in the art gallery—but by pursuing the reasonable Dahl got his results.

He had sent policemen out to shops, asking whether they'd sold wigs. When he heard that a tall elderly lady speaking German had bought such an object, he'd got interested.

The plan was simple and bold—deserved to succeed, really. Leroux, on the run, took refuge with Wanda, whose presence nobody had suspected. Castang—it seemed a long time ago—had a strongish idea that she was involved in some racket. Why else the pretty brutal nudges to see him off and out of district? Now, indeed, one could make the guess that Wanda took a strong interest in the girl-traffic and maybe more than that, but what evidence was there?

To keep a man in her hotel room overnight is no great matter. A good tip to the chambermaid. Longer, and the housekeeper will likely discover what the French call the "pot aux roses" but for a few hours the risk is minimal.

Isn't this just the sort of adventure to appeal to Wanda? Make her feel herself young again? The girl who had hidden an out-of-bounds soldier in her room?

Next morning she hung around the hotel desk—choosing picture postcards—at the moment when there is a lot of coming and going. The staff is distracted by people paying and leaving, while others are checking in. Filling in registration forms; they ask one's passport number, and some people write down anything, since who's to know, while others are law-abiding, and look it up—and relatively few people know it by heart.

Wanda knows that quite often people busied do not put valuable papers away that same instant, but tuck them into a pocket or a handbag. And she was lucky; she got a woman's passport, and not at all bad for her purpose. Fat and middle-aged, but who looks at an old woman travelling with her daughter? She could get the wig to match the hair, a few sloppy sort of clothes—Castang had to laugh but . . .

"But this was insane."

"They were desperate, and it might just have worked. How long would it be before the loss was reported? Some damn cop writing it all down on a slate, might well have got it on the computer only by the next day. They had only to get through the middle of the night, and those guards can be

sloppy, if the number of passports tallies with the number of
passengers they barely glance, and once you're in Germany . . . Get out of the hotel fast, sure." Dahl nodded.

"Where she was unlucky was in getting a whole fat wallet,
money, credit cards up to here, missed at once and before
you can turn round, there's an uproar, American Express and
practically the whole State Department and this would end
up by reaching my ears. We think they went to another of the
big hotels, the ladies' lavatory down there in the basement
where it is pretty well deserted in mid-afternoon. The wig
was signalled all right but after my man had been in there;
the shopgirl only phoned in later. Found the note on my desk
when I got back here, and that might only have been next
morning. You see?—they might have made it."

"I thought at first of those Czech girls' passports—did you
recover them?"

"Sure. That greasy chap had them. Nice piece of evidence,
conclusive, judge can't overlook that—they were to be co-
erced into prostitution. Now I'm sorry about that business in
the station. It's not a complicated place as a rule but there are
the two entrances on opposite sides, and all that building
going on in the middle, and I found myself on the wrong
side."

"One always is," said Castang with feeling.

"You know," said Dahl apologetically, "it's true Frost
made a balls-up falling down the stairs that time, but in fact
he's good. Now there's this second thing, the judge is going
to take a dim view of people getting shot, because they always do where police weapons have been used, but it wasn't
his fault and I'm going to stand up for him."

"Happens all the time," sympathetically. "Cop gets sus-
pended but always ends up whitewashed. 'I thought the chap
had a gun. I felt threatened—it was really self-defence.' "

"Chap *did* have a gun. So did the other chap, we thought,
but it turned out to be the woman." Said Dahl, defensively,
and Castang had nothing to say.

"We still don't use guns with much conviction hereabouts." He didn't want to, it sounds plaintive. "This must be

one of the very last places on the earth's surface where that can be said to be true. And I'm glad of it. I'm even proud of it. There've been moments in our past when we've been bellicose, but this last couple of hundred years we've been a pacific crowd on the whole."

"And *be* proud of it," said Castang.

"When the Germans invaded us, back in 1940, we didn't make much active resistance. It's a guess that there were memories of the sixties of the century before—when we lost Schleswig and Holstein, our two pretty southern provinces which we couldn't defend adequately—there are too many goddamn islands here and we couldn't mobilise troops fast or efficiently.

"But it's generally admitted that our passive resistance was pretty good, and we got nearly all our Jews away."

"We know all about guns," said Castang. "I carried one for twenty-five years. Had I been in your shoes, on duty, I'd have used it. But isn't it odd?—going back to those years of the forties, your record there's none better, and ours there was none worse."

"Are you actually French?" curiously. "Because you know you don't look it, and there's times you don't sound it."

"Born in Paris, brought up there, worked there, and proud of it. I don't know what I am, save anyhow I'm a European. But when I'm most ashamed of it then I try to be French."

"Fair enough," said Dahl.

"It's what?—it's a coincidence? Except as my wife says, there is no such animal. I was born in forty-five, never knew my father, my mother neither, just for knowing who she was. I could be thus anything—did some English soldier get there? So that when I came to look at this guy Leroux I felt some obscure sympathies, because of this much in common, if some wandering German soldier impregnates a Czech girl, isn't that me too? I go one way, he goes another. But aren't we basically one and the same would you say?"

"Too late to ask him," said Dahl in a police voice. These remarks of Castang's; they're no business of his. "Leastways, there in emergency they weren't all that optimistic.

When they cut those baggy women's trousers off him, three bullets there inside, didn't look too hopeful but he might make it."

("I hope and pray that he survives," Vera had said. Her stillest, smallest voice. "I'm thinking about his wife. I took the child away from her. That was right, nothing to say about that. But if she loses her man as well . . . poor wretch.")

"Have you got a drink in this office?" asked Castang.

"We have."

"My wife," ploughing on. "She's literary. Wants to go and look at this fucking castle up in Elsinore because of Hamlet. Shakespeare fan, you know," holding out the glass for more. "My English doesn't really run to this. And then there's another one. In which there's a seacoast to Bohemia, and a lot of idiots were laughing at Shakespeare for not knowing this, but she says he knew it perfectly well, but Bohemia is a place where magical things happen . . . Anyway, there is too a seacoast—I found one. But these stories—girls get their identities confused—there's a metaphysical side to all this. But what with Shakespeare, and Ibsen too, I found myself all at sea; happens to me more."

"Don't know anything about metaphysics; I'm a cop," said Dahl woodenly. "I know what Rilke said, though. That there aren't any victories: there are only survivors."

"That'll do to be going on with," said Castang.

He must go back to the evening before. It seems more than six hours ago.

The inside of the main railway station is a large square space. Lined, on two sides, by the familiar features; coffee shop or left luggage office. On the far side, escalators to trains. He was disconcerted because in the middle Danes have built a big cardboard shed. A new link to the Underground? That hardly matters, but it blocks all vision across. Against this, little stalls have become encrusted selling things to voyagers; books and hot dogs; flowers, fruit, or souvenirs. People coming from outside must plough round a large troublesome obstacle.

"I hadn't expected trouble," said Dahl. "My idea was simple. Intercept with a polite word. So just me and Frosty. No dramas. 'Are your papers quite what they should be?' Certainly, no guns."

Guns were far from Castang's mind too. He wanted an observation post from which to survey the two entrances. The best one was at the bookstall, which was on the corner of the interior structure.

Very good; one can read a book. That is a pleasant and a useful occupation.

Or would be, if anyone had ever yet found a readable book on a railway-station stall. He had quite forgotten what very peculiar reading matter is here if nowhere else available: Mm, *Caroline Chérie*, mm, *Forever Amber*. The nuance is perhaps subtle. Station platforms are thought a little more literate than those more horrible spaces in airports. This odd, oblong block of paper sheets with plastic publicity surrounding—what can it possibly be for? Covered in print so one can't write on it, nor could one blow one's nose; not with any feeling of satisfaction. The airport ones are perhaps a little more simple-minded and violent? The leg-over spelt out amid heavier breathing? But stuff there too for flowery old ladies. The thing turns round and he twiddles it, wanting to look like a man about to put his money down for Clothilde in the Cloister.

Vera has plunged right in among horoscopes and crossword puzzles, deep in the true-story of a football player as primitive in face as in thigh.

His conscience isn't very good and neither is his disguise. If Leroux appears, and Dahl fails to, then he's a clever cop. If neither appears, then he's an ass but there's no one to notice it. If both appear then he stays as unnoticeable as he can manage. What worries him is that if Vera got it right there's an unpredictable factor in these equations.

Should he have told Dahl what he thought or guessed at? He has no certainties, and no wish to make a fool of himself.

He had allowed, he thought, the right amount of time. Can't go on standing like a dick behind this bookcase.

*   *   *

"I'm still not altogether clear," said Dahl, pouring them both some more to drink, "exactly what you were doing there in the first place. Naturally, I'm not suggesting that you would have interfered with the course of justice."

"I thought I made that clear," said Castang who was feeling anything but. "I felt pretty sure I had the movements of those two worked out, and it was probable you had too. In case I was right but that you hadn't, those two would get on the train and I can't stop them; I've no status and no right to interfere. But I could give you a phonecall, couldn't I? How long does it take those trains to reach the ferry—hour or so? Plenty of time for you to intervene."

"That was being a bit too clever if I may say so. As you very well know. Furthermore that isn't quite all."

"No—well—I didn't see you," disingenuous. "You'd be tucked out of sight maybe, since Leroux would know you and Frost anyhow, and you'd want to establish their purpose, let them get well in, before intervening. Delict of flight— evasion of justice—as with any other criminal activity; got to have the beginnings of action, haven't we, before a judge will be satisfied."

"Come off it. They weren't going to the station to change money at the bank." Hey, thought Castang, that might have been it: the old man wanting to keep out of sight, he'd have found cover there in the cambio and he wouldn't have seen me, from there. "You recognised that old man," said Dahl. It wasn't far from an accusation of complicity.

"I was in a bind, I must admit. I couldn't know he was around."

"But having recognised this other man—who has disappeared but we've no good reason for holding him—you suspected it. You knew something of his motives."

"I met him once. I didn't see him anywhere here. If I suspected anything at all it was only here," pointing at his gut, "and not here," tapping his head which was muzzy from fatigue.

"I think a judge would find something to criticise in your

attitude. You withheld some pertinent information. But I'm not going to push you: what would be the point?"

"As for motives," slowly, "I'm a police officer or I have been, and one never knows anyone's motives for doing anything at all, and you know that as well as I do."

Castang took a piece of paper off the desk, borrowed some ballpoint pens. He made an effort at drawing. Vera is the one who knows how to draw. She is, I presume and hope, in bed and asleep. He had told her to take a taxi back to the hotel and make it snappy. Fade right away out of sight because this is strictly police business and nothing for you.

Laboriously he made a plan, much like those made to illuminate an enigma by Miss Christie: here's the body, there's the desk where the coffee cups stood.

"This great big square, what is it, a hundred metres? And inside that this other square where the building's going on, protected by partitions, so you can't see and you can't cross over, you've got to work all the way round. All these people with their luggage, obstacles everywhere. You were on the wrong side, so even when Frost tipped you with the walkie-talk it would take you a minute to get round all that. Here this dotted line they came in, past Frost and he didn't want to make a peremptory challenge right there and he made the mistake of waiting for you."

"I bumped an old woman," bitterly, "and she spilt a cup of coffee on me. She thought I was trying to snatch her handbag . . ."

"And of a sudden here from this direction somewhere the old man came storming at them." There were only a few seconds all told.

Castang, lurking inside the bookstall, made what speed he could, stopping only to say to Vera 'Stay there' but distracted enough by this to stumble over a revolving display—they have wire shelves and to stay firm they have metal legs which protrude . . . The bookstall girl caught him by the arm; he'd been hanging about there too long. He said 'Police!' roughly and shook her off but precious seconds were lost.

So that he had to shout. "Klaas. Klaas!"

The old man stopped for a fraction, startled. But not enough. All round, a fatal hesitation, and then a fatal precipitation.

Frost, walking faster, breaking into a run when Dahl failed to appear, shouted "Police. Halt."

Wanda wasn't looking at him. Perhaps she heard, and that confused her further. Klaas was running, bellowing at her. "Ingrid!"

Never mind the motives. What people in a fluster do is perfectly illogical. In a crowd, if somebody runs, a lot of people start to run. For no reason at all. Maybe a bomb has fallen, and maybe the dam has burst.

Wanda trying to look in two directions at once did the most foolish thing she could have done. It is strange—or is it?—that Leroux, awkward in his disguise, did nothing whatever but stand and stare. She slipped her hand into her bag and came up with a pistol; a 7.65 Sauer as it proved, not a big gun but efficient. Woman's hand or not.

Castang froze; no wish to get shot by anyone. Because Klaas didn't hesitate at all. I don't know what he thought; probably thinking didn't enter into it. He had that big gun Castang knew about. Sheer instinct? As a young man he'd been taught to waste no time on other people's hostile movements. It came out of his belt like lightning.

No, I don't think he intended to shoot anyone. There at last he had the two of them. He knew the police would arrest them. And then he could not say what he had to say. I don't know what this was. Something about betrayal, something about his lost honour. For years everyone had diminished and despised that honour. He had lived with that. But his girl, his son—he wasn't going to stand for that. So that he had come here, to make himself known to them, and make himself felt too, I've no doubt.

He was reacting to a threat. Wanda was reacting to what she thought a threat.

Frost, down on one knee, followed his training. Pointed his gun and bellowed, "Halt or I fire."

But Wanda, frightened, fired. You know, people *shouldn't*

carry loaded automatic pistols. You can't tell if the slide has been worked or not, but if the damn thing is cocked, it fires at a touch. That's why I always carried a revolver, with its hammer down on a spent cartridge. Yes, you are slower in an emergency. But you do have time to think of what you're at, huh?

She fired off half a dozen. How many of them went wide I don't know. I have the utmost dislike for these things at the best of times. Stay where I was? You bet, and wishing I had a barricade composed of two thousand telephone directories.

I suppose she thought he was going to kill her. We won't know, will we? She's not going to answer the judge's questions.

Two hit him anyway; the rest went all over the shop. In that big stone hall, even the popgun slams like a bloody cannon shot. Maybe those strawboard partitions deaden the acoustic a bit. By this time, people were running about like rabbits.

"Not two," said Dahl. "Three. One fatal. Big vein, or artery, I don't know which. And the people running, delayed me further."

"Yes, a seven sixty-five, it kills you but it doesn't stop you. Used to be standard issue for the gendarmerie—not any more and for just that exact reason. Hit, and badly, the old man took one pop at her. I'm glad I was never at the other end in Russia."

"By that time I was there," said Dahl sadly. "I can't blame Frosty at all, we just haven't been trained for that sort of thing. Book says of course you fire a warning shot in the air."

"Book's written by bureaucrats," said Castang, "never even shot a clay pigeon."

"The boy's never fired a shot in his life except on the police range. He saw her gun, he saw her fire it, he had to act, he tried to put it low to knock her leg out, the way one's taught."

"Those things throw high when one's not used to them."

"I *saw* it," said Dahl. "He aimed, at that moment the old

man put her down. Took her straight between the eyes—that thing was an old army-issue Luger." Castang didn't say 'yes, I know . . .' "She went over backwards like a—like a . . ."

"Doesn't matter. I understand. In that fraction he fired she was no longer there. But Leroux was standing exactly in line."

"If it had been just a single shot . . . but on automatic . . . he triggered in a panic and held it. We'll just hope Leroux survives.

"You better get home. Have anyhow a few hours of sleep, and me too. You do realise that you'll have to come back, in office hours. Between your statement—I'll want you to dictate that to the stenographer, the way you've told it me—and mine, and both of us experienced senior officers, I think we'll get Frost clear, I had to suspend him of course pending enquiry. The old man and the old woman both dead: on top of the medical evidence I think our joint statements will pull the judge clear. Oh you can go home tomorrow, I'll have to stay and face a week of paperwork and a press outcry about a great big police cock-up endangering the lives of innocent citizens in the middle of Copenhagen Central Railway Station."

"I've been there myself," said Castang bleakly. Ambiguous remark.

Chapter 20

Well yes, there are often Epilogues, spoken in Shakespeare by Time, or Chronicle, or someone; help show that years have passed, other necessary explanations for peculiar goings-on.

So I suppose—said Vera—this one is as good as any, spoken by me.

For the day dawned bright, beautiful. Sunshine, just a little breeze. Little 'mouton' clouds wandering like sheep about a lovely rain-washed sky. On the spring grass and the budding trees raindrops like dew glittered in tiaras, necklaces, eardrops and pendants, clips and brooches and more diamonds than the Royal Family even if you say add in all the others, can't be bothered working it out, Queen Victoria was related to Absolutely Everybody.

Around nine—Castang very bleary indeed—Dahl phoned: Danish, polite, considerate.

"It's a lovely day. Didn't Madam want to go to the castles? Just that there's so much mess here that on the whole I'd prefer to have you tomorrow morning instead. So take the day off."

And now they are standing on the battlements of Elsinore.

There aren't any battlements: Shakespeare didn't know and didn't care. Much like the seacoast of Bohemia. He got the important part, the metaphysical part right. That's all that matters. He had some vague notion of a Norman castle. Mit battlements. Like the ones in *Macbeth*, Inverness or what-

ever, very primitive, very Fortress. Ghost carting about on
battlements, not possible.

This is a lovely Renaissance château, delicious fantasy architecture. Sure there are fortifications—we are walking on
them. Three concentric rows, but these are the highly sophisticated 'Vauban' star-shaped embrasures and bastions, from
three centuries later. One walks upon these earthworks, there
are cannons and things and a pretty lighthouse. No ghosts.

When she's like this Castang feels very fond of her. That
he loves her, he is never in any doubt. Passion, yes, still, very
much so, and after all these years: the old girl can be extremely moche (untranslatable word—dull?—plain?—
dowdy?—all that) and wildly sexy. There's also love-pride,
and love-vanity, and a lot more. Also there is boredom, fury,
exasperation; that whole stolid row of soldiers which form
rank and you've marital affection, an awkward squad.

A tremendous ragbag of love, illuminating even when superficial and inaccurate. She's didactic, pedantic but not in a
pejorative sense. She is too astonished at what she knows,
too interested; too amused.

Now she doesn't want to talk about this; wants to talk
about Admiral Nelson!

"Look, across the strait, that's Helsingborg." A lot he
cares. "The Danes had a big fleet anchored here, powerful,
well armed, protected by one another and all the guns of the
fort—quite impregnable. Nelson came slipping round the
corner there, slid himself in between, taking immense risks,
of going aground as well as getting shot to pieces, and they
all stood there with their mouths open while he blew them to
buggery. Amazing man . . .

"Not at all nice in private life, in fact an appalling
calamity. Behaved very badly in Sicily. But one can't resist,
the going in with all his medals on and the imagination
telling him, he knew perfectly he would get killed.

"Cape Saint Vincent is a fine name, isn't it? And Trafalgar
even better. You wouldn't want to be called Lord Isle-of-
Wight or Start Point. Austerlitz sounds just like Auschwitz."

"Yes. Tell me about *The Winter's Tale*."

"True. There's a long speech by Time. I had to learn it by heart at school.

"Children always remember the gentleman who exits, Pursued by a Bear. He gets eaten by the bear too, poor man."

Castang waits patiently. It'll come.

"The winter's tale means a tale told by the fireside, tol' by les-bonnes-femmes. That's me, I suppose. But it has to be magical. For me it's the best one—better than *The Tempest*. The story's ridiculous, jealous fathers and pious wives."

Vera's voice, deep and a little hoarse. She's in her middle forties, thought Castang astonished. Our children are grown up.

"The King of Sicily is suddenly insanely jealous—one is never told why—and accuses his wife, who is the soul of virtue, of adultery. Her baby is taken away—by the fellow who's eaten by the bear—and abandoned on the seacoast of Bohemia. I always saw Sicily as grave, austere; there you had castles like in *Macbeth,* and all of them Norman knights, in full armour, with those masking helmets. Now I think of it I'd like to do some pictures of all this. But Bohemia—this is quite right—is oriental and altogether magical. Exactly like in Browning in *The Flight of the Duchess*—'Commend me to Gypsy glassmakers and potters'—fortune-tellers, and tinkers. Autolycus is a pedlar, fiddles all the peasants, a wonderful talker—and a notorious pickpocket too. That's you, I think—'the snapper-up of unconsidered trifles'."

"I feel much complimented," said Castang.

"The baby is found and brought up by the peasants. And she grows up a true princess, immensely pretty of course, marvellously bright. Perdita, the lost one. Naturally the Crown Prince meets her and they are madly in love, the King is furious but it all comes right in the end, her father acknowledges her, she's the true princess. How dull it all sounds, doesn't it? Perdita's lines, which are very beautiful, are extremely odd in the voice of a modern actress. All about virginity and purity. My sentiments, I may say; I took her very seriously when I was a girl. Any actress who's any good knows them to be real, and gives them full value. The beginning is tragic and the ending is comic, everything is inside out, all very Bohemian. And inside this absurd entertainment you'll find everything in life that is most serious. Birth, and maturity; innocence, and experience; evil, and repentance. How time passes, and how it acts. And the end—the end of it all—is harmony."

Her voice trailed away: from starting out to sea he turned round, to look again at the unreal, pretty, Bohemian castle. He will like Frederiksborg too; the courtyards and fountains, the bells and clocks, the aery baroque soap-bubble on its island.

"Shot through," said Vera's voice, "with that irony, so English. The silly tale, told at the fireside by some silly bonne femme, is a profound—a universal—masterpiece."

They walked down the slope and the cobbled path, under the triple fortified gateway, towards lunch.

"You see—there is a seacoast to Bohemia and they sail back to the real world, to Sicily. Perdita gets sick, on the boat."

"Sooner them than me," said Castang.